BORDER
MUSIC

Also by Robert James Waller

THE BRIDGES OF MADISON COUNTY
SLOW WALTZ IN CEDAR BEND
OLD SONGS IN A NEW CAFÉ
IMAGES
JUST BEYOND THE FIRELIGHT
ONE GOOD ROAD IS ENOUGH

BORDER MUSIC

ROBERT JAMES WALLER

WARNER BOOKS

A Time Warner Company

Warner Books, Inc., 1271 Avenue of the Americas, New York, NY 10020

ⓦ A Time Warner Company

Printed in the United States of America
First Printing: February 1995
10 9 8 7 6 5 4 3 2 1

Library of Congress Cataloging-in-Publication Data

Waller, Robert James
    Border music / Robert James Waller.
        p.   cm.
    ISBN 0-446-51858-1
    I. Title.
    PS3573.A4347B67   1995
    813'.54—dc20   94–29350
                                                          CIP

Book design by Giorgetta Bell McRee

For the sound of distant trains
And passengers left at the station.

We'll sing one ol' song
For the girls of the summer,
We'll smoke cheap cigars
And wear secondhand clothes,
We'll do that one time
Before the moon comes around
And runs with our lives
Down the West Texas roads.

"Last Waltz for Texas Jack"
After-Supper Songs
Bobby McGregor

CHAPTER ONE

Northern Minnesota, 1986—
How free
they were.

When this nameless piece a' shit tore off Linda Lobo's G-string instead of sticking money in it like he was supposed to, Texas Jack Carmine went crazy-over-the-edge and hit him with a pool cue. Four hours later and two hundred miles down the road, Jack bought coffee and sweet rolls in Chisolm for him and Linda. After that they headed up to Ely, then cut southeast down through the Superior National Forest. Not moving too fast, understand, Jack more or less letting the '82 Chevy S-10 have its own way.

And the day itself, something like Jack Carmine: one of those mid- to late-autumn jobs, uncertain about where it was headed early on, starting out yellow gray at sunrise, then eventually struggling up to the middle sixties and staying there through early afternoon before the night cold would come settling in again. Jack's favor-

1

ite driving songs, what he called his "road tapes," were coming out of a little tape deck sitting on the dash. He'd won the deck in a poker game without knowing it was the wrong size for the slot in his truck. Worked out anyhow, and the music blasted out of two little tinny speakers resting on the seat back, tied down there in a loose rattly way with leather boot strings so they wouldn't pitch forward when he hit the brakes.

On that day in that hour of the lives of Jack Carmine and Linda Lobo things were going about two big jumps past okay. Linda . . . Linda . . . what was her last name back then? Some know, others don't. Bobby McGregor, Jack's old traveling partner, has always been haunted by it. And by her. Bobby turns the question in his mind: Adkins? Archer . . . maybe Archer? No, A-something, but none of those.

"Doesn't matter, gets less important as time goes on, and I forgot it anyhow." That's what Jack said to Bobby the last time they talked, some years ago.

Bobby didn't believe him. Jack knew her name, but he wasn't telling Bobby or anyone else who asked. He'd mentioned it once in a casual way, but never again, especially when Bobby had asked him straight out.

He'd said, "Now listen, ol' buddy, I know you, and you're probably goin' to write all this down in some song and make money off it. That's okay, I don't give a damn one way or the other. Write what you want. But I can't come up with her last name for you." He'd grinned peculiar at that point, kind of a sideways grin with what Bobby knew had serious pain hiding inside it. "Besides, when it comes to pullin' things out of the past I like to concentrate on the melody, not the words. Even if I did remember, a man's got to have some secrets. No secrets, no mystery. No mystery, no life worth rememberin'. No life worth rememberin', no life worth goin' on with."

Anyway, Jack and Linda were heading in the general direction of Lake Superior, weather good, windows rolled down. They started drinking beer in late morning, Linda pulling long-neck bottles out of the cooler on which she was resting her feet. Jack had a long-neck balanced between his legs, leaning against the door and slapping the side of the truck in time with the music. He was steering all the while with one hand and tapping the wheel on the off beats. When Jimmy Buffett came on singing, "I ate the last mango in Paris . . . ," Jack took his right hand off the wheel, turned up the volume to max, and went into honking the horn and singing and slapping the truck door all at the same time.

Linda started laughing and stretched out her long, long—longer than long—left leg, trying to steer the pickup with the heel of her old cowgirl boot. That didn't work, and the truck drifted over the center line toward a ditch shallow enough that it was nothing more than a little depression in the grass.

Jack laughed, too, hit the brakes, and got the Chevy stopped a yard off the blacktop. He shut down the engine, stood on the running board with the tape still playing loud, and screamed at the forest right over the top of Jimmy Buffett: **"Hear me out there! I ate the last mango everywhere . . ."**

Linda spilled out the other side of the truck and started doing a little fandango across the road and into a small meadow directly opposite of where the trailer hitch pointed. Jack climbed on the truck hood while Jimmy Buffett was hammering up toward the noonday sun and maybe reaching it, ". . . took the first fast boat to China." Linda was shaking her hips, bending way back, her hair the color of wet blacktop and hanging down and nearly touching the ground. She wasn't fly-me-to-the-moon beautiful, but she was fine looking in her own special way. The kind of look that makes you think bad thoughts—or maybe good ones, depending on how you see the world. Bad or good, wet thoughts in any case.

Bobby McGregor only saw her twice up close, plus one other occasion that would count mostly as a glance. But each time he remembers thinking if there was ever a woman who could go down the road with you and never get tired or start complaining, she was it. Before all the good, fundamental images got winnowed out of the language, she was what used to be called high-assed, her bottom tucked up real tight above her legs. And Bobby also remembers those nice breasts—big, round ones, he guessed—trained right at you if you were looking close, which Bobby was doing the first time he met her, until his wife caught him at it and he went on to something else. He's never forgotten her, thinks about her now and then, mostly now. Linda . . . Linda with her last name gone and a body for which you'd ride the long freights home. Reality seldom bears the promise of imagination, but when it comes to her, Bobby McGregor's never had any doubts it would. No doubts, and no chance at finding out back then. She was with Jack Carmine.

> Jimmy Buffett: singing loud about eating mangos and last planes out and Third-World girls who backed you up when times got hard.
>
> Jack: waving a long-neck beer and trying to do sort of a Latin shuffle on the truck hood in his old lace-up boots, which was pretty funny since Jack never could dance worth a crap, though he liked to do it and made up

in energy what he'd been shorted in grace and rhythm.

The meter of both music and life in the particular times through which he was living somehow eluded Jack Carmine, even though most everybody else seemed to feel the pulse. Or maybe they didn't really feel it; maybe they just had it memorized like they'd been told. He'd thought once or twice about joining up with the armies of conformity, then reconsidered and went on being a seldom hombre, dancing to some other song nobody else ever heard or even dreamed about hearing, living his days in a fashion that made Henry David Thoreau look like a regular citizen. Henry David spent only two years staring into the waters of Walden Pond, Jack Carmine had spent a lifetime doing something like that and never once saw anything resembling a reflection looking back at him.

Jack's Wrangler's had a small tear along the left thigh where a piece of sharp pipe had ripped through and cut his leg a little bit. Had on a red-and-black flannel shirt with the sleeves rolled up to the elbows, showing the leather band on his right wrist. No watch, though. Jack Carmine didn't believe in watches. Never wore one, never owned an alarm clock. Jack's attitude was you woke up when it was time to wake up and you worked like hell until it was time to quit. The only time he was late for work was around April 1 every year when the switch to daylight savings time occurred. That always screwed him up for a day or two, time springing forward and all that. The bosses put up with it because Jack outworked any two men and made up for being late by staying late.

Jimmy Buffett: still shaking the little ratty speakers, sounding as if he were trying to bust out and join the fun.

Jack: still on the hood doing his worse-than-awful version of some kind of foreign dance.

Linda: singing about the road life and all the while still dancing. She ripped off her old denim shirt and got her bra undone in less than one-half of half a second, moving to the music while she did it and then swinging both items above her head, glad to be in the sun again.

Jack: still screaming Jimmy's lyrics and watching Linda shake it real good in his direction and then watching her some more when she turned and faced the forest so all the black bears or whatever was in there could get a good look, too. He noticed, among other things, how nice her back was. The sweet arch of it running down to where her rear curved out just so pleasantly and her vertebrae etched real clean against good skin.

He jumped down from the hood with Linda moving toward him, music still pounding out of the truck cab. They started dancing right on the highway, him looking down at her chest now and then, since a man couldn't help looking down now and then if he had anything at all going for him. Sunlight was falling late-October hard, but still yellow and warm, and Jack Carmine and Linda Last-name-A-Something went on dancing along the road in the direction of Ely. She told him later on it was the first time she'd really been happy in a long while.

"Took the last plane out of Saigon . . . ," which was exactly what Jack did in '75. They were dancing back toward the truck when Jack looked over her shoulder

and saw a car coming toward them with a top-heavy
profile indicating serious law. Jack flipped the long-neck
into some brush while Linda wriggled into her shirt no
more than eighteen seconds before the trooper pulled
up beside them. She was holding her bra behind her
where Jack was standing, squiggling it back and forth
like a raggedy doll. He took it from her and stuffed it
down the front of his jeans.

What the trooper saw was this guy with long brown
hair that was turning pretty gray and hanging two inches
over his flannel shirt collar. And he also saw this interesting-looking woman who was kind of flushed in the face
and had nice black hair hanging halfway down her back
and filled out her jeans like she'd been born in them.
And he could have sworn she didn't have any shirt on
when he came around the curve less than a half mile
back. And what he heard was the tape deck moving into
Waylon Jennings doing "Rainy Day Woman."

The trooper was looking at the front of Linda's shirt,
underneath which some pretty wonderful stuff had obviously been liberated and was pushing against the
denim as if it were seeking even more freedom. He
switched over to looking at the front of Jack's pants.
Kind of a funny-looking hump under the zipper. The
trooper had seen about everything in fourteen years on
the northern roads, but the high-up bulge in Jack's
Wrangler's was something a little different.

"Everything okay here?"

"Everything's A-okay, Officer. A-okay and a little
better'n that," Jack said, smelling the scent of conifers
and watching some kind of big bird land on the highway
behind the trooper's car. Bird started pulling and tearing
at a piece of something dead and smashed, stopped for
a moment then and looked in Jack's direction, as if Jack
might be next somewhere down the hard miles of all

the highways that ever ran toward sad-eyed endings. The bird was in no hurry; it all came down to blood on the pavement eventually.

"Where you from?" the officer said, glancing at the truck license plate.

Jack grinned. "Alpine, Texas. Up here layin' gas pipe. All finished now. Me and the missus, we're sort of takin' the long way back home, seein' the sights a little, as it were."

Hard to say if the trooper grinned back or sideslipped into something else a lot closer to benevolent doubt. He'd heard Texans were crazy and figured he'd come across a good example of that, so maybe it was best to let the garden grow as it grew and not fuss with it. The trooper glanced at his watch. His oldest son was quarterbacking the Two Harbors football team that night. If he was going to make the game, it was time to get moving. Nothing too harmful going on here anyway, nothing that would disrupt the general peace and tranquillity in a permanent way.

"Well, take it easy, and drive carefully."

"Will do, Officer, will do. Turnin' south for Alpine pretty soon," Jack said.

The law went down the road, but the moment was broken. Back in the truck, Jack and Linda moved on southeast through an afternoon with its own virtues if you knew how to appreciate them, which Jack did for certain and Linda was trying to do all over again. About a mile farther on he raised off the seat, reached down inside his jeans, and yanked out Linda's bra.

"Careful there, mister. It's the only one I've got except for the tassels stuck in my purse, and they ain't gonna take me too far in polite company."

She pulled out two more beers while Jack hung her bra over the rearview mirror and pointed at it swinging back and forth. "Speakin' of tassels, this is a whole lot better than a damned string deal from a Hibbing High graduation hat hangin' off your mirror," he said. "We'll get you some extra equipment first town we hit. And considering we left . . . where'n hell was that we pulled out from in a shower of parking lot gravel, you carryin' your boots and duds in both hands?"

"Dillon."

"Considerin' we left Dillon, Minnesota, eleven hours ago in a fever, we ain't doin' too bad."

Linda stuck her right boot against the wing window support and tapped it to Kenny Baker fiddling his way into "High Country." Eventually they started getting back to where they'd been pretrooper and prerules and pre- all that stuff making up organized living. She took a swallow of beer and looked over at Jack Carmine. "Wonder how that guy's feeling you whacked with a pool cue."

"He's feelin' hard, I'd guess. Probably shouldn't have done it, but it's a difficult time for tryin' to be a reasonable man. Never hit anybody with your fists. They only do that in movies and certain doghole saloons in Texas. Breaks up your hands and you can't work. Can't work, can't eat. Can't eat, can't work. Can't work, can't buy beer. Can't buy beer, can't dance. That's the way it runs. And speakin' of runnin', how about runnin' that tape back to Jimmy Buffett's last-plane-out song. I need to hear that one again, real loud."

"I gotta pee," Linda said.

Jack slowed down and stopped along the road. "Watch out for moose, they're in rut this time of year. They see your bare bottom, there'll be a stampede of bulls down through those white birch trees with the yellow quaverin' leaves. And I ain't got no pool cue this time." He was beating the heel of his hand against the steering wheel, pretty close to keeping time with the music.

"I've had worse happen," said Linda. "On the whole, I'll take a moose in rut over men every time. 'Least you know what they're after for sure."

"Some truth in all that," Jack said. "Think maybe I should wander into the trees also, 'long as we're into bodily functions. I'll take a different route and promise not to look."

"Suit yourself. Won't bother me one way or the other." She walked up a mild slope into the birches, talking over her shoulder. "Better watch out for moose yourself, since I'm not certain they know anything about human differences and might not care in any case. I saw an article while back about orangutans in Borneo or wherever trying to get it on with both men and women."

"No kiddin'?" Jack said, angling off from the direction Linda was heading.

"That's what the article said," her voice coming from somewhere off in the trees. "What's your name, anyway?"

Jack was peeing on a log, trying to write the first letter of his first name on the log with what he was doing at the moment.

"True name's Jack Carmine."

"I thought you said it was Eric something-or-other." She was buttoned up and walking. He could hear her boots coming through the leaves toward him while he was finishing the crossbar on the *J*.

"That was last night, when I didn't know whether you might have second thoughts and decide to turn me over to whatever version of a posse the Norskies could rustle up. For some reason all I could think of was Eric the Red, so I said my name was Eric Redder." He zipped his jeans and walked back to the truck, where Linda was leaning on the door with her arms folded, looking at him through the open window frame.

"Who's Eric the Red?"

Jack started the truck and got it moving. "Norwegian navigator about a thousand years ago. Discovered Greenland, as I recall. My high school history teacher back in Alpine had the hots for ol' Eric, talked about him all the time. Figured these Norskies up here'd be aware of their ethnic legends and so on and would cut me some slack if it came down to it. On top of that, thought I'd found a useful application for history there for a moment. As I see clearly now, that was drunk-thinkin' and wouldn't have done any good. But somehow it seemed like a good idea at the time."

"How come you swatted that guy when he pulled off my G-string? He wasn't the first that tried it."

"Just didn't seem right, that's all . . . him doin' that. Tell me, how come you were dancing all but naked in a place called the Rainbow Bar, anyway?"

"Beats workin' at the chicken-processing plant, which is what I was doin' before takin' up a new profession at the Rainbow. I was makin' five fifty an hour at Northern Food Processors, workin' in somethin' approximatin' forty-eight-degree temperatures and well on my way to carpal tunnel syndrome. The supervisor used to come down the line while I had my hands in chicken guts and run his hand over my rear when I couldn't fight back. One day he whispered in my ear, 'You ought to go down to the Rainbow when they have amateur night and show 'em how it's done.' Next time he put his hands on me about two months ago, I let him have it with a load of cold chicken guts right in the face.

"After that I went down to the Rainbow, bypassin' amateur night altogether. The manager was a bag of poultry guts himself, like somethin' out of a real bad movie. 'Cliché' is the word, I guess—sloppy fat, cigar, big pinky ring. Leaned back in his office chair and said, 'If you're gonna be a strobelight-honey, I gotta see what ya look like; take off your clothes.' So I took 'em off. He said, 'Ya got great tits and legs, sweetheart, and ya ain't bad lookin', either. Turn 'round for me coupla times.' I did just that, and he started kind of drizzlin' and said, 'Not bad for an older gal, not bad at all.' Then he told me I was hired and the pay was seventy-five bucks a night for what he called 'three performances of exotic dancin' per evening, startin' at eleven.' A girl's got to live, so I decided right then and there to give the gin-and-skin routine a try. He said, 'Good, we'll call you Linda . . . Linda what? . . . Linda Lobo. That'll look good in newspaper advertisements.' "

"Probably a dumb question here, but how'd you know what to do . . . up on stage, I mean?" Jack was taking the truck around a long curve past a small lake on the left, yellow leaves scattered on the smooth brown surface. Four does and a pair of yearlings were drinking fifty yards down the shore and lifted their heads, watching two pieces of flotsam drift past in a Chevy pickup with dented fenders.

"Like you said, dumb question. First off, the Rainbow crowd was a whole lot more concerned about quantity than quality. In case you haven't noticed, I've got a fair amount of the former, and that's what counted in the Rainbow. Beyond that, it don't take no trainin', all women know how to shake it hard if they want to. Nature gave us that ability as a way of attracting you wonderful things called men. I just kind of pretended I was all wound up and . . . you know . . . doin' it."

"Doin' it," Jack said flatly, a little grin coming over his entire being. "As in doin' it with a man?"

"Man, another woman, moose, all the same. It don't require any heavy thinkin', Texas Jack. You just pretend you're doing it."

Merle Haggard jumped into "I Take a Lot of Pride in What I Am," the electric bass shaking the little speakers almost to bits.

> I keep thumbin' through the phone book
> Looking for my daddy's name in every town.

Linda reached over and fished Jack's cigarettes out of his shirt pocket. She tamped one on the dash, lit it, and settled back. "Older woman named Carma showed me how to twirl my tassels."

"I saw you do that. Pretty fast . . . I remember thinkin' how fast you could make 'em twirl. Your friend, the one who taught you, she spell her name with a C or a K?"

"C. Why?"

"Just wonderin'. Whatever happened to your supervisor at the plant? He ever wander down to the Rainbow to get a better look?"

"He sure did. That was him you cracked with a pool cue last night after he tried to improve his view by tearin' off my G-string."

"C'mon . . . that was him?"

"Yep. Floyd Rattler. Ol' Floyd the Void, as we used to call him."

"Guess I helped you lose your dancin' job. Sorry about that."

"Not too much of a loss; I always viewed it as a temporary thing till somethin' better came along. Anyway, they were thinkin' about switchin' over to a new entertainment deal, somethin' to do with dwarf tossin' or female mud wrestlin' or topless women sploshin' around in creamed corn, some kind of variation on those things, maybe all of them together at the same time."

Jack Carmine lit a cigarette and shook his head, trying to imagine what combinations could be developed from mixing half-naked women, dwarves, and creamed corn: (1) dwarf refereeing match between mud-wrestling women; (2) half-naked women tackling naked dwarf eating creamed corn; (3) dwarf in bikini . . .

Merle kept digging himself a deeper hole in the tune.

"I always liked that song," Linda said. "Kinda sad in a way—guy lookin' through the phone books, no matter what town he's in, tryin' to find his daddy. Got 'Pancho and Lefty' on these tapes anyplace? I like that one, too."

"So do I. Think it's comin' up pretty soon. Look in the glove compartment, see if there's a Minnesota map in there. I've got no idea where we are."

She unfolded the map and studied it. Jack looked over at Linda Lobo. Her long hair was messed and wind-blown, but she still looked good to him—a long way from perfect, but high cheekbones and nice lips, re-minding him vaguely of how the actress Barbara Hers-hey looked in her salad days, back when she was doing *Boxcar Bertha* and other antisocial gems Jack liked. Linda was holding the cigarette in her left hand, staring at the map, and tapping her boot toes on the cooler.

"Lake Superior's straight ahead. Road stops there, dead-ends on 61 runnin' along the lake shore. Goose the truck a little and we'll hit the water. Turn right at the lake and Silver Bay comes up. Left is a place called Little Marais. Where we goin', anyway?"

"Don't know. Somewhere, I guess. Texas eventually is where I'm headin' after I visit my uncle, Vaughn Rhomer, in Iowa. Always stop and see him when I can. He's one of the best people I know. Wanna go to Texas?"

"Just like that . . . go to Texas with you? I only learned your real name a few miles back. On the other hand, my options are somewhat narrowed down at the moment. Let's see how things run for a while. Maybe I'll just have you drop me off in Altoona, Iowa, if you don't mind. Got family there. It's not much out of your way if you're headin' for Texas and if I'm rememberin' the maps in my head correctly."

She looked out the window. "Keep thinkin' I ought to get organized, make somethin' out of my life. Doesn't seem to happen all by itself, though."

Jack scratched his cheek. "Been my experience that randomness takes on its own forms if you leave it alone long enough . . . 'course you may not like the shape of things that come from doin' that, but it's one way of behavin' among all the rest."

The rubber tires hummed toward the waves of Lake Superior, the road ending there while October was thinking about doing the same.

At the intersection with 61, Jack cocked a quarter between his thumb and forefinger. "Call it," he said.

"Heads, we go right." Linda was taking her bra off the mirror and stuffing it in her purse.

The quarter spun. He caught it and slapped it on his wrist. "Tails." He turned left with the sun running low behind them. "Hey, here come Merle and Willie with that song you wanted."

Jack and Linda both waited for the chorus, then came in singing together, as if on cue. They turned toward each other and laughed and kept on singing about bandits and the road, about letting old friends down and slipping away to places where nobody could find you.

Ten miles farther on, Little Marais showed itself,

nothing much beyond a liquor store and mom-and-pop grocery. Jack and Linda went into the grocery store. He bought a loaf of bread, had the woman tending things cut an inch from a round of sharp cheddar cheese, and picked up a jar of honey on impulse, figuring it might come in handy in ways still undefined.

"See anything you want?" he said to Linda.

She was in the rear of the store and didn't hear him. He walked over an aisle and peeked down it. There were a few racks of clothing against the back wall, and Linda was fussing around, looking at things.

She walked toward him with four small packages in her hand.

"Find what you need?" he said.

"Yep." She grinned, dangling two plastic-wrapped brassieres in front of her while she walked. "I'm amazed they had my size. Must be some pretty healthy women in these parts. Got a couple of sets of things for farther down, also."

"See any sweaters or jackets back there? You're going to need somethin'. It's getting cold, nights."

The woman in charge said, "We got some denim jackets and sweaters on sale over in the corner there."

Jack and Linda walked to the clothes, which were all sized for men. Linda pushed hangers around until she found a smallish Levi jacket. Jack was looking through wool sweaters piled on a table. He pulled out a black turtleneck and held it up. "This might come close to fittin' you."

She took the sweater and looked down as she held it against her. "It'll work. Think I'll wear the jacket; I'm already feelin' chilly here in the late afternoon."

"Anything else?" the proprietor asked. She glanced at the front of Linda's shirt, then at the packaged bras

on the counter. About time, she thought, still not understanding the imprudent and unapologetic generation
coming along behind her.

Linda picked up some toothpaste and a toothbrush,
a stick of deodorant, and a pair of boot socks. She stood
looking at a cardboard display of razors and blades.
"You use this kind?" She pointed at the razors.

"Yes, ma'am, when I'm shavin', the inclination for
which kind of comes and goes."

"I'll borrow yours; no point in havin' two of everything." She went back for a tube of shampoo and a
few items of makeup and laid the whole works on the
counter.

The woman behind the cash register rang up the sale.
Jack pulled a money clip from his left jeans pocket. The
clip was sterling silver with a curlicue turquoise design
embedded in it and was something of a mystery. It'd
shown up in his pocket one morning after he'd stumbled
north across the border from a wild night in Ojinaga
back in '78. He peeled off three twenties from his roll
and paid the bill. Linda pulled on the denim jacket and
buttoned it, and they went over to the liquor store.

"Howdy," an old man said when the bell above the
door tinkled and they walked in.

"Howdy back," said Jack Carmine. "Need some
beer."

"Cold stuff is over there in the cooler." The old man
flipped his head. "Warm stuff is next to it along the
wall."

Jack picked up three six-packs of cold Moosehead and
walked to the cash register, his chin pressed down on
the top six-pack to steady the load. "Pretty quiet around
here," he said, grinning.

"Gets quiet after Labor Day. Personally I like it quiet.

Better class of people come through after the summer tourists are gone. Upper-shelf people come around this time of year."

"Yeah, like us," Linda said under her breath. Jack smiled. The old man was punching the cash register and didn't hear.

"Want some peanuts?" Jack grinned at her.

"Sure."

"We'll take five packages of those mixed nuts and two packages of the beef jerky."

The old man pulled the packages off a rack and totaled the bill.

"Anyplace to stay around here?" Jack asked, handing over some bills and change.

"Best Western just up the road. Right near the Onion River. Too early for skiing, so they'll probably have some rooms."

Back in the truck, driving north, Jack chewed on a stick of jerky and hummed. Linda opened two beers and a bag of nuts. Night was coming fast.

"I've got a little money in a Dillon bank. I'll pay my share when I get a chance to send for it," she said, dumping peanuts down her throat and following that with a wash of Moosehead.

"Don't worry about it. I just collected nearly six months' wages before stopping in Dillon. Had 'em hold most of my summer money so I wouldn't piss it away."

"Well, I do worry about it. So I'll pay you back when I can. Used to payin' my own way."

"Okay, it's up to you."

The Cliffside Motel sat on the lake shore, balconies jutting over a slope running down to the water and a parking lot filled with cars.

"Want me to check on the rooms?" Linda asked.

"Fine with me."

She came out of the office a minute later. "Here's the deal. The man has a pair of rooms left. One's got two double beds at forty-six fifty but no lake view. The other's got a queen-sized bed and a lake view, but it's fifty-four bucks."

"Want your own room?" Jack looked at her.

"No need to spend that kind of money. You seem okay to me. We can work it out." She smiled. "I've spent a night or two in these places with people I didn't know half as well as I know you. Besides, any man who'd coldcock someone to defend a lady's honor when her clothes are being torn off probably can be trusted."

"Let's go big-time, then, take the one with the lake view." He pulled out his money clip and handed twenties to her. "Ask him about somewhere to eat."

"You figure on staying one night, or two, or what? The man wants to know that."

"Tell 'im one. I've never been much for plannin' ahead, less so as I get older."

Linda nodded and walked to the office. When she opened the door she looked back at Jack Carmine and smiled, moving her head from side to side in a quick little way as if some hidden song were beating its way through her brain.

They carried their gear into the room in one trip. Jack had an old blue duffel bag, which he put on top of the cooler for the portage. Linda carried a brown paper sack with her essentials.

She pulled the drapery cord, showing Lake Superior thirty feet down the slope. "Hey, this is real nice, balcony and everything, just like the man promised," she said, opening the sliding glass door.

Jack went out on the balcony and leaned on the wrought-iron railing. Two-foot waves were slapping the rocky shore. Off to the left was a stand of trees holding on to the last red-and-yellow things of autumn, leaves rattling in the lake breeze. They stood there for a few minutes, not saying anything, both of them squinting into a thin, diagonal strip of sunlight running across the water from somewhere down toward Duluth.

"Jeez Louise, I need a bath," Linda said. "Where's your razor?" She went into the bathroom with a beer, her brown paper sack, and Jack's razor.

In fifteen minutes the room started smelling good, the way it always does when you're traveling with a woman. Jack sat on a corner of the balcony rail, drinking Moosehead and swinging his feet. He rubbed his cheek, felt three days of new black whiskers poking at him. A young couple dressed in perfect L. L. Bean came out on their own balcony two rooms away. The man looked over to Jack and nodded.

"Evenin'," Jack said, trying to remember the last time he'd felt young. Long time ago. Long time.

He went back in the room just as Linda walked out of the bathroom with a big towel wrapped around her body and another one wrapped around her head the way women know how to do it after washing their hair. Jack wondered how old she was. Early thirties, he guessed, and holding up extraordinarily well, about as well as the towel was being held up by her breasts, which was a first-class holdup. Her legs weren't as long as they looked in her jeans and boots, but they were still long and just fine or a cut better. He'd always noticed that, how women seem bigger when they're dressed and a lot smaller and a lot less formidable without their clothes.

She turned on a little radio by the bed and moved the dial until a country music station homed in. Jack went in the bathroom, shaved, and got into the shower. Linda knocked on the door.

"Come on in," he said over the noise of the water.

"Mind if I brush my teeth while you're doin' what you're doin'?"

"No problem." Steam pouring over the top of the shower curtain, water driving into his neck, soap running down his body. Jack Carmine was starting to feel somewhat younger. Somewhat.

"What's this thing lyin' here?"

"What thing?"

"Thing with a strap and zipper pocket."

"Shoulder holster, where I carry my serious money, except for that which I already wired to my bank in Alpine. Got my pocket picked of seven hundred dollars in Vegas some years ago. Got the holster right after that. Don't like checks; like cash." He barely heard the door shutting as she went out. He combed his wet hair straight back and wrapped a towel around his hips. Linda was lying on the bed, looking out through the sliding glass door, chin on her folded hands.

"What'd the man say about a restaurant? Anything?"

"Says there's a restaurant here at the motel and a place or two about forty miles up the road in Grand Marais." She said it pensively, in a way indicating she was thinking about something else, slowly kicking her feet where they hung over the edge of the bed.

Coming up on the late middle of his life, Jack Carmine leaned against the frame of the sliding door, one ankle crossed over the other and arms folded. It all fit—wearing a towel in a room on the shore of Lake Superior, sharing a room with a woman about whom he knew nothing. It fit perfectly, all of this, the woman and the situation. It fit the life of a man who never could decide on where he was going next and didn't much care one way or the other.

"Most people don't do things like this," she said, coming out of whatever she'd been in.

"Do what?"

"Run out the back door of a place called the Rainbow Bar in Dillon, Minnesota, with someone they don't even know and get in a truck and drive all day and end up here without any clothes on in a motel room."

"That's true. If you read it in a book, you wouldn't believe it. Country'd probably collapse if everybody behaved like this."

She was still looking out the window at Lake Superior. "Sometimes you . . . you just got to go, just got to get out of wherever you are. Catch the last plane out, like the song says, know what I mean?"

"Gotcha. Think about all those dumb bastards suckin' each other's exhaust fumes in the Holland Tunnel about now or ridin' some clackin' commuter train out to the suburbs. I think about that a lot and swear I'll never ever come close to doin' it. Made that decision thirty years ago. Think they're any better off with their mortgages and retirement plans and full medical coverage than we are right now? Hell no, unless we get sick or old or need a house real fast."

"Your name really Jack Carmine?"

"Yep."

"And you really live in Alpine, Texas, right?"

"When I'm there, which I hardly ever am, 'cept winters."

"Jack Carmine from Alpine . . . people say that? Kid you about the rhyme?"

"They used to, not so much anymore. I sometimes introduced myself as Jack Carpine from Almine, just to confuse the issue. Want a beer?"

"Sure. I'm gettin' the bed damp with this towel. Can you handle it if I take it off?"

"Yep, if I suck up a little discipline, of which I ain't got much, but some. You'll have to put up with me glancin' your way now and then, however. Maybe every fourteen seconds or so."

She rolled over, giving him a flash of her front side, and slid the towel off her body. "You look pretty good in a towel yourself, Jack Carmine. How do you stay thin like that, drinkin' beer the way you do?"

"Hard work and good genes. Mostly the latter, I'm guessin'." He was having a little trouble getting his heartbeat squared away. Linda was lying on her stomach again, arms curled around a pillow on which she was resting her head, looking back at him. Nice smooth body all clean and perfumed, her rear looking good and breasts pressing into the bed.

"I think I better sit down, if you don't mind. I'm havin' just a bit of trouble keepin' things under control. Don't get me wrong; I'm not pushin' for anything, just talkin' truth. There's certain involuntary aspects to being a man sometimes, some parts kinda takin' on a life all their own."

"Don't worry about it. I'm reasonably familiar with the idea. Nothin' to be embarrassed about." She patted the bed beside her. "Sit here if you want, I'm not worried. You know what the girls used to say in high school about boys?" She giggled into the pillow.

"I'm half afraid to ask. Tell me anyway."

"If you ain't seen it, you won't know what it is. If you seen it, you won't be afraid of it. Bad, huh? We thought it was pretty smart stuff back then."

"There's some wisdom in that, somewhere. Think I'll let it pass for now, though."

A half hour later they were both lying on their stomachs, two feet apart. Jack had tossed his towel in the general direction of the bathroom ten minutes ago.

"You know," she said, "there's something real nice about lying here talkin' with a man, both of us naked and yet not trying to get crazy right off the bat. Most men couldn't do that, and I appreciate it. I think it's called bein' intimate without gettin' intimate. You done this before?"

Jack was tapping the lip of his beer bottle against the headboard and studying what he was doing as if there were some zenlike quality to it. "Well, for argument's sake, let's say I have. The trick is to get by that first surge of hormones and adrenaline and quiet down. Where'd you say you're from?"

"Altoona, Iowa. Right outside Des Moines. I was workin' on the line at American Battery till they up and moved the whole shootin' match to Dallas with one week's warnin'. I needed money and got word the chicken processor in Dillon was hirin'."

"What's your last name, if you don't mind me askin'?"

She told him and rolled over, looking up at the ceiling. Her breasts were every bit as big and nice as he remembered when he'd watched her dancing the night before in the Rainbow and along a country road a few hours ago on this day. She blinked her eyes twice, still staring up at the ceiling with little sparkly things embedded in it. The radio was playing one of those nondescript songs, good music for country dancing, not too memorable beyond that.

"What'd you leave behind in Dillon?"

"Nothin' much. Rent was paid up, so I'm square with the landlord. A few clothes, mostly jeans and work duds. One pretty decent dress I bought in a wild splurge last summer—sixty-two bucks, on sale."

"Tell you what," Jack said, grinning at her. "I'll buy you a nice dress—real nice one—and all that goes with it. If you're stickin' with me for a while, or even if you ain't, for that matter, we'll find a store in Duluth or Minneapolis or somewhere down the line, get you fitted out proper."

She rolled her head on the pillow and smiled soft at him. "You don't have to do that."

"Know I don't have to, but want to. Wanna watch you try on clothes. Something kind of sexy about watchin' a woman tryin' on new clothes, so I'll get my money's worth. I think it's because women like to do it so much. Makes you feel good just watchin'."

She put a hand on the small of his back and noticed an old, mean-looking scar on his right shoulder. "Jack Carmine, you're okay. How'd you learn so much about women?"

"Keep your head up, pay attention, things come along. Just know it, that's all. Gettin' hungry?"

"Yes. Wanna try the motel restaurant or what?"

"I'm votin' for the run up to Grand Marais. Somehow motel restaurants always seem about the same. I get this feelin' there's a cook and two waitresses followin' me around the country and go to work wherever I stop. I look up from a menu I'm sure I've seen before and there's a biscuit shooter in a black-and-white uniform and a pink hanky in her pocket, and I swear I seen her in another restaurant back down the line someplace."

Linda swung off the bed and padded toward the bathroom, grabbing her jeans and new sweater on the way. Jack liked to watch women walk away. "Somethin' good about that, not sure why," he once told Bobby McGregor. Some years later Bobby wrote a song around those thoughts.

Jack was never much into thinking hard about matters in general by the time Bobby met him, back in Saigon when things were going to hell. Said reflection did violence to the soul and did even worse things to the heart. Said it took away all the good warm feelings and replaced them with something he didn't like. Said everything worth knowing came out of doing, not thinking.

Bobby asked him once about his philosophy of life.

"My what?" he said.

"You know, how do you see humanity at rock bottom and your place in it."

They were leaning on a long wooden bar in Shreveport, out there just wandering around and awaiting career developments, like they used to do before Bobby more or less settled down.

Jack had studied the liquor bottles lined along the back side of the bar, then started tearing the paper label off his beer in thin strips, concentrating on what he was doing. "Survival first, procreation after that."

"What?"

"Just what I said."

"You mean that's it?" Bobby had started grinning and ordered two Lone Stars for them while he thought about what Jack had said. "Nothing more?"

"Just that. Comes down to hangin' on, and while we're hangin', doin' our best to keep our questionable species hangin' on also. We've turned the second part into kind of an art form when it's goin' well on summer nights like this, but it's all the same . . . all the same. We come, we do, we go . . . nothin' more, and that's about as serious as we ought to take ourselves."

"What about the great things we've created, rocket ships to the moon, Michelangelo, Picasso, all of that?"

"Fluff. Good fluff, maybe, and a way of escapin' from what's really pushin' at us down deep, but still fluff. You asked me about how I see things at rock bottom, and I told you. People keep tryin' to make us out as somethin' superior, as somethin' better than dogs and crocodiles, fish and flowers. We ain't, when you want to get real fundamental about it. We're all on the same ball of twine, all ridin' one goddamn single arrow— dogs, crocodiles, fish, flowers, us—out through wherever we're all goin', which is nowhere, and that's the heart of things as I see it. Believe what you want to believe, Bobby, all the same to me."

Jack dug in his jeans for change and walked toward the jukebox, doing a little Texas two-step shuffle as he crossed the empty dance floor. He put four quarters in, got the machine cranking, and went over to a table where three women were sitting.

Twenty seconds later he was dancing to "San Antonio Rose" with one of them. As they came past the bar, Jack was grinning at Bobby. "Survival seems well in hand tonight, so I'm workin' on part two of Jack Carmine's view of things."

He took the woman across the floor, a little out of time to the music, as usual, but she was compensating and making it work, looking up at the face under the Stetson and laughing at what it was saying to her. Women liked Texas Jack Carmine in the same way people enjoy sunshine and soft rain on their faces. He seemed to skate on the wind instead of letting it blow him around, and women sensed it. More than that, he genuinely liked women, not only in bed, but overall. Liked to watch them, talk with them, dance with them, and women picked up on it. They liked him because he liked them for all the things women are.

Linda came out of the bathroom, looking good. Her jeans were a little dusty, but the new turtleneck sweater fit her near perfect, a touch on the baggy side, but close. She'd tied her long hair back with a pink ribbon from her purse.

Jack was lacing up his boots. He'd put on a clean flannel shirt, blue-and-white plaid this time, and his other pair of jeans. "Ready, dancin' lady?"

"You see one of those shoeshine cloths here?"

Jack looked in the closet and found one, tossed it to her.

She put one boot up on the luggage rack, then the other, running the cloth over them, then stood with both feet close together and looked down. "Kinda pathetic."

"Kinda just fine, I'd say." He pulled on a leather jacket that'd been down the road some. "You're looking real good in all respects."

"Thanks. It's good to hear that once in a while whether it's true or not."

"It's true tonight, and that's all that matters."

They went out of the room, big moon three days short of full and temperature dropping fast. Jack started singing. "Crew-cabs in the parkin' lot and the clink of ol' pool balls. Lines of love and passion, written on the restroom walls . . . ," and the truck rolled north along the shore of big water, what the Indians called Gitche Gumee. Just under an hour later they came into Grand Marais.

"Man at the motel said there's a good pizza place and a roadhouse or something like that. Harbor's Edge, Harbor Somethin', can't remember," Linda said.

"There it is, Harbor Light. That okay with you?"

"Sure."

Jack swung into the parking lot. He opened the truck door partway, then stopped and said, "You hear what I hear? There's a band playin' in there. That's got promise, don't you think? Except they're playin' one of those new songs that strike me as a lot like what automobiles have come to be, can't tell 'em apart. Liked tail fins on cars, like the older songs better."

Linda smiled at him while they walked to the front door of the Harbor Light. "While you're on the subject of old, how old are you, anyway, Jack Carmine?"

"Lessee, forty-six right at the moment, and—uh-oh—forty-seven tomorrow." He pulled open the door and held it for her.

"Texas Jack turns into Birthday Jack. Why didn't you tell me?"

Jack started moving his hips and shoulders as if he were dancing. "Didn't think about it till you asked. Yep, tonight I'm doin' tangos and eatin' mangoes, grabbin' the last plane out. Goin' first-class in Grand Marais, insofar as that's possible at all."

The hostess came up to them, smiling and clutching menus to her chest. Jack grinned at her. "Best table in the house. It's my birthday tomorrow, and I'm suddenly near to out of control since I remembered it."

She smiled again and took them into the restaurant, gave them a nice table that looked out into a stand of conifers waving slow in the night wind, and laid menus in front of them.

"Something from the bar?"

Jack looked at Linda.

"Scotch on the rocks," she said.

"Give her the best Scotch you got."

"We have J and B."

"Okay. Bring me two Mooseheads."

"Two?"

"Yes, ma'am, two. Got a last plane to catch in a little while. Need a runnin' start."

"There's no airport here like that," the hostess said.

"Yes there is, only I'm the only one can see it, and the plane's leavin' shortly with the bandit-boy on board." Jack flattened out his hand and swooped it over the table.

She looked at the ceiling for a moment with "another drunk" written on her face. "The waitress will bring your drinks in a moment." She walked away.

"I don't think she likes me," Jack said, grinning.

"She's just not used to high flyers, Jack. She'll come around. She'll be beggin' for your hand in marriage before the night's over. Trust me."

The waitress showed up with drinks. "Our special tonight is fried pol-lok."

Jack looked at Linda, then back at the waitress. "*Pol-lok*? Those're people. You servin' parts of people here? Jesus Christ, I been in some tough towns, but this beats all. Fried Pol-loks tonight, next thing it'll be boiled Texans at Sunday brunch."

The waitress blushed. "No, I mean . . . it's fish. I've always had trouble sayin' it right."

Linda looked up at her, smiling gently. "Oh, pollack, that kind of fish."

"Yeah."

"Who's playin' here tonight?" Jack asked.

"The Rusty Cadillacs. They're real good. 'Least I like 'em."

He looked over at Linda. "Whaddya feel like, dancin' lady?"

She looked good. Face made up just a little, black hair all shining and gathered in the back with the pink ribbon.

Last night she'd been swinging her breasts, flaming orange tassels twirling around when she did the thing Carma had taught her.

"If you're worried about price, stop worryin'. You like lobster?"

"I love lobster. Hardly ever had it in my life, though. You sure?"

He looked at the menu, talking to the waitress. "Says here you got lobster tails at market price, which is the price set by those boys up in Maine with all their holdin' ponds where they keep the lobsters so they can keep the price up, like diamonds. Farmers been tryin' to do the same thing for years, but they're too dumb or stubborn to get organized." The waitress was nervous, pad and pencil ready. "Two big ol' lobster tails at market price is what we'll have."

"We're outta baked potatoes, but we got hash browns or fries."

"I'll have the hash browns," Linda said. "Italian dressing on my salad."

"Same thing here." Jack grinned.

"Two lobster tails, hash browns, and Eye-talian dressing. I'll be right back with your salads."

"Havin' fun?" Jack asked after the waitress left.

"So far, so good." Linda smiled and looked at him, tapping her knife to the Rusty Cadillacs playing somewhere in another part of the building. "This the way you do things most of the time? Drivin' around in your truck, eatin' lobster?"

"Sometimes, sometimes not. Depends how my moods and money are runnin'. Never solve anythin' just drivin' around in the truck. On the other hand, if that don't solve problems, not sure what does." He surveyed the big dining room with open rafters showing above them. "This strikes me as a real old building. Kinda like it. Like old things in general, things with a little livin' rubbed into 'em."

Linda tapped her knife and looked up at the ceiling. "That sort of fits us, doesn't it?"

"Me, not you. You're not old. These deep ol' lines in my cheeks ain't all due to hard wind and burnin' sun."

"Well, I'm thirty-seven and startin' to sag a little, mentally for the most part. But I'm also noticin' a little droop here and there, enough so that my career as a strobelight-honey wouldn't have had long to run"— she spread her fingers, studied them—"except for my fingernails, which are doin' a lot better since I got outta the chicken plant."

"No sags or droops obvious to me, and I been lookin' pretty close for the last few hours. Besides, I like to think the gloss of age has its own charms." Jack grinned. "We goin' dancin' after the lobster, or you too tired?"

"Sure, let's go dancin'." Linda held up her drink, and Jack tapped a Moosehead against it. She said, "Here's to whatever, anything better than twirlin' my tassels in the Rainbow in Dillon, front of all those gapin' mouths and droolin' chins. It's a sad world, Jack Carmine, all those men so pent up they got to pay money to see a woman prance around in front of 'em. I was just earnin' a livin', but they was all just livin' a dream that'd never come about."

"Okay, we'll drink to anything better'n that, and we'll try to improve on things as we go along. But I gotta say, with some small amount of both truth and regret, you mighta become the all-time world-champion tassel twirler had you stuck with it."

"Well, thank you . . . I guess. Probably not the same as being a great violin player, but skill comes in all forms, and a lady's got to make the best of what she has." She started laughing.

"Let me in on the joke," he said.

"I was just thinkin' about how attendance at football games'd probably go through the roof if we substituted my kind a' twirlin' for baton twirlers at halftime."

"Hell, I got a better idea. Put you and Carma and a few others out there on the field. People'd come from all over just to see that and forget about football altogether. As a matter of fact, you could probably carry it off on your own. Want me to start workin' on it, take over as your bookin' agent? See it now, don't you? Fifty thousand people at ten bucks a head doin' that thing called 'the wave' and eatin' hot dogs while they're watchin' Miss Linda Lobo twirlin' her tassels. I could stand out there on the field with a number twenty pool cue and act as your protector. We could retire after one performance."

Linda got the image of Jack swinging a pool cue as thousands of fans charged on the field and laughed harder. "Well, that probably sounds better to you than me. But it'd make more sense than watchin' a whole bunch of big ol' men tryin' to push each other around while chasin' a little ball."

The butterflied lobster tails came along, slightly curled and bright orange red. After the waitress set two cups of melted butter over warming candles and left, Linda said, "This is real nice. Feels kinda fancy and all, more'n I'm used to, at any rate." She smiled at Texas Jack Carmine through the candlelight, and Jack was happy because Linda Lobo was happy.

When they'd finished eating and the waitress had cleared away their plates, Jack leaned back in his chair. "Well, how'd you feel about the lobster?"

"I felt like I was watchin' *Lifestyles of the Rich and*

Famous, only I was in it this time. It was real good, Jack. I'm glad you suggested it. Oh, oh, look what's comin' your way, I bet." She pointed toward the kitchen.

The waitress was carrying a small cake with a single candle stuck in the frosting. She marched up to the table. "Happy birthday from the Harbor Light. I'm supposed to sing the song, but I don't sing too well, but I will if you want."

Jack squinted at the waitress's name tag. "Pam, everybody sings good when they warm up to it. Just gotten so most people got so cold they can't get warm, think they can't sing. Don't worry about it, I'll do the singing if you promise to hum along. Deal?"

She nodded.

Jack started singing in a croaky baritone, "Happy Birthday to Jack . . . ," then stopped. "C'mon, Pam, you promised to hum along."

The waitress blushed and faltered into a low hum, standing there with her hands clenched together and pressed against her stomach. Linda smiled and sang along with Jack. When they finished, Jack dipped his fingers in the water glass and pinched out the flame. "My granddaddy always shut down birthday fire that way. 'Fight fire with water, Jack,' is what he used to say, 'and save your breath for runnin', 'cause you're gonna need it.' When he got to be around seventy, it took a lot of pinchin' to get all the candles out, and I'd near die waitin' for him to get done so we could eat cake."

Four people sitting at a nearby table applauded. Jack turned in his chair and bowed to them. "Like some cake? I'll cut it thinner'n West Texas rain, make enough for everybody." They said no, since they were waiting for their steaks, but thanks anyway. So he cut it in thirds

and insisted Pam take her piece along for later on when
she might have a chance to eat it.

Jack paid the restaurant bill, and they went down a
hallway in the general direction of the music. At the
end of the hall was a crowded bar, and beyond the bar
was a door opening into the dance hall portion of this
more or less total entertainment complex in the north
woods. Above the Rusty Cadillacs was a red, white,
and blue banner:

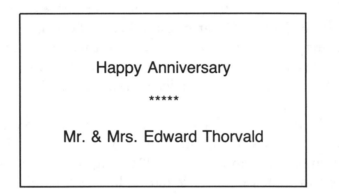

Jack pushed up to the bar and got two beers, and they
went into the dance hall, which was about seventy-five
feet long and fifty wide, with tables around the edge
and a low stage at the far end. The band was playing
"Me and Bobby McGee."

> Freedom's just another word
> For nothin' left to lose . . .

"Well, take . . . it . . . a . . . way . . . *Leon!*" Jack
was clapping along with the music. "You do the Texas
two-step, Miss Linda Lobo?"

"Never done it, seen it done on TV. Who's Leon?"

"Bob Wills's steel guitar player in the old days. Bob used to say that when it was time for an instrumental break." He gestured toward the dance floor. "Wanna give it a try?"

She cocked her head, held out her arms, and grinned at him, "Teach me, Texas."

"See, there's this little kind of shuffle-skip thing you do. . . ."

Two minutes later Linda Lobo was doing the Texas two-step better than Jack had ever done it in his wildest dreams. That doesn't mean she was great, it means Jack wasn't so great. But fun was the mission, and having wisdom of a kind that's pretty much been lost overall, they didn't let technique get in the way of pleasure.

When the Cadillacs finished "Louisiana Saturday Night," Jack's flannel shirt was soaked, sweat running down his chest and forehead. Dancing was a lot of work for him. Linda was a little red in the face but still looked cool as you please otherwise.

Around eleven the band played a country version of a fanfare. "Like to bring Mr. and Mrs. Thorvald up here, so we can give 'em a proper salute," the band's guitar player said over the microphone. Everyone clapped, and the Thorvalds came up in front of the stage.

"By God, isn't that somethin'?" Jack said, looking down at Linda, who was about seven inches shorter than his six feet one. "Forty years, for chrissake . . . forty years they been married. Hell, if I added up all the married years of everyone I know, includin' seconds and thirds, it wouldn't total forty."

The Thorvalds were short and stout and standing with their arms around each other's backs, waving at the crowd. Linda was looking at them, looking sadlike in her own way. She tilted her head toward Jack, and he could see her eyes were wet. "That *is* somethin'," she said. "Takes a lotta carin' and patience to make it that far in one piece."

"Lotta love, too, don't you think?" Jack was smiling nice and easy when he said it.

"Lotta all those things, Jack. All those things that kind of got away from some of us."

Jack put his arms around her, then reached up and brushed away a tear that had run down out of her left eye. She put her arms around him and stood on her tiptoes, kissing him soft and warm for a few seconds, then laid her head on his chest and watched the Thorvalds lead off the "Anniversary Waltz."

"C'mon," Linda said quietly as other people moved out on the floor to join the Thorvalds. "Let's do the anniversary waltz." And they danced, as the others danced, with the Rusty Cadillacs playing the very best they could for this song and Jack dancing the very best he could for this song. He and Linda moved around the floor in waltz time with the others who had come to honor the Thorvalds and the night and all things caring and patient and loving in a world that was moving otherwise, all those things getting away from Linda Lobo and Texas Jack Carmine.

Later on Jack danced with Mrs. Thorvald. Linda could see them over Mr. Thorvald's shoulder while she was dancing with him, her left hand on his white shirt where the red-and-black suspender came over it. Mrs. Thorvald tilted her head back, laughing at something Jack was saying to her. He was grinning and looked over at Linda, wiggling his eyebrows, just before he took Mrs. Thorvald into a wide turn near the stage. She was still laughing.

When he brought her back to where Linda and Mr. Thorvald were standing, she said to Linda, "You got a real prize here, honey; hang on to him. I declare, he not only dances pretty good, he's got a fine sense of humor, and that's necessary in any marriage, more so nowadays than ever. Good thing I didn't meet Mr. Jack Carmine when I's younger or the mister here might have had some competition."

The mister was bald, but the mister was grinning, and he swept Mrs. Thorvald into his arms and danced her away as the music took up again. Linda put her arm around Jack Carmine and watched them go, saw how the Thorvalds smiled at each other, saw on their faces all the years of working it out and making it work. In a world getting more and more used to losing, Mr. and Mrs. Edward Thorvald had won big.

When the song ended, the guitar player stepped up to the microphone. "Listen, everyone, it's prize time. We're givin' away something good for the person here who's the longest way from home. Grand Marais doesn't count. It's a long way from anywhere, but it's where most of you're from. Okay, let's hear it—where you from that's some distance?"

"Rochester," said Mrs. Thorvald's brother.

"St. Paul," said Mr. Thorvald's sister.

The drummer hit a rim shot and yelled, "Oil Trough, Arkansas."

"You ain't from no damned Oil Trough, Arkansas, Billy." The guitar player was turned around, looking at the drummer. "You're from right outside Ely. Everybody knows that 'cause you keep tellin' 'em Ely's more superior than the lake across the road from where we're standin'. Besides, it's well-known your mother used to look the other way when your daddy'd introduce you as his son."

The crowd roared and applauded. They'd heard the same routine before, but it didn't matter.

"Well, hell, then, Alpine, Texas!" Jack shouted.

The drummer hit another rim shot.

"Foreign countries don't count," said the guitar player, and the crowd laughed.

"Anybody here beat Alpine, Texas? . . . Goin' once, twice . . . Come on up here, Tex, and get your prize."

Linda gave Jack a little push. He handed his beer to her and climbed on the stage, looking tall and lean beside the short guitarist.

"Say somethin' to the local folks, Tex."

"Howdy, local-folks-from-way-up-here-in-the frozen-north. Last time it got as cold in southwest Texas as it is outside here tonight was when the melt from a previous ice age ran downhill from your place here. And it ain't even serious winter yet. I can see why you don't run cattle up here; they'd walk themselves into nothin' just tryin' to keep warm and you wouldn't be able to see 'em if they's turned end-on to you."

The crowd hooted good-naturedly. Someone shouted, "Looks like that little lady you been dancin' with is keepin' you warm."

Jack looked down at his shirt that was sticking to him and pulled it away from his chest with a thumb and forefinger. "I'm afraid she'll not be comin' close to me anymore tonight," he said.

The guitarist jumped in. "I think we oughta bring up Mr. Tex's lady and let her give 'im the prize, whaddya think?" More applause and yelling.

The guitar player helped Linda onto the stage while a few wolf whistles came from the bar area. She stood there blushing a little, clutching the necks of her two beer bottles in her left hand.

Jack bent over and whispered to her, "Got your tassels along? We could create endurin' legends here tonight."

"Where you from, ma'am?"

"Originally from Altoona, Iowa," Linda said softly into the microphone the guitar player had tipped toward her. Dancing all but naked was one thing, talking to a crowd of people was a lot harder.

"Iowa?" the guitarist said, and the crowd booed. "That's known up here as the gateway to Nebraska, but we'll let you stick around just for tonight. Now ol' Gordy here's got a present for Tex, and we're goin' to let you give it to him."

The bass player had been hiding the beanie with a propeller on top of it behind his back. He handed it to Linda. She laughed and placed it on Jack's head, then spun the little propeller while everyone in the place applauded. She leaned back, smiling, and looked up at him. And . . .

always . . . always . . .

she'd remember Texas Jack Carmine standing there with his long brown hair turning gray and brown eyes and suntanned face with serious lines cutting into it, grinning and looking silly as the propeller turned.

"That's so you'll have a way of getting back home if things go bad," the guitar player said.

Jack recovered his style, took a beer from Linda, and held it high, shouting over the microphone: "*Somos pocos, pero estamos locos*—We are few, but we are crazy!" The crowd roared as Jack waved and stepped down from the stage, still grinning. He took hold of Linda's hips and swung her down beside him while the Rusty Cadillacs rolled into an old Hank Snow tune, "I'm Movin' On."

That big eight-wheeler movin'
  down the track
Means you're true-lovin' daddy
  ain't comin' back . . .

Jack and Linda took off dancing, her reaching up now
and then to spin Jack's propeller. The conifers swayed
outside, the big lake where the ore boats went was cold
and getting rougher, and Texas Jack Carmine danced
with Linda Lobo while winter started moving south out
of Canada toward Grand Marais, Minnesota.

Linda drove them back to the motel. Jack had tossed
her the keys when they left the Harbor Light, saying,
"If you don't mind drivin', I'd appreciate it. I may be
crazy, but I ain't foolish, and I'm just about one too
many tokes over the line for safety's sake. Get stopped
and some trooper'd see this new hat of mine, sayin',
'Well, ain't that a cute thing,' then make me stand on
one leg with my eyes closed and count backwards from
ten. After that it'd be twenty years of hard labor fillin'
up all the big holes left by ore minin' over around
Hibbing."

She put on her glasses and took the Chevy south
along the shore, through a light rain that caught them
ten minutes out of Grand Marais. The oncoming truck
lights were bright and hard in her eyes, so she kept it
slow and rode the right side of the pavement. The
radio was turned down low, Jack monkeying with the
dial.

"Sometimes you can get XERF, Del Rio, Texas, all
the way up here, if the planets are just right. Not tonight, I guess." He leaned back and lit a cigarette, listening to the swish of tires on wet concrete, looking out
the side window at the wall of dark forest moving by.

"Not tonight, I guess," he said again, speaking to the forest and nobody else in particular, talking kind of sadlike and quiet as if pulling in a border radio station would have filled in the last word of an unfinished song he couldn't quite remember. He reached up and spun the propeller on the beanie he was still wearing. The propeller slowed down, and just as it stopped, he whispered, "Take it away, Leon . . . for chrissake."

"What'd you say?" Linda asked.

"Nothin'. Mumblin' about how the northern lights interfere with gettin' Texas radio stations."

> In the forest, then,
> Or the window reflection,
> As always:
>> suddenly.
> As always:
>> unexpectedly.
> . . . babies
> On the wire,
>> Concertina wire,
>> Razor wire.
> And a *thuk, thuk* of
> Turning rotor blades,
> And turbine engine roar
> And the same in your head.
> And twisting, then,
> And turning,
> Coming in low
> Through the smoke—
>> Jack Carmine's old stories,
>> The chop–chop chronicles,
>>> His .50-caliber tales.

Jack Carmine didn't say anything more. Neither did Linda Lobo as she bent over the wheel and drove the pickup south through the cold rain of a Minnesota autumn, toward a room with one shoeshine cloth that couldn't make any headway on old boots, but had a nice balcony overlooking the water.

CHAPTER TWO

New Orleans, October 27, 1993

And what would it be like then to lie with a woman as black and far-off strange as this one? She was sitting two tables over in the Cafe Beignet. Vaughn Rhomer drank the first espresso of his life and tried not to be too obvious in the way he looked at her. Still he looked. And he imagined. Naked and spread-eagle wide on ivory silk, she would be the eleventh Rorschach, though finely etched. A figure of steaming skin and coursing blood in the X position. Until she began to move under your touch, that is. Until she began to slowly twist and turn and rise toward you like the night itself, some long and forever night from which you could never escape even if you wanted to. A woman such as this one could snuff the light and take you into darkness.

The light early on, darkness later. Vaughn Rhomer was ready for some darkness. He'd seen enough light in his years to last a thousand lifetimes. Back in Iowa the Rotary was light. So was the First Lutheran Church. The VFW? . . . He wasn't sure, tinged with gray but belonging in the same general category as Rotary and church. Earlier this same evening he'd visited Marie Laveau's House of Voodoo and counseled with Miss Blanche, who was holding down the psychic's chair. They'd sat in a stuffy little room behind the shelves of potions and charms, talking above the roar of a window air conditioner, talking about darkness and the good things it carries. New Orleans understands darkness.

So did Thomas Martin, consummate traveler, rider of the far places. On page 148 of *Journeys, Vol. II* (London: Empire Publishing Ltd., 1932), he continued thusly:

> *In the Caverns of Rokay there is no light. There is life, however, tentative life: blind fish, a colony of bats, and rustling evidence of something I cannot identify by the sound. But no light. This is a place deep in the Earth's heart where no man should ever willingly go, and each second I wonder why I have come. There is the low growl of something here, inaudible, but here nonetheless—Earth itself speaking. And the words of Earth, they are couched within the growl, and the words say, "Go back, stranger. Go back, Thomas Martin, go back to the light where humans are meant to live." Even so, the rumors of treasure persist, diamonds or spilling handfuls of something unthinkably better, cached here by the wandering La-Koos-Koos when their accumulations became too heavy for the daily portages of their lives. Somewhere below me I hear the sound of falling water, though the sputtering candle on my helmet has not found it yet. I am afraid, yet I cannot turn back and*

remain the man I am. And so the press is on-
ward, farther down I go and farther yet. . . .

Fine and fair were the traveler's words, so thought
Vaughn Rhomer, and worth remembering. Six years
back, in a hand that was practiced and pure, he'd set
down those words of Thomas Martin exactly as Thomas
Martin had written them. One should be true to things
of worth as they originally had come, and only in that
way do they survive the punishment of modern times.
Vaughn Rhomer believed that. So the passage was cop-
ied into a spiral notebook, with neatness and fidelity,
with lingering concern for the placement of each letter
and comma. Originally he'd considered using three-ring
binders for his notes but decided on spiral notebooks
after concluding things have a natural order of occur-
rence that should not be tampered with.

After the writing, repetition. In the winter nights of
Iowa, Vaughn Rhomer traced his finger down the notebook pages—word and word, line and line—until he
had tooled that passage and others into his memory.
Out loud he said the words, giving them the kind of
turn he imagined Thomas Martin would have used in
the saying of them: "There is life, however, tentative
life . . . tentative life . . . tentative life."

He tapped the middle three fingers of his right hand
on the marble tabletop and looked at the black woman
again. The weather in New Orleans was warm for late
October, a humid eighty-three at six o'clock in the evening, and the Cafe Beignet sat open to the streets around
it. Mardi Gras and other spring celebrations were way
out in front. Vaughn Rhomer had arranged his visit that
way, avoiding loud parades with people vomiting on
your shoes and doing unspeakable things to one another

on Bourbon Street. There was a time, he supposed, when it had been different, when Mardi Gras had been brushed with a gloss of stylish decadence that made it sensually intriguing. Now, as with almost everything else in America, decadence had been heightened and taken to extremes, style abandoned.

"Extremes lead to extinction, the middle borders are where truth lies," so said T.H.K. Masters in his classic essay on the subject. Vaughn Rhomer had memorized that line, too. It was in the fourth of his spiral notebooks, third page from the beginning.

On the sidewalk outside the cafe, Ariendo Vincent played alto saxophone. Played it solo while the black woman listened intently, nodding and smiling in the way of remembrance when he rolled into "Stars Fell on Alabama." Ariendo Vincent took it slow, gave it a texture that was round but never fat, sometimes staying true to the melody and sometimes only licking at it.

Vaughn Rhomer knew the song. Art Whalen's Rhythm Kings had played it at the Friday night fish frys before the VFW switched over to booking country bands. He let the words turn over in his mind: "We lived our little drama, we kissed in a field of white . . ." He and Marjorie had danced to the song in their dancing days, their yesterdays, olden days.

The black woman raised her right hand and signaled to a waiter. Vaughn Rhomer panicked, believing for a moment she was asking for her check. But as the waiter approached she casually bent her wrist and pointed toward the empty brandy glass on the table before her. The large white sapphire on her index finger might have come from the Caverns of Rokay, Vaughn Rhomer thought. Thomas Martin could have carried it out and sold it to a gem merchant in London, where it could have been purchased by a wealthy tourist who had it mounted and later died and left it to a niece, who possibly came upon hard times and sold it yet again, until the black woman found it in one of the pricey antique shops along Royal Street.

"Another, if you please." She smiled at the waiter as she spoke, and the sound of her voice was like the curl of woodsmoke on a rainy night in deep autumn.

Her skin was smooth and pure, her blackness even deeper than Ariendo Vincent's, running straight and true out of Olduvai, with no dilution along the way from Arab slavers or plantation men who strolled down from the big house on summer evenings. Yet her facial structure belied that initial judgment; there was a hint of something in the nose and lips. Caucasian, maybe. Possibly from a Creole gentleman who had met her mother's great-grandmother on a Sunday afternoon in Congo Square, just north of the French Quarter. More likely, though, something farther back, a ship's captain, perhaps. Rhomer knew she would taste and smell of Africa and chains and long marches to misery ships that sailed for de land of cotton when old times past were still in progress.

Ariendo Vincent moved into a Duke Ellington song. Vaughn Rhomer knew it by melody, not by name. It was a good song, better than what was playing in the car going by on Decatur, the street to his left. The car's windows were rolled up, but Vaughn Rhomer could hear the thump of a powerful stereo system inside. The evening he'd first descended with Thomas Martin into the Caverns of Rokay, an identical sound had been coming from his son's room two floors above in the house on Trolley Car Boulevard. *Bum, bum, bum . . . bum, bum*— a *bum* a *bum*— Vaughn Rhomer had felt the bass more than heard it. The lowest notes caused a loose fitting on the basement heating ducts to jingle. He'd known without inquiring what the album cover lying on Nathan's bed would look like: satanic, half-clothed men clawing at strange-looking guitars and biting the heads off wrens or wrapping barbed wire around tormented women trying to escape. Maybe something even worse, whatever that could be.

On that night six years ago, a year to the day after nephew Jack had passed through with a woman named Linda, Vaughn Rhomer had put down his notebook and glanced at his genuine military watch (water-resistant to twenty fathoms) lying on the table before him. It was late in the dark of an Iowa autumn, past 2300 hours, 11:18 civilian time. Tomorrow was a workday, but his custom was to catch the opening summary of the BBC's morning news, which would be coming up in twelve minutes. It was good to know the BBC was out there tracking things—the disposition of a king in Thailand, riots in Bombay, striking miners in Russia.

He'd long since given up on Nathan going to bed at any decent hour. "Dad, I'm a senior. No class till nine, and nothing after lunch except optional study hall. I can come home and nap before going to work. No sweat, Dad, ease off."

Right, no sweat, ease off. "I've never eased off, Nathan. How do you think your mother and I are putting two sons through college and supporting another one at home?" Roll of insolent teenage eyes and silence after that. The words of his father were part of a droning litany Nathan endured with something less than forbearance.

At dinner that same evening, Vaughn had said, "Take off your cap at the table, Nathan. We have the heat on, your head won't get cold." More rolling eyes and after that a hostile, pointed look at the bogus old man who ran the produce department at Best Value and was always reminding people who got it wrong that his last name was pronounced with a long *O*. Nathan slowly twirled a spoon on the table and left the red *Chicago Bulls* cap on. He stared at the spoon as if it were a talisman, as if he were making ready for a trancelike state that would lift him high and far into realms distant from the blather enveloping him, into places where people were current with what was obviously good and lasting and meaning-ful, far from outworn tradition and into the contempo-rary world he and his friends inhabited.

"Nathan, your father's right. I don't understand this need for wearing caps all the time. I even see grown men doing it in restaurants. I feel like asking them if they're hiding something up there."

Cap still on, spoon twirling, Nathan glanced with zero-level tolerance at this plump, gray-haired woman named Marjorie who claimed to be his mother.

"Take the goddamned cap *off*, Nathan. *Now!*"

"Vaughn, please don't use bad language," Marjorie said.

Cap off, slapped down on the table, sweat-stained and with a yellow blotch of something on the curled bill. Nathan looked at his plate of vegetables, then at the ceiling. "God, deliver me from fools such as these," he mumbled, thinking he'd heard that somewhere, maybe in English class when he was quasi-somnolent on a spring afternoon. Nathan wasn't a word man, so it didn't matter where he'd heard it. He was going to be an accountant, and accountants didn't need to know about words, only numbers, as Nathan was fond of stating when explaining his miserable grades in English lit.

"What did you say, Nathan?" There was a loud clink

of metal against orange Fiesta ware as Vaughn dropped his fork, put both elbows on the table, and rested his chin on his folded hands.

"I said I'm not hungry. I'm going up to my room."

"Finish your dinner first, Nathan," his mother said.

Nathan pointed the teaspoon at his father, "Just because *he* works in the produce department at Best Value doesn't mean the rest of us love vegetables as much as he does. God, we never have regular food, just vegetables in about every dumb combination you can think of. Plus soybeans and rice and the rest of that monkey food."

"It's not monkey food, Nathan. It's good, healthy food. And remember, your father is *manager* of the produce department, he doesn't just work there. It took him a lot of years to become manager."

"Okay, *manager*, then. So what does that make me, son of Celery Man?"

"Nathan!" his mother said.

At that moment and in many such moments before and after, Vaughn Rhomer had imagined a poisoned dart from a Jhivaro blowgun quivering in Nathan's throat or maybe the handle of a Russian bayonet protruding from just under the boy's rib cage. But he finished chewing his steamed broccoli with marinara sauce and said, "You're right, son, I think you ought to go to your room."

Nathan swept his cap off the table, put it on backward, and went up the stairs in a measured stomp mirroring the pattern and bulk of a silverback gorilla. Ten seconds later the *bum, bum* began. The bass sounded like Nathan's footsteps when he'd gone up the stairs.

Vaughn had helped Marjorie clean up the dishes so she could get to hobby club on time. Thelma Swan had been in charge of the night's program, where they'd made snowmen out of popcorn balls. One of the snowmen had been sitting on the kitchen table when Vaughn Rhomer ate his breakfast the next morning. The raisin eyes seemed focused on his oatmeal.

He'd liked hobby club nights. He'd liked any night Marjorie was gone. That way he didn't feel guilty about spending the entire evening in his room. The room where he kept his gear. The room in the basement of a house on Trolley Car Boulevard. The room where all things were possible. The room—his keep.

He'd built the room in 1981, ten years before the Cafe Beignet. Self-defense had been his motive, dreams had been his goal. At one time his gear had been displayed around the house, where he could see and enjoy it during the everyday movements of his life. But Marjorie complained about his "junk scattered all over" and how much he spent on it, even though he bought almost all of his things at garage sales and auctions or found it on his walks along an abandoned railroad right-of-way near his house. The previous year's expenditures had been less than $300, mostly on used books.

Marjorie was tired of his gear, he was tired of Marjorie's complaining. And the kids never stopped their teasing, their well-honed ridicule, when he was sitting at the kitchen table practicing the ten basic calls of the Royal Navy on his genuine bosun's whistle or looking through his brass telescope at the neighbor's English spaniel, Barney.

"Going out for a trip to the Pillars of Hercules this weekend, Dad?"

"What's the commie situation out there on the boulevard, Colonel Rhomer?"

"Hey, Dad, tell us again how to find water in the desert."

Vaughn Rhomer had grinned and endured the harassment for a long time, then finally said to hell with 'em all and had built what Marjorie and her friends called "Rhomer's Room" in the northwest corner of the basement, behind the furnace. He'd laid down two-by-fours and bolted them to the cement floor. From those he'd run more two-by-fours to the ceiling as framing studs. Knot-free #1 pine covered the exterior and interior walls of the room, with fiberglass insulation jammed in the wall cavity for heat retention and sound control. Inside, the north and west walls were floor-to-ceiling bookcases. Along the east wall, to the right of the door as you entered, were oak-veneer, two-drawer filing cabinets stacked three high.

The eight-by-twelve room had two lights. One was an overhead bulb hanging from the ceiling by a black cord, with an eighteen-inch green metal shade in the shape of a coolie's hat covering the bulb. The other light was designed for reading, an old gooseneck floor lamp with a shade that was yellowed and fringed in red. The only table was round and four feet in diameter, covered with green felt. The only place to sit was a forty-year-old wooden desk chair with a slatted back. It rocked on metal springs and had a small pillow on the seat.

The combination to the room's lock was 2 left, 9 right, 19 left—the date when Thomas Martin first discovered the true headwaters of the Varagunzi River. Nobody could ever forget that. Marjorie, the children, and the cat, Razberry Rhomer, were all curious about the room in varying degrees, but only Vaughn knew the combination. Sometimes he let Razberry in when she scratched at the door after everyone else had gone to bed. Razberry never made fun of him. She just lay on the green felt, tending to herself at first, then sleepy-eyed and purring afterward, while Vaughn read or sorted his gear and sometimes absently reached out to pet her.

He could spin the lock and enter another world. A world of ancient thoughts and distant drums. A world of firelight and fast guitars and gypsy-sad music played near the wheels of painted wagons that would roll at dawn. A world of dust in your face and rain on your hat and ships beating their way around the Horn, where icebergs floated, where sleeting winds in the Drake Passage could drive a good man blind and a good ship backward. A world of

One French paratrooper's rucksack containing bottles of quinine and water-purification tablets, a rain poncho, and canvas pistol belt, among other things.

One black-powder rifle.

One N-1 U.S. Navy foul-weather deck helmet.

All six volumes of The Journals of Thomas Martin *(being the complete chronicles of Martin's legendary travels in the late nineteenth and early twentieth centuries).*

One kerosene lantern, circa 1925, filled and ready to light.

One jungle hammock.

One replica of a battle sword from the armies of Genghis Khan.

The complete works of H. Rider Haggard.

One signal mirror.

An old World Traveler radio wired to an aerial stretching from the roof to a tree a hundred feet out in the backyard.

One two-quart canteen with a red-and-gray blanket cover from the Spanish-American War.

Two mosquito head nets (he'd only wanted one, but the catalog sold them in pairs).

One pilot's survival knife with sawtooth edge and sharpening stone.

A reasonable collection of Rudyard Kipling.

Two hollowed-out pineapple hand grenades.

One machete in a brown leather scabbard.

One compass in a metal case, including induction damped needle swing plus degree and millimeter scale. On the side of the case was a straight edge calibrated in centimeters.

One pair of military-issue, speed-lace boots with nonslip lug soles, plus one pair of ultralight-weight boots with padded suede collars and steel shanks, advertised as being ideal for correctional facility workers and SWAT teams.

Two bandoliers, each containing fifty rounds of dummy ammunition.

One copy of The Standard English-Swahili Dictionary.

One Israeli gas mask offering excellent face, eye, and respiratory tract protection against all riot control gases.

One GI field pack issued to Vaughn Rhomer during his Korean War days. (He'd enlisted, hoping for an overseas assignment, but had spent his entire tour of duty as a cook at Fort Leonard Wood, Missouri.)

Twenty-three years of National Geographic, carefully disassembled, clipped, and filed. A local librarian had given him hints on cross-referencing, with particular emphasis on gaining quick access to his favorite world-class photographers, such as Robert Kincaid and Jeremiah Slocum.

And more. There was a lot more stashed in wooden peach crates and vintage detonator boxes left behind by the British army in the Verdun campaign of World War I. If you were going to go out there, equipment was important. You had to be ready. Vaughn Rhomer was ready.

The south wall of the room was his display area, a place for the things he liked to see every night. Such as the print of a voluptuous Mexican woman in a red skirt and blue off-the-shoulder blouse, dark hair blowing. She sat with a rifle between her legs and a guitar leaning against the adobe wall beside her, looking dead straight at him, ripe in the mouth and full unafraid. He'd found the print at a garage sale over on Oak Park Lane and bought it for fifty cents. It was spotted in two places with what looked like green liquid of some kind and torn at the corners, but he could make out the signature of somebody named Marta Gilbert and the word *Bandida*. The print led him to Alonzo Patterson's *History of the Border Wars* (El Paso: A. G. Witherspoon Publishers, 1937). On page 148 Patterson quotes one Howard Mims:

We were more afraid of the women than the men. They were absolutely ruthless, shooting and laughing as they held up the genitals of the

*men they killed. One of our comrades who had
been taken prisoner and subsequently escaped
told of a beautiful woman who danced in front
of a thousand men, wearing only twin bandoliers
crossed between her substantial breasts and nothing else on her body. She held a bottle of tequila
in one hand and a carbine in the other and pro-
ceeded to make love to the rifle in front of the
entire gathering. It drove the men wild, and they
ran toward her, lifted her up, and carried her
shining body around and around the fire and
finally into the darkness, where I could no longer
see what happened due to the inadequacy of my
viewpoint from where I was held captive in a
crude stockade.*

Vaughn Rhomer longed to have been there. In the
stockade or carrying the woman, it wouldn't have mattered. Just being there would have been enough. And
to have fought beside a woman named "Bandida" in
the border wars and, even more, to have loved her in
Chihuahuan nights when the fighting was done . . . for
that, he would have cut any deal with any satanic presence happening by. He'd accidentally left the book on
the kitchen table once, open to the scene with the woman
dancing. Nathan had found it and yelled, "Hey, Mom,
Dad's reading pornography." And Vaughn Rhomer had
called up again the maxim that got him through those
moments: Life is never easy for those who dream.

Next to Bandida hung a *tronchete*, a mean-looking
Mexican version of a jackknife with the curved blade
folding into a yellow-white bone handle. It was in a
boxful of junk Vaughn Rhomer had bought in 1985
when they auctioned off ol' man Kaplan's stuff over on

Fourth Street. At the auction someone had said Kaplan was something of an eccentric. Vaughn Rhomer wished he'd known him. Anyone who lived on Fourth Street in Otter Falls and owned a *tronchete* would have been worth knowing. Vaughn Rhomer had never seen such a knife, but he'd discovered the name and a photo of one in his copy of *Knives Around the World*.

Near the *tronchete* was a pair of old spurs. And next to the spurs was a gray, rotted board with a latch fastened to it. Vaughn Rhomer had found the board out behind the house. It apparently had lain there for years in high weeds, ever since the two-story white house with a forty-five-degree roof and dormers on both sides had been built in 1961. He'd asked around and discovered the house sat on what used to be a meadow where horses ran. The spurs and board fit with one another in some hazy way. Something to do with contradictions, with men pushing horses to run, then boxing them in with fences so they couldn't run at all. Something to do with the way Vaughn Rhomer felt inside himself, gut-level instincts spurring him on while the barriers of convention held him fast. Sometimes he'd step over to the board and fiddle with the rusty latch, making sure it still opened.

And fiddling, and thinking, Vaughn Rhomer would look over at the picture of Jack Carmine in full battle dress with a bush hat raked on his head, hoping things were going well for him wherever he was. Nephew Jack, who'd broken all the latches that had ever got in his way. Jack Carmine, who knew how to live sweet and free in the years given to him, in the years going by that would never come again. When Vaughn Rhomer changed the display on his south wall from time to time, the picture of Jack stayed where it was, near the latch and board. And the letters Jack had written from Asian jungles, those were kept in a file and read once a year, on the Fourth of July. Jack Carmine, son of Vaughn Rhomer's older sister, Lorraine. *Texas* Jack Carmine, God's only free-born soul, rider of the summer roads, traveler of the far places.

CHAPTER THREE

Northern Minnesota, 1986

On his forty-seventh birthday, seven years before
Vaughn Rhomer would sit in a New Orleans cafe and
long for darkness, Jack Carmine awakened just after first
light and looked at Linda Lobo sleeping beside him. Her
hair fanned out promiscuously on her pillow and the
sheet around it. Outside, the wind was up, blowing cold
rain against the windows. Linda had wanted the drapes
left open so she could see the lake from their bed.

Jack rolled over and looked out, glad the last section
of gas pipe had been laid two days ago. He'd worked
in this kind of weather before, those times when winter
came early, and he didn't like it—the cold, the mud.
He lay there and remembered nine years ago when he'd
rolled north with a custom wheat-harvesting crew,
hammering a combine all those months, all the way
from Texas to Weyburn, Saskatchewan. Thirty miles
below the Canadian border the sky had turned cobalt
blue, stayed that way for almost a week, then gone to
black gray. It had begun snowing when they were half-

way through the final job. He'd pulled on an old leather vest lined with sheepskin and a mackinaw over that, pushing the big orange machine hard, running through snow that was picking up in intensity minute by minute.

The rancher had been out of his mind with worry, and the crew boss had shouted over the CB, "Wiley, Bobby, Jack—keep goin'. *Push* those sonuvabitchin' combines; we're cuttin' all night."

Jack had listened to the crew boss, tugged down his black ball cap with the *Cat* logo on it, and gritted his teeth. It had been an ethereal, dreamlike world out there in his headlights: blowing snow on yellow grain, Wiley Hobbs behind him on the left, Bobby McGregor up ahead on the right. That night Jack Carmine had knocked down more grain than he'd harvested, worried all the while about getting off the cut and ramming one of the other combines.

The big machine had rumbled beneath him, grain trucks pulling alongside and emptying his hoppers. They'd kept on going through the night. The crew boss had come on the CB every so often and yelled, "Punch her home, boys. We're headin' for Texas after this."

Hour after hour in the dark, white snow blowing and yellow wheat blending, radio playing music and every thirty minutes announcers saying things in the Middle East were a mess and Guy Lombardo had died. At dawn they'd towed the combines out of the mud and loaded them on lowboy trailers, three hundred uncut acres still out there buried in drifting snow.

Now Jack Carmine was lying quiet in a motel by the Onion River and studying the back of Linda Lobo's neck. That's another thing he'd always liked, the way a woman's neck looks when long hair is swept away from it, with only a strand or two still lying on the skin. Jack Carmine's Eighth Conjecture: Slightly flawed perfection, in the context of long hair swept away from a woman's neck, has a peculiar force of its own.

But he had to make water and deferred his studies while he slid quietly out of bed and headed for the bathroom. Jack had an exceptional resistance to hangovers, and aside from his bladder needing relief and his mouth needing a toothbrush, he was in good shape. "Bad sign," Bobby McGregor once told him. "People who don't get hung over are more likely to become alcoholics. Heard that somewhere." Jack and Bobby had been heading west, out through the high plains on their way to California to scout around for work in an airplane factory or something along those lines. That was eight years ago, and their exact mission at that time escaped Bobby later on. But it had something to do with building airplanes; he'd always been pretty sure of that.

When Bobby had mentioned the hangover issue, Jack had grinned and said, "We ought to drink to that bit of knowledge, Bobby McGregor. I'm always in favor of learnin' new ideas, 'long as they don't interfere with the way I already view things."

Just then the old Coupe de Ville's hood ornament had pointed them down the main street of a town named Salamander. They'd gone into a place called Leroy's, where Jack had three beers in exactly thirty-eight minutes. Bobby had timed him. Somewhere back down the line they'd seen a billboard, MEXICO CALLS TO YOU. Why it was there, way out in the middle of nothing, Bobby never quite figured out. His guess was Jack's demon had placed it there for Jack to see, a way of diverting him one more time from the task at hand. Jack had started talking about going to Mexico after that.

He'd pulled a silver dollar from his jeans and said,

"Heads, we go to Mexico and tease the señoritas, Bobby. Tails, we go to California and work our asses off."

Bobby never forgot it. The silver dollar spun around, bounced twice on Leroy's bar, came up on its edge, and went into a lazy wobble before staying there. In the world of Jack Carmine, that was some kind of omen one would ignore only at considerable risk.

"I think it's talkin' to us, Bobby. It's sayin' the choice is ours and is not to be decided by any piece of crap metal from the U.S. official government. Me, I'm sayin' Mexico."

"Jack, I'm out of money, got to work," Bobby said.

Jack pulled out his wallet and riffled through the bills in there. "I got three hundred eighty-two dollars, Bobby. Two hundred of 'em are yours to do with as you wish."

"Jack, that's just about gas and meal money to Bakersfield."

"Fair enough. Let me off at the first south-runnin' highway we come to. You take the car and go to Bakersfield; I'm headin' for Mexico."

Bobby tried to talk him out of it. But Jack had Mexico on the brain by that time. He insisted Bobby take the two hundred dollars, and three hours later Bobby let him out at Cheyenne where Route 85 went south.

He was carrying an old duffel bag from his military days, tossed it over his shoulder, and said, "I'll send you a Polaroid picture of me and half a dozen dark-eyed nubiles. That'll take care of Bakersfield, and you'll be on the first conveyance south."

Jack never sent the picture.

The rain of late October sounded like an automatic weapon on the sliding glass door when Jack came out of the bathroom, almost bumping into Linda Lobo. She gave him a little wave, mumbled, "Uhh," and went into the bathroom. He heard the toilet flush and the water come on. She was in there some amount of time.

She came out wearing only her oversize black turtle-neck sweater, which reached down just far enough to cover what needed covering, though the margin for error was slim. She looked around. No Jack.

Two minutes later she heard his boot quietly tapping the outside door. When she opened it, he was standing there in his jeans and leather jacket, no shirt and no hat, Styrofoam cups in his hands. Rain dripped from his shoulders and hair, steam rose from the cups.

"Coffee, dancin' lady? Couldn't remember if you used condiments, so I brought some."

He tossed creamer and sugar packets on the table, grabbed a towel from the bathroom, and ran it over his wet hair.

"Just what I needed," she said. "I take it straight, but thanks anyway for covering the possibilities. It's not a happy body this mornin', think we could use a little heat in here?"

She leaned against the window frame, watching Lake Superior getting itself more and more worked up. The water was colored dark green running to black.

Jack squinted at the wall-mounted thermostat, adjusting tiny levers, and mumbling, "Heat up, fan on, maximum comfort ahead . . . town in Texas called Comfort"—he was still examining the thermostat—"just down the road from another called Welfare. I always thought that sounded like a good region in which to retire, if the town names are at all indicative of the climate and attitude."

"You don't seem the retirin' type to me, Jack." She was still staring at the lake.

"That's true. Never be able to afford to retire anyway.

I'll probably die with my boots on, running off the cut on a big orange combine or in some damn gas pipe trench somewhere, probably on a day like this. Die standing straight up and have a cheap burial . . . let the mud just kind of suck me down all the while some crew boss's yellin', 'Point your toes!' and poundin' on my head with a scrap of pipe.''

Linda laughed softly at the image Jack painted. She looked around at his feet. "Speaking of boots, how come you don't wear cowboy boots? I thought all you Texans wore 'em.''

"Well, them high-heeled ones like you wear are only good for three things when it comes down to it: ridin', diggin' your heels in corral dirt, or hoppin' around when you're feeling hot and got your Saturday night clothes on. Hate to destroy all the myths and legends, but one of the last real cowboys I know, guy named Sam, wears old tennis shoes most of the time when he's workin' stock. I got some good boots of the type you're talkin' about, custom-mades, only they're livin' in Alpine, Texas, right now. Earl and Hummer are down there keepin' an eye on 'em so they don't go out when I'm not in 'em. That's why I couldn't dance up to perfection last night, didn't have the correct boots on.''

"Earl . . . and who?''

"Earl and Hummer. Earl's a Mexiroon, 'least that's what he calls himself—three-quarters Mex, a quarter Anglo. Looks after my place while I'm gone. Hummer's the dog, sort of your basic yellow brown and lookin' like he crawled up from Chihuahua after a bad night. Hell of a cattle dog, though. Don't know which one's older, Earl or Hummer. Even-up tie, I'd say.''

Linda took a sip of her coffee, brown eyes looking at him over the edge of her cup. "Why's the dog called Hummer?''

" 'Cause whenever someone gets ready to go some-where—to town or the moon, doesn't matter—he lies flat by the door and puts his head on his paws, makes kind of a sad, hummin' sound. Always has done that, so we call him by the noise he makes. He seems to like his name well enough, though nobody's asked his opinion about anything for some time, come to think of it."

Jack turned on the television to the Weather Channel, then went over and stood beside Linda, both of them holding Styrofoam cups in their right hand. She switched hers to the other hand and put her right arm around Jack's waist, hooking her thumb in one of his belt loops. He looked out at the rain, touching the back of her head, stroking her hair. Jack Carmine's Seventh Conjecture: Stroking a woman's hair while looking out at a rainy day is 92 percent of as good as it gets.

She studied the side of his face. Jack Carmine—fast on his feet, light with his words. Something else, though, behind the quick grin. Something he wasn't talking about. . . .

Something dark back down the road.
Or: Still up ahead.
Or: None of that.
Or: All of it.

When he got his face in a certain way and looked out windows, Jack Carmine struck her as some kind of old brown and crinkled envelope, licked and sealed, things inside. Dangerous things, maybe, if the envelope came unglued. It made her a little uneasy.

Last night, after they'd returned from Grand Marais, he'd stood looking out that same sliding door. Linda had lain in bed, watching him, exhausted from lack of sleep and hard traveling. He hadn't made any move toward her or even touched her at all except for the dancing, but she'd have taken him in if he'd wanted. She'd felt like it, in a way—the night, the dancing. She'd have taken him in as some kind of finish to a nice evening if nothing else, as she'd done before with other men. But it would have been more than that. She liked Jack Carmine from Alpine. He was good to her, seemed respectful, and that was different, a man being good to her, and respectful.

Fatigue had caught her, though, and when she'd lulled off to the place where sleep was about to come, she'd heard the sliding door open and raised up on one elbow. The lights were off in the room, but she could see his figure out on the balcony. He'd been standing there, naked. Standing there in the cold rain and hard wind, head bowed. That had scared her, the feral quality of a man doing that, and if she hadn't been so tired, she might have made a run for it. But she chalked it up to the kinds of demons she herself understood, and had gone to sleep.

Jack took a sip of coffee and looked down at her looking up at him. He smiled and tightened his hand around her hair. "Hell of a mess out there," he said, turning back to the lake.

After a cruise-line commercial promising sun and more food than could be eaten in a lifetime, the announcer came back on with the Five Day Business Planner, promising dire consequences for anyone stupid enough to be living north of Iowa.

> You folks up in northern Minnesota better get out your shovels and mittens. Up to twelve inches of snow—the first major storm of the season—is heading your way. That'll be followed by a bitter cold, arctic air mass and high winds. Look for chill factors down to thirty

below by Sunday. The snow is expected to start later this morning along the Canadian border and move rapidly south throughout the day.

Jack canted his head toward her, half grinning. "Well, Miss Linda, I think it's time for Texas Jack to be makin' a dash for home like an old tomcat when the garage door's comin' down and the dogs are runnin'. I'm extendin' the invitation again: Want to gather up your possibles and come along? Texas first, maybe head on down to Mexico and lie on the beaches after a while."

"Things've been movin' pretty fast in the last thirty hours for a country girl. I'm still tryin' to get a handle on it. You really serious . . . about me comin' along?"

"Yep. Dead serious. I ain't known for bein' overly polite and coyotin' around the rim of things."

He turned toward her, gave her a solemn, kind of wistful look she'd see again in times to come. "I'll cut the deck a little deeper and just say I'd like it very much if you'd come with me. The place in Alpine ain't much, a little one-horse spread, but it's real pretty there in a spare kind of fashion and a whole lot warmer than it's going to be up here. I think you'd like it. However, if you've got something or somebody keepin' you in the north country, I could make sense of that. Wouldn't care much for it and be somewhat disappointed, but it'd be understandable. Got no claim on you, anyway."

She walked to the bed and sat on it, knees together, cup clutched in both hands and looking down at it.

"You need to know some things, first. We'd have to stop in Altoona and . . ." She paused, looked up at him.

Jack moved in, grinning. "No problem. Gotta say hello to my uncle Vaughn Rhomer in Iowa, anyway. Just for a few minutes. Des Moines is south of where he lives, right? And you said Altoona was next to Des Moines, ain't that right?"

"Jack . . ." Linda Lobo stared down at her cup. "Alpine, Texas, sounds pretty good. But here's the deal, straight out: I've got a three-year-old daughter livin' with my mother in Altoona. She'd have to come along . . . Sara Margaret, not my mother."

Jack was thinking, serious at first, then grinning again. "Well, Jesus *Key*-rist . . . well, so what? Never figured on a baby, but what the hell. Got a pickup out there'll carry babies, diaper pails, playpens, and a lifetime supply of them plastic things babies suck on. Your mother can come, too, but she'll have to ride in back with the diaper pails. Either that or she can drive while I ride in back with a bottle of Wild Turkey and one of those plastic things rammed between my teeth."

Linda flopped back on the bed, looked at the sparkly ceiling, laughing. Her sweater pulled up to just below her belly button, but she paid no attention to it and laughed harder. Jack paid some attention.

"Jack Carmine," she said, talking to the ceiling, "you've got no idea about children—Sara Margaret's pretty well past all that baby stuff. And you've also got no idea what you and Earl and Hummer are in for. Sounds like a bunch of good ol' boys hidin' low out there in Alpine, and now you're goin' to be seein' female things on the clothesline and little hands foolin' around with mashed potatoes at the supper table."

Jack flipped his empty coffee cup behind his back. It hit the side of the wastebasket and bounced to the floor.

"Earl and Hummer ain't no problem. They're livin' like a couple of buck nuns down in the high desert, been so long since they seen a woman or a girl-child, they'll think you're both something drifted down from Pluto or whatever. Even if they don't like it, I'll beat on Earl and Earl'll beat on Hummer till we get the chain of command back in order."

She sat up and smiled at him. He looked out at the wet. "In any case, we oughta get fixed for high ridin'," he said, tilting his head toward the rain and the lake, wind blowing harder. "Two more degrees downward and that shit's goin' to turn into ice, turn the road into one long skatin' rink all the way south. The pickup ain't real good on ice, too light in the rear, kinda like me."

Twenty minutes later they were headed south, both of them singing along with the Marshall Tucker Band:

> It ain't gonna be the first time
> This ol' cowboy's spent the night alone . . .

Forty miles down the road at Castle Danger, a sign screeched BEST CINNAMON ROLLS IN THE WORLD.

Jack looked at the sign and shook his head. "Don't believe it, Rainy Carmine makes the best cinnamon rolls in the world, and she ain't workin' up here," he said as he pulled off the highway and stopped in front of the restaurant.

Linda looked over at him. "There's a lot of names I got to get used to—who's Rainy Carmine?"

"Rainy's my mother. Better'n average poker player, world-class maker of cinnamon rolls, when she was cookin', which occurred about every third Wednesday. Good dancer, too. Taught me and my brother to dance after she taught us to play poker. She even tried to teach Earl some dancin', but he wasn't inclined to fast footwork, except when he'd walk in the barn and find a rattlesnake smirkin' at him from behind a wheelbarrow."

Jack turned off the ignition and grinned at Linda Lobo. "Let's run in there and see if all that braggin' about cinnamon rolls has got anything to back it up."

He reached under the seat and pulled out a cap carrying a *Minnesota North Stars* logo. "Here, this'll keep your head dry. Won it shootin' pool out in Fergus Falls, from a guy named Worm. Don't know why they called him that. Didn't want to find out, either."

They jogged through hard rain and hustled in the front door of the restaurant. Jack flapped his leather jacket, shaking water off it, and looked around. It was a Sunday morning crowd, north country people. A few young folks, but mostly old ones. Mostly old men with hands permanently scarred and swollen from a lifetime of abuse in the ore pits.

The kitchen was serving up eggs and sausage, pancakes and potatoes, and the local specialty, boiled whitefish.

"Want breakfast?" Jack asked, looking at what was left of somebody's toast on the oilcloth in front of him, scraping crumbs into his hand and dumping them in the ashtray.

"Nope. Not a breakfast eater, ordinarily," Linda said. "More coffee'll do it for me."

A waitress, wearing jeans and a sweatshirt, carrying a coffeepot, came over. "Good morning," she said.

"Mornin' back." Jack grinned. "Two coffees and one of them unequaled cinnamon rolls the sign outside proclaims. And if it ain't as good as Mrs. Rainy Carmine's, you gotta take the sign down. Okay?"

The waitress smiled. "The cinnamon rolls aren't done yet. Be about another forty-five minutes. Cook had some problem with the oven this morning, first thing."

Jack frowned and pouted. "Way the world's goin', overall—rain on the road and broken bakin' ovens."

"Want me to bring out a roll when they're done?"

"We'll be thinkin' about that. Got to put Minnesota in my rearview mirror before all that snow gets here and forces us to winter in."

The waitress walked over to the next table with her coffeepot, asking about refills. Jack tapped his right boot against a table leg and looked at Linda. Around them was the quiet rattle of coffee cups and conversation. Back in the kitchen, the cook yelled, "Two over easy with sausage and biscuits."

"Like your hat, where'd you get it?" Jack grinned at Linda Lobo.

"I got it from a cowboy who won it shootin' pool with a guy named Worm," Linda said, smiling at him.

"How'd you get it, sweetheart?" Jack was talking out of the side of his mouth, trying out a C-minus imitation of W. C. Fields. He wiped the steam off the window next to him and looked out.

"Can't remember," Linda said. "One of those deals where you wake up in the mornin' with a hat on over a brain that's thinkin', Now where'd this come from?" She took off the cap and looked at the logo. "And you're hopin' it didn't come from some hockey player, 'cause you don't even like hockey, let alone hockey players, last you remembered. How's the weather?"

"Bad and turnin' to worse. We got better things to do than lay around Castle Danger waitin' for cinnamon rolls to get done. Like gettin' down the road and outta here."

"I'm with you, bandit, ready when you are. By the way, happy birthday. I almost forgot."

"So'd I. Thanks. Forty-seven years old and shinin' like the sun, of which there ain't any today . . . bandit?"

"Heard you call yourself that in the restaurant last night. It suits you, somehow. Mind?"

"Nope. Kind of like it, in fact."

Kenny Rogers was singing "Ruby" on one of Jack's road tapes when they went past Knife River: "It wasn't me that started that old crazy Asian war . . ." Just south of there the rain turned to snow mixed with sleet. About every quarter mile the truck fishtailed. Jack hunched forward, fighting the wheel, coming in and out of controlled skids.

"Jesus Christ," he said, tapping the brakes. "Gotta be crazier'n an ax murderer to live up here. Don't even need any diagnosis by psychiatrists—open-and-shut case—you live up here, you're crazy and ought to be put away pronto, with no legal formalities gettin' in the way of it."

Two miles farther on the visibility dropped to a hundred feet, snow blowing around the small world of Jack Carmine and Linda Lobo.

"Jack, I think we oughta think about stoppin' somewhere. This is gettin' pretty bad."

"I'm hell-in-the-neck stubborn about that kind of thing, take on a Mad Max mentality. Keep thinkin' we'll drive out of it, keep seein' that last sixty miles of long, smooth, desert road west of Fort Stockton down to Alpine. Besides, I can't wait to see the look on Earl and Hummer's faces when I pull in with a truckload of baby gear and dancin' ladies. We'll see what it looks like when we hit Duluth. How far to there?"

Linda studied the Minnesota road map. "Not far. Twenty miles, maybe."

"That'll take about two years, way things are goin' at the present," Jack said.

A semi truck blew past them, doing at least fifty in the opposite direction. Bad visibility turned into a whiteout for a few seconds.

Linda looked over her shoulder through the small

window behind her. "I'll bet he's got a sign on the back of that rig sayin' 'I'm a professional driver, call one eight hundred somethin' if you don't like what you see.' "

"Yeah, he keeps drivin' that way, he's goin' to end up bein' a derelict ore boat when he hits those curves by the lake north of here. What'd that sign say we just passed?"

"Fifteen miles to Duluth."

A half hour later Jack pulled into a supermarket parking lot. "Be back in a wink," he said.

He came out of the store pushing a grocery cart loaded with sacks of dog food. Behind him was a boy pushing a second cart loaded with the same kind of sacks. They tossed the sacks into the truck box, snow blowing around them, and Jack slid into the cab, snow on his shoulders and cap.

"Twelve sacks of Purina dog food equals six hundred pounds of weight in the back, reduce the slidin' around. We get stuck, use the dog food for grit under the tires. What we don't use, ol' Hummer'll be eatin' for the rest of his natural life and well into eternity."

"Well, that much is brilliant, Jack Carmine. I'm not sure goin' on in this mess is all that brilliant, however."

"I never been accused of brilliance in anythin'. Besides, ain't a question of brilliance, question of heatin' the axles and gettin' there. Question of snaggin' little Sara Margaret and movin' on to sunnier lands and better things."

They went through a weather curtain just past Moose Lake, snow gone, hard rain again.

"Made it," said Jack. "It's money from home here on out. Give me a little Merle Haggard in the way of celebratin'. There's a wider selection of tapes under the seat in a shoebox."

"Where's your mother now, she still alive?" Linda

was sorting tapes, looking at Jack's scrawl on the labels. She pushed one labeled *Merle* into the tape deck.

"Lives with a guru-type fellow in Taos. They meditate on the moon and howl at the sun. Eat nothin' but vegetables and wear plastic shoes."

Jack lit a cigarette. "After ol' Edward Polynice Carmine died—that was my dad—she pulled out for parts unknown. Couldn't blame her; wasn't easy livin' with Poly."

"Was your dad a rancher?"

"Well, it started out that way and finished different. Poly inherited fifty thousand acres of decent grassland from Grandpa Smyler Carmine. But, see, Poly had gone up to Austin and got himself a law degree. Spent the rest of his life and most of the ranch fightin' one environmental battle or another. Like the time they was goin' to dam up Pinto Creek—only a little trickle of water there anyway—and create some kind of desert spa. Gotta hand it to ol' Poly, though, he fought 'em to a standstill and made enemies out of everyone who thought condominiums and golf courses were to be paid the same respect as the American flag, which included about everybody and still does. Poly's ace in the hole was an old law about water rights in desert arroyos. Anyway, he never did earn much of anythin' from his law practice, so he kept sellin' off pieces of the ranch to finance his private wars."

"Who took care of the ranch while your father was off doin' all that?"

"Rainy and Earl and me. We'd look out every other year or so and see the boundaries closin' in around us like the walls of one of them rooms in a horror movie. Poly sellin' off ten sections here, fifteen sections somewhere else. Got too small eventually to graze any amount of cattle at all, at most a hundred and fifty or so as they ran. Jesus, it came down to real hardscrabble, pinto beans and cactus greens. Rainy went to work in a restaurant in Alpine. I started workin' on the oil rigs up north around Odessa when I was sixteen, tellin' those doin' the hirin' I was older. Earl minded what was left of the ranch while Eddie, my younger brother, practiced his oboe and eventually made somethin' of himself from doin' that."

Jack grinned over at Linda. "Then there was Poly's oil-drillin' scheme. The ranch, what's left of it, is just off the southern edge of the Permian Basin, a hundred and fifty miles below the Odessa-Midland fields. One of Poly's crazy friends, Fine Daley, was a diviner—you know, held a forked stick and claimed to be able to find water. He witched around on the property, telling Poly afterwards there was something black and thick swirlin' underground."

"How'd it work out? Find oil?"

"Nah. Too bad. Poly was down to his last chip, and that hole was his main hope for financial resurrection, his big casino. Said it was goin' to bail us out. We had a party the day drillin' got under way, Poly sayin' words over the spot where the drill was goin' down. Earl stood off to one side with me and Hummer, shakin' his head and sayin', 'This crazy sheeit, Jack, your daddy's barkin' at a knot.' "

Jack Carmine lit a cigarette and cracked the truck window, took out his bandanna, and wiped dust off the tape deck. "You'll see the old derrick when we get ourselves into deep Texas. The family's always called it 'Perry,' which is short for *perezoso*, which is some kind of Spanish for lazy, since it never did do any serious work. Poly ran out of drillin' money long before the bit got down to serious oil-findin' depths. That venture pretty much blew out Poly's candle, died of a heart attack not long after."

Linda Lobo was looking south through the slap of wiper blades. "So it just sits there, the derrick?"

"Yep. Earl and Hummer have developed themselves a ritual over the years. Every day, about noon, they go out there and piss on ol' Perry, both of 'em simultaneously. Kinda their way of sayin' Earl was right all along."

"Too bad about the oil. You Carmines might've had a real Texas kingdom if there'd been any."

"Well, justice takes kind of a waverin' route sometimes. Family tradition has it that we got the land originally through the mischief of one Ben Carmine, who migrated out from Tennessee and engaged in scalp-huntin' for the governor of Chihuahua back in the middle 1800s. Ol' Ben was said to cut quite a figure in his silver-buckled leggin's and moccasins, with a lace mantilla looped around his waist and a somewhat dirty red-and-black serape slung over his shoulder. So it's clear to anyone who's payin' attention that we later Carmines have failed to uphold the sartorial standards originally set by Mr. Ben."

Jack braked for a slow-moving car ahead of them, adjusted the defroster, and went around the car on a straight piece of road, mumbling about Sunday drivers and goddamn cold rain.

"Want to hear the rest of it, the family story?"

"I'm on tiptoes and waitin'."

Jack tugged on his right earlobe and looked over at her. "By the way you said that, I have this feelin' you're not buyin' this handsome tale."

"Well, I want to, but I keep thinkin' it starts off like somethin' I saw late one night on TV."

"Listen here, dancin' lady, what I just told you and what I'm about to tell you is what's left over after Poly sorted out the truth from corral dust when he got serious about our genealogical history. I've never much trusted those lookin' back down their family trees, figurin' they're always tryin' to find they're descended straight from royalty and'll select just the right branches to get them there. But Poly was hardheaded and pretty good at that kind of sortin' when he put himself to the task. Besides, as Poly used to say when he discovered somethin' outrageous back along the bloodlines, it's one of those things that if it ain't true, it ought to be just for purposes of addin' color and entertainment to a somewhat dreary universe. Therefore, you can take it or leave it; me, I take it whole and feel the push of Ben Carmine's genes just about every moment of my wakin' life. Longer you hang around me, more you'll see that, though I recently have drawn the line at scalp huntin'."

A Camaro doing about eighty and driven by a young man barreled past the pickup in a wave of road water. "Don't you just admire the children and the cars their parents provide for 'em?" Jack said, watching the Camaro fishtail down the road in front of them.

Linda Lobo lit a cigarette. "Rave on, Jack Carmine. I'm listenin' and tryin' my best to believe all you're tellin' me."

"All right, I'll do that. Now ol' Ben gave up his scalp-huntin' ways when he married a Mexican widow named Chata Valenzuela. Chata already had a couple of kids from her previous marriage and had inherited a sizable chunk from her husband's estate, which as a woman she couldn't legally hold and needed a husband. She staked Ben to a tradin' post east of Presidio on the Rio Grande, where he swapped liquor and guns to the Indians for horses stolen from Texas settlers. He then sold the livestock to various army posts in and around the area. Had kind of an intricate circle goin': guns to Indians for horses, sell the horses to the cavalry so they could chase the Indians, who was stealin' more horses usin' the guns Ben sold them. When people started catchin' on to his loose doin's and things got too hot for him, he sold out and bought the land where we're headed. That is to say we're headed for what's *left* of Ben Carmine's property after Poly got through with it a hundred or so years later.

"Ben had therefore decided to take up the quiet life, but that didn't work out. Some old enemy from the past, apparently an hombre he cheated in a border land deal, rode up with four amigos and blew hell out of Ben while he was eatin' supper one night, right in front of Chata and the kids."

Jack looked over at Linda Lobo. She was smiling about halfway and shaking her head. "The only trouble I'm havin' with all this is that Iowa seems pretty tame compared to what you're tellin' me. Mostly a history of hardworkin' farmers from Germany and places like that, from what I know."

"Well, Miss Linda, there's Iowa and there's Texas, which ain't like nowhere else anywhere, and it gets even better. See, the widow Valenzuela already had two sons when she married Ben Carmine. Had two more children by him, girl and a boy. Gave all the kids the Carmine surname. A few days beyond when Ben got himself curled up, the boys, who were in their late teens by that time, hauled out and ambushed all five of the hombres who'd shot their father.

"After that, things get a tad hazy as to just who cranked up the basic urges and got the rest of us Car-mines here. Best bet, accordin' to what Poly used to say, is that one of Ben and Chata's boys, Larkin, married a Mexican girl of the line from one of the border cribs. Larkin kicked the other two boys out—one got hung for horse stealin', the other became a high-grass constable and eventually joined up with the Texas Rangers. It ends up with Larkin takin' over the ranch, all the while fatherin' four sons and two daughters, himself.

"From that caboodle came the bandit you're presently travelin' with, so you might say my past is a little checkered, not only in this life, but also back down the bloodlines. Bein' I'm a descendant of scalp hunters, back shooters, and ladies of the night, I always figured that excused my irregular behavior somewhat, sort of a genealogical whitewash for what I am and mostly for what I'm not."

Linda Lobo was shaking her head again, looking over at him.

"So there you are. We originally got the land by the dubious activities of some real practical folks and lost it to Poly's idealism. Like I said earlier, some kind of complicated justice in all that, which I'd sort out if I was into thinkin' hard, which I'm not at the present time and hardly ever am. In all events, I'm just repeatin' what Poly found in his researches, and when Poly put his keen legal mind to a problem, he shook it like a dog shakin' a rabbit skin, got down to the nub of whatever he was after, and looked it straight in the eye till it rolled over and surrendered.

"Rainy had the final word on all this, like she usually did. She's always said that when it came to bein' born, the Carmines were gate crashers, that we got here in spite of nature's undyin' attempts at gradual improvement."

Below Hinkley the rain let up, sky turning silver gray, some promise of watery sun way south of the Chevy's nose. Jack Carmine looked over at Linda Lobo, grin-

ning. "We'll make Otter Falls by evenin'. See little Sara
Margaret tomorrow. Snatch 'er and run like smoke for
the high desert. Hey, look!" He bent forward and
pointed at the sky. "See those Canadas beatin' their way
south? Just like us."

The geese were in a riffling skein off to the right, high
and moving fast.

"They're headed for the ponds of East Texas, dancin'
lady, travelin' by the stars, got some kind of interior
guidance system tellin' them when and how to go, don't
need no goddamned five-day business planner from the
Weather Channel to help 'em out. Always said, if there's
anything at all to this reincarnation thing, I'm comin'
back as a Canada goose named Raymond. Fly point just
one time like that fellow up there, instead of ridin' drag
the way I been doin' my entire life."

Linda Lobo smiled warm at the man descended from
scalp hunters and girls of the line, whose mother wore
plastic shoes and lived with a guru in Taos and used to
bake the best cinnamon rolls in the world every third
Wednesday, whose father fought weary battles for the
land itself and drilled for oil where a diviner said it could
be found, who wanted to be reborn as a goose named
Raymond and fly point through the autumn skies. She
didn't say anything, didn't have to. She just kept smiling
warm at Jack Carmine while he grinned back at her.
He'd look at the highway, then up at the sky, then back
at Linda Lobo, and she'd be smiling at him, and they
kept doing that for a long time down the road.

CHAPTER FOUR

New Orleans, October 27, 1993

Looking back, as he often did during long nights in his basement room, Vaughn Rhomer would grade the days of his living, sorting them like green peppers from a late shipment. A few good ones, some bad ones, and the rest falling into a grayish category most of us would call a decent and productive life. Decent and productive, those days, but nothing anywhere near what they might have been to his way of thinking, nothing like the days and years of nephew Jack Carmine. For Vaughn Rhomer, the quintessential Jack was the one who had passed through Otter Falls years before on an autumn evening, when the north country was battening down the winter hatches. Jack and the woman named Linda, both of them wearing real traveling clothes, had stopped for a little while before heading on to the far places where real travelers went.

Vaughn Rhomer had looked at Linda A-Something that evening years ago and wished he could have a woman such as her just once in his life. Well, something like her, maybe not quite so much woman to start with. That Linda was nice, but she had a world-class sense of carnality about her that said if you were going to ask her to dance, you'd better know what you were doing when the music started. Linda A-Something was territory far too wild for those who had never been out there.

But that was a different Vaughn Rhomer back then. Not the Vaughn Rhomer who sat in a New Orleans cafe seven years later. The new Vaughn Rhomer was evolving, unfolding, and beginning to reach out. He listened as Ariendo Vincent, in sunglasses and red beret, glissandoed upward and ended clean on the highest note his alto saxophone could reach.

"Damn, I got it, I hit it!" he shouted, satisfied and grinning and walking fast off the sidewalk and into the cafe, passing between Vaughn Rhomer and the black woman, waving one arm in celebration. "This is a new horn, and I'm still figuring it out. Be right back, folks, need cigarettes." The woman casually flopped the palm of her left hand upright, letting Ariendo Vincent slap it gently as he went by. As he touched her palm, he said, "How ya doin', Gumbo, been a while."

Gumbo—a name now. Vaughn Rhomer knew about gumbo because he knew about okra. He'd tried stocking okra at the store, but it didn't move well. Iowans didn't eat much okra. He wasn't sure why.

She reached slowly forward then, yellow sleeve moving like sunlight across the porch of a tin-roofed house in the delta lands, and took a thin cigar from a package on the table, holding it in the V formed by the first two fingers of her left hand.

Fingers: long.

Nails: red.

She raised a silver lighter and touched flame to the tip of the cigar.

> *. . . to do it all over, to live again. Be born once more, and do it differently. All of it. Not settle next time for less than what could have been. Not suffer here in our latter days the fitful dreams of the things we should have done but never have and never will. None of us should exist as men living out our fathers' plans and our fathers' lives instead of our own. Even when we revolt against our fathers' ways, the rebellion itself is a mirror image of those ways, becoming an imitation of its own kind. The dreams, then: saddling your pony in soft, evening snowfall— high, high Asia and twilight in a mountain village, a desolate place of mud and straw and cooking fires, where the universe slides together. Or, in the low country and moving like a bowman's arrow, quick and silent through long grass, spear in your hand and gazelles on your mind. Or casting nets where the bait fish gather, going where the dolphins run and one, lone pelican flies. All of it far from commuter trains, far from meaningless retirement plans we will never get to use and bequeath to someone else, far from the vacuous roll of ordinary commerce. We should have done those other things, the dreams tell us all of that, and the dreams never lie. But we erase them with morning light and return to the lives our fathers chose for us. If you had done them, if I had done them—done the real things—we might have had a woman such as the one I now look upon here in Mombasa. Yet*

if we cannot have her, at least we have seen her dancing, a yellow feather in her hair. But that was in a night fancy somewhere, though it seemed real enough at the time. And the fancies of all men so become the dreams of each man becoming in turn the dreams of all men. There are shadows from evening firelight and men in black robes, chanting, a circular sitting of them, knee to knee on a long sandbar. We have been telling old stories and singing old tales of dreamtimes past, giving old warnings of women who dance and turn through the firelight and leave only their footprints for the mornings that follow. And we clap our hands in ragged unison while the woman dances while the river flows and turtles sleep, smelling her body as she comes near to us, and we reach out, touching her smooth legs, listening to the sound of her feet on hard-packed sand as she moves past us into riverine darkness. But all of it . . . all of it . . . has disappeared in the wash of work and responsibility and might-have-beens, and it all went by while nobody was watching, not even the sons of the fathers.

> *From S. J. Walk,* The Things We Should Have Done *(Fargo, North Dakota: High Plains Imprint, 1954), page 178. Read and copied in V. H. Rhomer's Notebook #6, 8/1/85.*

Vaughn Henry Rhomer, the son of a small grocer who had fought his way through the Great Depression, survived it, never forgot it, and counseled caution, marking a boy with his words: "Go with one of them

big firms, Vaughn, where they got retirement plans and
health insurance. It's too tough doin' it all on your own.
Be sensible, be careful; it's a mean world out there.
One day things are okay, next day the planks are being
yanked out from under you."

So did Vaughn Rhomer live true to his father's words
and suffered all the while the old pull of old ways, of
the hunt for gold in far Borneo, of doing whatever lies
in the bones of all thin young men who long to go
and then return to the home fires with stories they can
remember, stories they can tell in their latter days, dangling their blue-veined feet in old brown rivers and looking down at scarred hands as they talk. And feeling their
souls grow pure and warm with the recollections, with
the telling, with the simple knowing they chanced it
and went far out there while the others stayed.

The father, Albert, approved of Vaughn Rhomer's
life choices. The wife, Marjorie, approved. Their friends
approved. And Borneo was left to others, to the Thomas
Martins who dared to go. And the woman in Mombasa,
what became of her? And what became of all the young
women who passed the Best Value produce counters in
their halter tops and shorts cut so high and pulled so tight
that the flesh of their buttocks could be seen? Vaughn
Rhomer had smiled pleasantly at them through all his
years, growing older and saying "Good afternoon" and
trimming lettuce while looking at each of them only
once as they walked away—gold, far Borneo, and the
flight of one, lone pelican—and wondering what it
would be like to lie between the suntanned legs that
walked your aisles and to look down at smiling faces as
you took them to the places you were sure they longed
to go but had never been. Or even just to touch . . .
that might be enough, only the touching. To put your
hands just one time on what thrust against those halter

tops and to gently cut the fabric of those shorts with your *tronchete* while a tanned young woman laughed in pleasure at your taking of her. He had imagined tossing a pair of tattered shorts over into aisle three and having them land in nasty Mrs. Butro's grocery cart or, even better, on her head, while he ravished and explored a tanned young body on piles of red tomatoes crushed and strewn on the floor, red juice squirting everywhere.

And now, here with music and the soft Louisiana night, and a woman such as this one called Gumbo eight feet away. And Marjorie dead these fifteen months from a female-specific creature that ate her while she was still alive. And the hard press of losing her, and missing even her complaints about his gear, and the guilt when he thought back on all those nights when he wished for time alone in his room, time away from her. Time away from her when they could have been together, should have been together. The sensuality between them had never been of sky and thunder. What there had been, what precious little there had been, expired in a long, downward slide into mutual celibacy in the years of their marriage. Neither of them said anything while it was happening. It was . . . well, to be expected—wasn't it?—not to be talked over and examined. He watched the sixties go by, saw the liberation, the possibilities. But he and Marjorie remained the way they were. Why? The whys ran like insects with fire-feet through his brain when he tried to think about it. Until he stopped thinking about it altogether and let it die long before Marjorie died.

The road, he had fought for the road in his own quiet way. Not the Big Road—not India or the Borneo rivers—but at least some roads, something to ease the feelings inside him and keep him from just hauling off and pulling out on his lonesome, which he wouldn't have done anyway. The Yellowstone vacation in '82 had been a disaster. He'd read everything he could on the place, planned it for months. One of the highlights was supposed to have been a stop at the Little Big Horn on the way, and he'd studied the dying of the general they called Yellow Hair until he knew every square foot of the battlefield before they arrived.

But Nathan had caught something and thrown up four times in the Buick. Laverne had watched game shows on a portable television, and Louis had read a textbook on computers. Marjorie thought the scenery was pretty, but she was worried about Nathan and really couldn't concentrate on what Vaughn was saying about Custer sending Benteen and Reno off like he did, splitting up the party, and why the general shouldn't have done that, according to military strategists. Vaughn Rhomer had stood there, trying to tell his family what had happened in these valleys, trying to recapture for them the shouting and shooting . . . the riders beneath high plains sunlight, the clarity of purpose in the minds of Sitting Bull and Crazy Horse matched against the arrogance of Custer. He'd stood there, pointing and talking to himself.

Marjorie had said she couldn't handle another family vacation, in spite of the romance of the road, which Vaughn Rhomer believed she didn't quite grasp anyway. Yet there was another chance, the Big Road this time. The grocery chain had run a contest to select the employee of the year throughout all its twenty-seven stores. Vaughn Rhomer was something of a quiet legend in the corporation among the head office boys. "You want to see how a produce department ought to be run, go up to Otter Falls and see ol' Vaughn Rhomer's operation. He's a little strange, wears some kind of military boots to work, and clips up bad lettuce with what somebody said is a Mexican throat-slitting knife. Even carries his passport to work for some reason. But he knows the name of every regular customer, and his produce aisle looks like a gardener's wet dream. He's got to where he's doing catering for us, custom vegetable platters for the university president's wife and other celebrities. Only store that has a catering service out of its produce department."

VAUGHN RHOMER OF STORE #17
SELECTED AS EMPLOYEE OF THE YEAR

That's what the monthly *Best Value Bulletin* had said. Three days and four nights in the Sheraton British Colonial, Nassau of the Bahamas, that was the prize. Plane fare for one included. Problem was the trip fell in March, and Marjorie was working for a local attorney part-time to help with the boys' present and future college expenses. She couldn't go just then at tax time. She'd encouraged Vaughn to go alone, saying he deserved it. But that hadn't seemed right to him; after all, they were married, and those kinds of things ought to be for both of them.

"Go do it, Vaughn. It'll be a chance to wear your new pith helmet the kids gave you for Christmas." (When the family had asked what he wanted for Christmas that year, he'd smiled and said, "Big forearms." They'd looked at each other and ordered a pith helmet.)

He'd thought briefly about what Marjorie had suggested, then shook his head. "Not without you, Marjorie. If we're going to travel, then we should do it together. Besides, you've been talking about new carpet for the living room."

So the prize had gone to the runner-up, Arch Williams, meat manager at the Webster City store. Arch sent Vaughn Rhomer a postcard from Nassau, an aerial shot of sailboats and green, translucent sea. For reasons known only to accountants and chief financial officers, the big guys at headquarters decided not to run the contest a second year.

And then—Marjorie . . . Marjorie—at the very time two of the boys were finished with college and Nathan was ready for his CPA examination, she was gone. The neighbors brought covered dishes and covered words to the house and stood in new-mown grass by the gravesite. Pastor Larson praised Marjorie, calling her a caring wife and loving mother, which, indeed, she was.

At the cemetery, the boys beside him, Vaughn Rhomer had raised his head for a moment and seen Jack Carmine's dark, sun-worn face three rows deep in the crowd. Dappled light came through the branches above Jack's head and skittered across his face, fell upon the white shirt and tie he wore. It was the only time he'd ever seen Jack wear a tie. And Vaughn Rhomer was moved by that, by Jack Carmine's presence, by the fact he wore a white shirt and tie out of respect for the death of Marjorie and the grieving for her on a summer morning. Vaughn had wanted to say hello, but Jack didn't attend the lunch afterward.

Marjorie had never liked Jack and declared the house on Trolley Car Boulevard off-limits to Lorraine Carmine's eldest son.

"He's a bad influence on the boys, Vaughn, and I won't allow him in my house."

"Why is Jack Carmine a bad influence, Marjorie?"

"He just is, that's all. He's part of the rough element, crazy and irresponsible, ramming around the country in old pickup trucks, drinking and swearing and God knows what else. I can't imagine what Lorraine was thinking of, raising that kind of boy, even though she *is* your sister, Vaughn."

Marjorie had first said that back in 1980, and now Marjorie was gone, and there was traffic out on Decatur, tourists strolling. A heavy-set woman waddled up to Ariendo Vincent and asked if she could have her picture taken with him. He nodded, and she turned toward her husband, who lifted a point-and-shoot Minolta. Flash—horizontal shot; flash again—vertical shot. They walked off without leaving any money in Ariendo Vincent's box on the sidewalk.

Vincent looked down at his money box and watched them go, lit a Salem, and took two long drags on it. Shook his head slowly and stuck the cigarette in a space between his saxophone keys. He pulled the horn to his mouth, took it out again, and said to the crowd of two— Vaughn Rhomer and the black woman—"Do a little Charlie Parker, here."

Vaughn Rhomer didn't know who Charlie Parker was or might be. The black woman seemed to know the tune, however, clapping her hands twice when Ariendo Vincent mentioned what he was going to play and then fishing around in her purse after that.

She wore an expensive linen suit of luminous canary yellow. The skirt came to just above her knees, with a slit in the back he'd noticed when she went to the restroom earlier. Her jacket had a flared hem with a single, fancy white button that kept it closed. The back of the jacket was pleated, and soutache trim lay along the shoulders.

All of that would have been quite enough to satisfy Vaughn Henry Rhomer from Otter Falls, Iowa. Quite enough. But her hat—my God, he was thinking, why don't women still wear hats such as hers and tuck their hair up under them as she had done? The hat was fine yellow straw, exactly the same color as her suit, with a low, rounded crown and a wide, wide brim, organza ruffles draped off the back. Around the edge of the brim was white grosgrain ribbon binding, matching her white gloves on the table and her white purse on the chair. She wore the hat tilted slightly forward, the effect being one of modest insouciance.

And the pearls—around her neck, a strand of small ones, and a single pearl in each of her tiny earrings. Her shoes were the same yellow as her dress and hat, and her stockings were sheer. Her lipstick matched her nails, vivid red, but not too much so, not flamboyant or even close to it. And her umbrella, of the same luminous yellow, coupled with a white lace shawl hanging over a chair back next to her. Summed or parceled out, either way, she amounted to perfection. Vaughn Rhomer tried to imagine Marjorie in the black woman's clothing, tried that for only a second and gave up on it.

She found the hanky she was looking for in her purse and raised her head. Rhomer went back to fiddling with his coffee cup. It was almost empty, so he ordered another. When he motioned to the waiter, the black woman glanced at him, and for a moment, a heart-tearing-all-is-possible flutter went through his chest like a moth around a street lamp. She didn't smile, though it seemed as if she might before she looked away, looked away.

The waiter returned with another espresso, and Rhomer thought for a moment about Marjorie. She would have complained about the coffee. Not only the second cup, but also the first one. "Vaughn, you know how coffee upsets your stomach if you drink it in the evening. Then you won't be able to sleep, and you'll be tired and out of sorts all the next day."

Marjorie,
O Marjorie,
You did the best you could
But now I have no need for sleep.

When the waiter set down the espresso, Vaughn
Rhomer's voice, with no instruction from his mind,
said, "I'll have a brandy, too."

"What kind, sir?"

Vaughn Rhomer didn't know anything about brandy
and flushed when he realized that. The waiter stared
politely at him.

"El Domingo," he blurted, making up a name on the
spot. It sounded as though it might be the name of a
brandy.

"I'm sorry, sir, we don't have that."

"Then . . . anything, whatever she's drinking." He
nodded toward the black woman, who was again listening to Ariendo Vincent.

The waiter looked in the woman's direction, said,
"Yes, sir," and walked off.

Her second brandy, delivered a few minutes ago—he
could have offered to buy it for her. Why didn't I? Why
didn't I lean forward when she was rummaging through
her purse and say, "May I have the honor of paying for
your drink, madam?"

He supposed that kind of move would have been
called an approach. An approach . . . how would you
approach this woman? Vaughn Rhomer didn't know.
He'd never known how to do that sort of thing. It's
bloody shameful and sad all over—he was beating on
himself again—being over sixty and not knowing how
to say something to her.

Nephew Jack Carmine would know. Jack always was
comfortable with women. He'd simply step over to her

table and say, "Howdy, ma'am. Jack Carmine, here, from Alpine, Texas. Mind if I join you?" If she said yes, fine. If she said no, nothing was lost; you were simply back to where you'd been before. Such was the logic of it, but there was logic and there was inexperience, the root of fear. And there was shyness. Vaughn Rhomer was inexperienced and shy.

So he was left there, confused and wondering and wanting, engaged in the mechanics of paying the waiter and arranging his round wool hat with the short bill and a button on the crown into a symmetrical design with the coffee cup and brandy glass. He looked at the hat, the cup, the glass, all resting on the marble tabletop, and the harmony of the layout suited him. After that exercise in keeping busy, he used a paper napkin to wipe white doughnut sugar off the table, being careful not to get any on his tan pants and dark brown jacket and medium brown walking shoes he'd bought for this trip. While he tidied up, he watched the woman surreptitiously. Ariendo Vincent was playing "Morning of the Carnival." She rocked her head slowly to the samba rhythm.

Back to the problem: How could it be brought about, the touch of this woman's skin against his, a border crossing just once in his militantly conventional life, a high, arching bound into provinces where all that mattered was sweet abandon? Nephew Jack would know; he understood the art of public seduction. But Jack was somewhere else. Texas Jack Carmine was always somewhere else.

CHAPTER FIVE

Western Vietnam—1972

Dear Uncle Vaughn,
Hunkered down in a hootch near the Cambodian
border, drinking warm beer and waiting for or-
ders. Hot and wet here again today. Always
hot and wet, been raining just about all the time
for six days. Goddamned unbelievable deep mud
everywhere, got to walk on planks just to cross
the compound, to keep from being sucked under.
The Shitburner (a little Vietnamese guy we pay
to do exactly that and probably is a VC in
disguise) is hauling out oil drums from the latrine
and burning off the crap with diesel fuel. A
buddy of mine's carving tigers out of scrap wood,
and three guys at the other end of the tent are
racing cockroaches and betting on them, radio's
playing the Doors and Jefferson Airplane.
Speaking of planes, or choppers to be more ex-
act, I flew an early morning mission, took off
when it was still dark and right in the middle

of a gook mortar attack on our position and got back before sunup—dropped off a captain, a spotter, and a real cobra named Clayton Price in some godforsaken stretch of jungle. I didn't know where we were going, still don't. But it took us a while to get there, and I had this feeling we were crossing into Cambodia. Saw this Clayton Price once before. He's got strange eyes, kind of blue or gray, can't figure out which. Moves real slow, hardly says anything, heard the captain call him "Tortoise." They tell me he's a sniper and can put one right up your nose at 1,500 yards. He was carrying a Remington 700 with a Redfield scope, a flat-shooting sonuvabitch so clean it looked like it just came out of the crate. I'd hate to be on the other end of the barrel, looking in the direction of a killer named Tortoise but not even seeing him lying all that distance away in heavy jungle. Those snipers are a breed all their own, keep to themselves, think of themselves as some kind of artists. For some reason, my chopper didn't fly back for the dustoff. Heard there was some kind of trouble, the chopper that went came back with only the crew. I'm wondering what happened to this Clayton Price. Another man done gone. What else is new?

Guy over in the hootch next to me is a journalist named Sean Flynn, son of Errol Flynn (no lie!). He's wild as hell, takes all kinds of chances, OK guy, though. I've come to hate most of the goddamn journalists. A lot of them go out and cover the war during the day, asking stupid questions such as, "Are you afraid?" Then, come evening, they sit on the patio of the Continental in Saigon and drink—a regular day job. Shit, they've got maids and everything else. Think they're real tough guys—like to tell each other they've got "brass balls"—what a goddamned joke. Screwing Vietnamese girls and saying they're going to take them back to the States after the war. First time I saw this Clayton Price, some asshole journalist was hounding him for a story on snipers. Kept following him around, wouldn't let him alone. After about an hour of that bullshit, Price pulled out his bush knife, grabbed the asshole's hair, and stuck the knife point in the asshole's nose. Couldn't hear what Price said, but the note taker turned white right under his suntan and got the hell out of there, pronto— There it is!

A fellow over a few hootches got hit by a bamboo viper two days ago in the latrine and died one hell of a mean death—word is you have time to light a smoke and take a couple of drags before the put-me-out-of-my-misery agony starts. But something kind of fascinating about all this; think I might re-up for another tour. Beats laying utility wire back in Brewster County, Texas.

Take care, Uncle Vaughn—keep the vegetables fresh.

Jack

CHAPTER SIX

Otter Falls, Iowa, October 1986

The Chevy pickup with dented fenders came down
Route 63 and nosed into town, late afternoon in a time
of days growing shorter. Almost dark. Vaughn Rhomer
was finishing up before going home, fussing with red
onions. There was a correct way to arrange produce,
to make it more appealing to customers. Some of the
younger people didn't grasp that and simply put vegetables onto shelves with no concern for appearance and
design. He'd tried to explain proper arrangements to
them, but they didn't seem to care and continued in
their careless ways, leaving Vaughn Rhomer, produce
manager, to straighten things out.

"Howdy, Uncle Vaughn."

Vaughn Rhomer turned, knowing the voice and smiling already as he turned.

Jack Carmine, grinning and standing there in an old
leather jacket and a cap with *North Stars* logoed on it,
tossing a Granny Smith up and down in his right hand.
Off to one side was an interesting-looking woman who

glanced at Vaughn Rhomer, then looked away and fiddled with a package of radishes.

Jack had a sense of how it lay with Marjorie and, coming through Otter Falls every few years, had either looked up Vaughn Rhomer at the store or called him at home from a pay phone. If Marjorie answered, she'd put the phone down and say, "Vaughn, it's Lorraine's boy. I don't want him around Nathan."

Next to Best Value was a shopping mall. Vaughn Rhomer and nephew Jack talked about the weather and the price of lettuce while they crossed the parking lot.

"Hear it's snowing hard in Minnesota."

"Yeah, we came that way, running ahead of it."

Linda Lobo was lagging a step behind, and Jack waited for her. He took her hand, smiling at her—he'd been smiling at her all day, as if he had secret plans he would disclose at the proper time.

Vaughn Rhomer liked Jack, admired him, but always felt a little tongue-tied around him. After all, Texas Jack Carmine was one of those who went out there, who knew the Big Road and should be accorded respect because of that. They sat in a restaurant open to the mall, near a fountain whose white noise was too loud. Jack was answering Vaughn Rhomer's questions about the road, about where he'd been, what he'd done. Linda drank a small root beer and listened, smiling now and then at Vaughn Rhomer.

Vaughn Rhomer asked about his sister. "How is Lorraine? Have you seen her lately?"

"Nope, not since she went to California and took up with Mr. Baba or whatever he calls himself and added primal screamin' to her repertoire just before they moved to New Mexico. She writes now and then, asks about you and Earl and Hummer."

Lorraine Rhomer, the older sister in pigtails first and long brown hair after that, the older sister Vaughn liked a lot, who had rebelled early and married Poly Carmine at eighteen against her parents' wishes. Vaughn Rhomer remembered the shouting and screaming from upstairs when she was packing to go in '39: "For God sakes, Mother, I'm already pregnant with his child, and his dad's got a place in Texas. We're going there whether you like it or not." Mr. and Mrs. Albert Rhomer never talked to their daughter again and died in the conviction she was wayward and not of them.

Jack noticed his uncle's eyes go cloudy. "Rainy's all right, Uncle Vaughn," he said quietly. "She married into a wild old bunch of southwest Texas boys and lived a hard life, as I think back on it. Whatever she and this Bababoo are doin', she seems happy. That counts with me. She always asks about you and sends her love in case I run into you." Jack didn't say that Rainy always postscripted her letters, "Tell Vaughn to dump ol' Marjorie and come down here to the mountains; I know women his age who still dance naked in the moonlight and would love a good man to death." Jack never mentioned that to Vaughn Rhomer; didn't seem the thing to do.

Jack and Linda sat across from Vaughn Rhomer, who glanced now and then at Linda. She said nothing but smiled pleasantly. The thing he noticed was both she and Jack had the same worn look in their eyes. They laughed easily, grinned a lot, but still . . . still, there was something in the eyes of Jack Carmine and Linda Lobo, something old and more tired than Vaughn Rhomer had ever been.

While they talked, Vaughn Rhomer heard Nathan's loud, shrill voice out in the shopping center. Nathan and his friends were hanging around the fountain, anal-retentive but pretending they weren't. Vaughn Rhomer excused himself and went out to the fountain.

"Nathan, come meet your cousin, Jack Carmine. He and a friend stopped by for a few minutes."

Jack's mother was ten years older than Vaughn and had Jack when she was nineteen, so it was hard to imagine Nathan and Jack as cousins. It was even harder to imagine when you saw them sitting across from one another in a restaurant booth.

Nathan came unwillingly. Marjorie's propaganda about Jack had taken hold, and Nathan felt as if he were marching toward all the sins ever committed. Besides, Nathan didn't much care for old people, and Jack was old. And, as it turned out, Jack Carmine scared hell out of Nathan Rhomer without even saying anything. Jack stood up when Uncle Vaughn led Nathan into the restaurant.

They shook hands. "Nice to meet you, Nathan; heard Uncle Vaughn speak often and well of you."

Nathan grunted something and pushed his hair off his forehead, looking out at his friends near the fountain, who were laughing at him. He rolled his eyes in the direction of Jack Carmine and shouted, "Be right back."

"We're going down to the arcade, Nathan," one of them shouted. "Come by if you're not too busy." They walked down the mall, laughing and looking back.

"Jack and his friend, Linda, are on their way to Texas, Nathan. Nice, big country down there."

"How do you know that, Dad? Ever been there?" The ridicule of Vaughn Rhomer was a family tradition by now, to be done in private or public without consideration for whatever audience might be listening.

"No."

"Then how do you know it's big and nice?" Nathan

was picking at something in the back of his mouth, using his little finger.

"Well . . . people say that, people who've been there." Vaughn Rhomer was a little red in the face.

Nathan shook his head.

Linda Lobo watched Jack's jaw tighten up. He lit a cigarette and wiggled it between his front teeth. "What year are you in school, Nathan?" He was grinning the particular Jack Carmine grin that Linda Lobo would come to know later on, the one that said something bad was headed your way.

"Junior." Nathan looked at the ceiling and twirled Vaughn Rhomer's coffee spoon in his fingers.

"Nathan wants to study accounting in college," Vaughn said.

Jack scratched his cheek, still grinning. "How come you want to study accounting, Nathan? Nothin' wrong with that, of course, just wonder how a young fellow knows so early on what he wants to do with the remainder of his years. Always find it kind of strange a seventeen-year-old boy decides what a forty-year-old man is goin' to become."

Nathan didn't like philosophy; he liked numbers and said so. "I like numbers."

"Whaddya like to do with 'em? Touch 'em, count 'em up, run 'em through your head, sayin' 'One, two, three, four' all the while . . . or what?"

Nathan had this strange feeling, as if he'd walked into a box canyon full of rattlesnakes blocking his way back out, herding him toward the head snake, who was lying on a big rock and smoking a Pall Mall, grinning.

"I just like the fact you can add one plus one and get two." Nathan was now smart-ass sullen, looking at Jack, something pretty close to a sneer coming onto his face. Neither cousin Jack nor this piece of woman with him was to be accorded respect. "What did you want to be when you were seventeen? Did you plan on laying gas pipe or driving combines or whatever it is you do?" He glanced over at Linda Lobo in her jean jacket and baggy turtleneck sweater, certain she didn't do much at all worthwhile except hang around with what his mother called the "rough element."

Jack Carmine stuffed out his cigarette, looking straight into Nathan's eyes all the while. "Nope. I wanted to drive race cars and be a great lover of beautiful women. Never got around to the car business, but one for two ain't bad."

Linda pressed back laughter, smiled easy.

"I gotta go," Nathan said, sliding out of the booth. "Nice to meetcha," not looking at either Linda Lobo or Jack Carmine and walking away.

Jack got up and followed him. "Be right back," he said over his shoulder to Vaughn Rhomer and Linda. He caught up with Nathan near the fountain and tapped him on the shoulder.

Nathan turned around, surprised and out here on his own now without the safety of the propriety old people used when they were talking in groups. He'd learned you could say about anything and get away with it in those situations because nobody wanted to create a fuss. Now he looked up at hard eyes, hard brown eyes that weren't grinning the way the mouth was.

"Nathan, I do sincerely hope your dreams of bein' an accountant come to be. Furthermore, I suggest you and your friends stay away from spicy food; it won't agree with your tender assholes on its way out. But I got only one real meaningful thing to say to you. My ol' man, Poly Carmine, was nutty as hell in some ways, but we never treated him the way you treat your father, and we never treated other adults with the kind of superiority you do. Right now you feel all rosy and secure 'cause you're part of a protective system, your good, polite parents and your school, all nice and orderly. But in another year you'll be comin' into my world, which ain't all that nice and orderly. And if I've got the slightest notion that you've been insultin' my uncle Vaughn— one of the last good, gentle men around—with your smart mouth, I'm gonna wait till you're full-grown and then I'm gonna shove a bar of lye soap right down your fuckin' throat till you feel it comin' out the other end so fast it'll bounce all the way to the ceiling on its way back up. You're a twerp, Nathan. One more thing: Stay out of southwest Texas 'cause you won't do well down there."

Jack walked back to where Vaughn Rhomer and Linda were sitting. "Just wanted to tell Nathan he should be sure and stop by if he was ever in southwest Texas."

Vaughn checked his military watch. "Well, got to be getting home for supper. Marjorie doesn't like it if I'm not there by six." He wanted to talk all night with Jack, to drink the kind of good liquor he figured Jack would know how to order, and to hear about the road and the Vietnam days Jack had only sketched in his letters. But he couldn't do that.

"How late's this mall stay open, Uncle Vaughn?" Jack asked.

"Nine o'clock. Got to buy something?"

"Nah. Just thought I'd hang around the fountain out there and see if some interestin' young people come by. Talk with 'em for a while, pick up a little arcade wisdom, try to expand my knowledge of our country's future scientists and business leaders."

They shook hands, Vaughn Rhomer with Jack, then with Linda. "Sure glad you stopped by, both of you."

"Good to see you again, Uncle Vaughn."

"Nice to meet you, Mr. Rhomer."

Vaughn Rhomer walked down the mall, past the bookstore, past the shoe store, past the flower shop, and turned a corner in his tan windbreaker and military boots.

"He seems like a really nice man, Jack."

"Vaughn Rhomer's a Georgia peach, in his own way. Sometime I hope he finds a naked lady dancin' in the mountain moonlight who's been waitin' a lifetime just for him."

"Where'd that idea come from?"

"Just a wish I have for Uncle Vaughn, nothin' more. Now, we got shoppin' to do." He took Linda Lobo's hand and canted his head. "Got to get some nice things for another dancin' lady, while we're here in Otter Falls, Iowa."

"What?"

"C'mon. We'll talk about it on our way down this tunnel of America's bounty."

Spearman & Crawford
"Fine Women's Apparel"

Jack towed her under the sign and into the store. They walked into a world of perfume and jewelry and at least a half acre of clothing.

Jack spotted an elderly well-dressed clerk straightening clothing on the racks. "Wait here a second, I'll be right back," he said to Linda. He walked over to the clerk, took off his cap, and shook the woman's hand. Jack Carmine was grinning his friendly grin once more and nodding back at Linda Lobo. The clerk also nodded, smiling, and walked with Jack to where Linda was standing.

"Gonna get you fixed up, Miss Linda. This here's

Anna Wilhelm, so says her name tag, who knows everythin' there is in the store and where it's at. I'll sort of drift off while the two of you are dealing with the gentler aspects of ladies' clothing—never been comfortable hangin' around that particular department in clothing stores, feel like I'm spyin' on something private in public." He grinned warm at Linda Lobo. "Get whatever you need, dancin' lady, and double it. Cost is to be ignored. We all got to look good when we see little Sara Margaret tomorrow and go paradin' into Alpine a few days from now."

Jack went across the main corridor to a western store and bought a new pair of boot-cut Wrangler's, size 33 waist and 34 inseam, plus two flannel shirts. He looked at belts, but none suited him. The salesman handed him a gray Stetson and suggested he try it on. Jack did and said, "Nope, don't think so; got two of 'em at home already, hangin' on pegs and feelin' lonesome, waitin' as they are for my imminent arrival."

Back to Spearman & Crawford, where he saw Linda and Anna Wilhelm far across fields of racked clothing. They were holding up things on hangers and looking at them, laying various items on top of the racks.

Linda grinned at him when he walked her way. Stacked on a chair behind her were basic things featuring ribbons and lace in black or pink or yellow, not to mention turquoise, things that would go under other things yet to be chosen.

While Anna Wilhelm was taking slacks off hangers, Linda reached back to the chair and barely lifted up lace bikini somethings colored black and designed frilly, tilting her head in that special way of hers, saying, "Whaddya think?" without actually saying the words. Jack yanked his *North Stars* cap over his eyes and feigned a staggering swoon against clothing racks.

Anna Wilhelm turned, glancing at Jack, looking at Linda, then at the chair where ribbons and lace resided. She riffled the items stacked there. "All the young women are buying these cute and sexy styles now," she said to him.

Jack nodded, once.

Linda was holding slacks and sweaters. "Jack, I'm comfortable makin' my own decisions about life in general, but I'm goin' to need a little advice here. I'm not used to shoppin' in this way, gettin' overwhelmed by the possibilities."

Jack grinned. "I was hopin' you'd say that."

A strewing of wool and cotton in earth tones and colors brighter yet across the racks of Spearman & Crawford. Linda would go in the dressing room and come out, go back in and come out in something else.

Anna had a stock boy fetch a chair for Jack, who sat there, legs crossed, *North Stars* cap over his knee, smiling. "Havin' fun, dancin' lady? I am."

Linda blushed a little and shook her head up and down with the kind of emphasis that comes only from meaning a true and absolute *yes*. "I'm like a kid in a candy store. But this is going to cost a fortune. You better set some limits, cowboy."

"Lemme know when we get in the neighborhood of fifteen hundred or so. We'll kind of pivot off that number to start with."

Anna Wilhelm smiled and looked up at a store clock, this night hoping time would move slowly. "Here's something very nice," she said, holding a loose-fitting sweater in plum with a keyhole neck and one pearly-looking button holding the neck shut. "It looks very chic over the top of black leggings."

"Well, chic is what I've always favored, and chic is what we're after," Jack said, still grinning.

With the Rainbow Bar only forty-two hours behind her, Linda pushed back the curtains and emerged from the dressing room in a purple sweater and black leggings, neither of which she'd ever owned.

Jack flipped his cap into the air and said, "Southwest Texas, home of the last real unbonded men on earth, is castin' its only vote for that one. I like these leggin's deals on you. Need some high black boots or somethin' to go with 'em. Saw that in a magazine."

Anna Wilhelm agreed and sent the stock boy to the shoe department for various pairs of boots and loafers and high heels, specifying colors, styles, and sizes. The young man returned in a few minutes with a cartful of boxes and was sent forthwith to the jewelry department with new instructions.

A long white blouse with a big collar and floppy cuffs—what Anna Wilhelm called a "menswear big shirt that will also go with the black leggings and high boots"—drew applause from both Anna and Jack when Linda Lobo came out of the dressing room wearing it under a fancy black leather vest.

Jeans, tan and navy slacks, yellow and red and dark green sweaters, several pair of leggings in various colors, piling up on nearby racks. When Anna Wilhelm placed a wool felt top hat on Linda's head and said, "This is very stylish, if you think it's you."

Linda looked in the mirror and laughed. "I don't think so."

Jack put his cap on backward. "I don't think so, either. I know a dog named Hummer who's got an old heart, and he'd never recover from the shock. Now, you're goin' to need a swimmin' costume for reasons I'm not at liberty to disclose right this minute."

Anna Wilhelm went over to another department and brought back what looked to Jack like small pieces of cloth draped over her arm. Linda tried on the suits in the dressing room, refusing to come out for inspection. Jack protested, but she said through the curtain, "Awful public here. You'll just have to wait until the moment your undisclosed reasons are disclosed."

"Well, fair trade. No dresses? Ought to have at least one good dress, so I can take you down to the hotel in Alpine, lookin' like I had you flown in from Paris overnight for more or less illicit purposes."

Black—for some reason they were into black again when it came to a dress, the choosing of which took some amount of time. But there came a moment, a moment in Texas Jack Carmine's life when it all pulled together and he was whole for the first time in a long time.

Anna Wilhelm had smiled—"Let's try this"—and gone with Linda Lobo to the dressing room.

When Linda came out, she was no longer Linda Lobo, dancin' lady, but something else, something in the way of . . . something beyond something in the eyes of Jack Carmine. The dress came to just below midthigh and was of one piece and sleek with a V-neck that reached far down and had a wrap side tie cascading to the hemline. Linda's hair was down now and had been combed slightly off to one side by Anna Wilhelm. She wore black high heels, black stockings, wide pearl bracelets on each wrist, and dangling earrings matching the bracelets.

Linda stood there with a pouty smile, right hand on her waist, left leg splayed slightly out, as she'd seen fashion models pose in advertisements and as the Altoona home ec teacher had tried to teach the senior girls during the four-week segment on charm. And the odd thing—at that moment—the odd thing was that Jack Carmine felt insecure all the while he was feeling whole.

He'd never imagined Linda could look this way and suddenly saw her as maybe being more than he could possibly deserve or hold, if it came to that. She stood there and said ever so softly, "Well, bandit, how's this?"

Jack Carmine was seldom without words, but he was then. He sat very still, looking at the woman before him, the long legs looking longer than long again and her long fingers fanning out across her right waist. He sat there and shook his head slowly back and forth, some kind of stunned look on his face, like he'd been side-whacked with a tire iron and was trying to recover.

Anna Wilhelm stood to one side, smiling, knowing she had created a masterpiece there in the fading hours of a Friday night in Otter Falls, Iowa.

Linda looked at the tag on one sleeve and walked to where Jack was sitting stone-dead dumb in his chair. She bent over and whispered, "Jack, it's lovely, and I can't believe it's me when I look in the mirror, but it's six hundred dollars—that's too much. Besides, I don't have any need for a fancy dress right now, and it'll be sometime before I'll be able to pay you back for all this we've already got."

Jack Carmine got himself back together again. "I put in a lot of overtime on heavy machinery this summer; money's not a problem."

He turned to Anna Wilhelm. "We'll take the whole package, jewelry, shoes, everythin'. Also gonna need a nice, big suitcase. Just forget all about boxes, 'cept for the shoes. Get us a suitcase—a nice one, hear?—and pack the entire business in there. We're gonna drive 'em crazy at the Holland Hotel in Alpine, Texas."

After a stop at luggage, then at coats for a long wool number plus a light mountain parka, then the perfume and makeup section, Texas Jack Carmine reached inside his shirt and unzipped the pocket of his shoulder holster. He took out a handful of hundred-dollar bills and began counting them out.

"There ya go, Anna Wilhelm. Better double-count it and see if there's seventeen of them big fellows."

Linda Lobo couldn't remember when she'd seen a hundred-dollar bill, let alone seventeen lying in three piles of five, plus two extra, on the counter.

They went out to the truck, into a quarter-moon night, Jack whistling, carrying his sack of jeans and shirts plus a big suitcase, Linda Lobo carrying two coats in zippered plastic bags over one arm and shoeboxes under the other. The lights in the mall were flicking off behind them. And so strange it was, both of them still thinking and without knowing the other was thinking it, about Linda in the black dress. And neither of them believing for just that one moment it had been her looking the way she did.

Across the street—across the world, maybe—from the Otter Falls shopping mall, Jack Carmine leaned the top of his head against the wall of a Holiday Inn shower, holding a half-empty bottle of Rolling Rock beer in his right hand. The water beat upon his body and ran down to the tub where the dancing lady had bathed before him and now was dressed in new black lace, bare legs curled under her where she sat on a bed, lying flat and soft in a room where music played. There was no light in the room except for the silent flicker of two small votive candles she'd picked up when they'd gone back into Best Value for beer and potato chips and deli sandwiches they'd stuffed into the cooler along with new ice.

And she was thinking of the man who showered on

the other side of the wall, in a tub with a crack near the drain. And other men. At thirty-seven, the long years of boys and men, thinking about them. Gary, she'd married him five years ago mostly because she'd gone over thirty and was feeling some old push toward having children. In two weeks the divorce would come through, allowing Gary to live unencumbered with another woman he'd found in the office of the sheet metal plant where he worked. About the other woman, he'd said to Linda, "Nancy understands me better."

And Lucas Mathen, to whom she'd given her virginity in Hayes Park in Altoona, Iowa, in the dark of one summer's night when she was fifteen and he was seventeen, and how they had done it over and over in the grass of Hayes Park all the nights of that long summer when the town was sleeping. They'd started out clumsy but, using beginners' standards as a way of measuring, were doing it pretty well by late August. Lucas Mathen, who purchased condoms from a machine in the men's restroom at the Texaco. Lucas Mathen was no fool, and she remembered him well for it.

And the others . . . others, others . . . here and there in the random choosing that passes for courtship or desire or a thousand other words in language that escaped her now.

And her father, gone to the Korean War when she was only three. His letters came and then didn't come anymore after he was sent north to a place called the Yalu River. And the little house in Altoona, with yellow shingles on the side and gray shingles on the roof, that had belonged once to her mother's grandparents and had been passed to her mother through the long and complicated words of the grandparents' will. This yellow-gray-shingled place was were the boys of Altoona rapped on the door and were more polite when calling for her than they were later on in their cars with radios playing.

Wendell, in 1969. Just why they'd gotten married was never clear. It seemed the thing to do, since her friends were all getting married. Ten months later it was over when he brought home a dose of nasty business he'd caught from a drive-in waitress. She'd kicked out Wendell's butt and took in antibiotics. After that she was cautious for a while. Still, there were the country music bars after work, and there were other men, loneliness and alcohol and the slide of pedal steel guitars on Saturday nights overriding long-term considerations.

So before Gary and her second marriage bed, her long legs had gone around twenty or so of them who panted after what they imagined lay underneath her cotton blouses and tight jeans. And having found what lay there, had no real idea of what to do with it and seemed as if they were almost afraid of what they'd found. But after a few days, all of them were anxious to look again and see if it was all as nice as they remembered. Years going by that way, finally settling on Gary when nobody else seemed to want much in the way of permanency. And was it she who had let them all go by or they who had done it to her? In a time without codes it's hard to know who's calling and who's hanging up.

And poor Gary, whose approach to lovemaking was to say, "You hot yet?" and didn't have any idea at all about how she felt in those moments, not even wet and ready and him already trying to get it over with so he could play softball later on and go to the tavern after the game was finished. Not long into the marriage she had begun to dislike the idea of sex with Gary and did what she could to avoid it. She and Gary had separated

fourteen months ago, a little more than two years after
Sara Margaret had been born and named after Linda's
grandmothers.

Last year she'd gone three times to a Des Moines
motel with a man from American Battery, who was
some improvement over Gary, and she'd been grateful
for that. An older man at Northern Food Processors
had been nice to her and took his time with her. That
made her feel a little more female sexy again, and she
decided maybe it was worth exploring some more to
see if something was out there she'd dreamed about as
a young girl but never found.

In the light of two votive candles, with a fire siren
going by outside and fading west along University Avenue, she looked at the neatly packed suitcase lying on
the luggage rack. She looked and wondered about the
man named Jack Carmine. He was turning off the
shower in a small room next to where she sat on the
bed and where she could see herself in the mirror above
the dresser, her image gentled by candlelight.

"Thirty-seven, dancin' lady . . . thirty-seven . . . it'll
start to go fast now," she said out loud, still looking in
the mirror. She sat straight and her breasts sat high
beneath the wired black lace and fancy ribbons he'd
bought her, and her hair hung straight to the middle of
her back.

She could see it clear and hard, hard and clear out
ahead, the old women when the old men had died,
sitting in the nursing homes attached to churches and
the easy wave of their conversation falling through old
years like a coffin door falling from the mortician's ef-
fortless pull. The old women by that age would all have
watched the hand on the door as the times closed down
in a single, almost silent click and only memories were
left. The tribes had it right: If you can't keep up, die on

the trail and let the scavengers have you. Quicker that way, better.

> And ooohhh, ooohhh . . . went the last
> old song
> the old man ever sang
> And Nooohhh, nooohhh . . . went his last
> old wife
> when she heard the words go by.

She looked at the suitcase again and smiled. In there was pretty much all she owned, and it was all new, and Texas Jack Carmine had helped her pick it out. A peculiar man, Jack Carmine, who'd lived up to his earlier promises by having as much fun as she'd had choosing her new clothes. And when they'd come to the motel, he'd offered again to buy her a separate room if she wanted. She'd taken hold of his jacket collar and looked up at him, saying in quiet words, "Not on your life, Jack Carmine . . . not on your life. Not tonight."

Not tonight. New clothes and new perfume and candles burning. In a life that had been without romance in most ways—the summer nights with Lucas Mathen being the one exception . . . kind of—this wasn't bad, pretty close maybe to what it was supposed to be like. When they'd bought their beer and sandwiches at Best Value, she'd asked herself, What else, what else? At the express checkout counter, she'd thought of the candles and run back for them. When the clerk whisked them across the scanner, she knew Jack Carmine was looking at her, but she just looked at the cash register and smiled. Now she was wishing she'd thought of something besides beer to drink, such as . . . what? Champagne, she should have thought of champagne. Too late, never mind.

Seeing herself in the black dress had brought up curious feelings, almost sexual. No, not almost, that's exactly how she'd felt. Partly because Jack Carmine had been looking at her in the way he did, but, in truth, it could have been any interesting man and she'd have felt the same. Call it vanity, she thought, or some one of those words meaning the same and which good people are not supposed to feel. It was nonetheless there, a strange, narcissistic curling back to herself in her mind. For a moment, for the first time and never before, she'd seen herself as some incredibly female creature who could alternate between strength and submission. A woman who could rule men with her thoughts or her body, depending on the time and place and reason, or be dominated by them when it was of her own will and choosing. A woman who could dance naked on desert sand before a thousand soldiers in a firelit circle, hearing the metallic clap of swords against shields matched to the rhythm of her dancing feet, and relish their wanting of her, yet giving herself only to the dark warrior she would select out of all who watched and wanted.

In that moment, those strange few seconds of something she'd never experienced, she'd felt some basic thing that was beyond forming into words. As if she wanted to hike up the dress and straddle Jack Carmine where he sat, have him take her—or her take him—right there, performing intimate theater before the eyes of Anna Wilhelm and the stock boy and whoever else cared to watch. Texas Jack Carmine—he seemed about as good as they made them and even some better than that from what she could tell, but any man would have done at that moment. It wasn't how'd she'd seen herself before, but rather how she hadn't seen herself before. And from that singular moment on, Linda Something, whose last name was known by some and not by others, was changed.

Jack Carmine came out of the bathroom, towel around his waist and singing some old song half under his breath, a song she'd never heard, having something to do with long winding trains and starlight on western rails.

He stopped when he saw her. "Lord, I just knew you were going to look like that. Just like that is how I imagined it."

Linda Lobo held out her arms and spoke softly. "Come dance with the dancin' lady, bandit. Music's playin' and time's goin' by."

Her words, but in the roll of later years, it was the sound of his words she'd remember. On that first time and many times after, Jack Carmine had said soft words to her. Not the easy, clever words that were the words of his days, but the words he used in darkness cut only by the flicker of candlelight, and those words in darkness were some different from his day words.

He was the first, and the last, who had spoken to her in those moments, soft words and slow ways—slow words, soft ways. Her perfume was new and the black lace something was new and she was soft with oil and smooth and perfumed, grime from the Dillon nights washing from her skin by water and by him, by his laughter and his ways that seemed to teeter on a precipice only he could see and thereby find his balancing point on the edge of it.

The man she called bandit had loved her well and long that first night. His words . . . she could never remember afterward his words . . . it was the low whispering sound of them that mattered, not the words themselves . . . on his good nights, in his good times, words coming from his mouth and lips that touched her even while he spoke the words: first tangos and last planes out and getting rid of pain, words about those things, words such as those.

But he understood what a woman might want—what *she* might want—the way a desert magician can read the clouds and see in them what might be coming next. On his good nights, in his good times, the bandit was a wonder, and she had said as much and called him by his proper name instead of "bandit" or "cowboy," letting the words come out of her mouth over and over again without even knowing she was saying them . . . saying his proper name over and over again.

She'd had her fantasies about the way these moments ought to be, about how she ought to lose herself and her center in some whirling ride through high, cloudy places where she'd never been, the colors of life, and even death, forming and then dissolving in the cambers of her mind. And with him, on his good nights, in his good times, it had happened just the way the fantasies had promised, and she would beg him to never let it stop being like that, to stay close inside her and let those moments run forever.

And years later she remembers often the thin straps of a black lace something sliding from her shoulders that night as he said quiet words, sounding as if he would treat her well and putting his mouth on her even as he said them. And years later, running her hands across her breasts and other places, she remembers how the black lace came off her skin as Jack Carmine peeled it away before laying her down on a bed the shade of blowing sand and promising her all the other colors of the high desert along the road before them. She remembers the high, cloudy places where she traveled with him.

As for Texas Jack Carmine, he knew a lot about high,

cloudy places. Low ones, too. He lived on the bounce, mostly, on his way from one of those places to the other. Looked at another way, Jack Carmine was a high-strung bow, drawn back, released, pulled back again, day after day in a long life of drill rigs and fence lines, the rumble of big orange machines and the recoil of .50-caliber machine guns that could sweep a Saigon rooftop like a giant push broom. He'd spent most of a lifetime trying to get the damn bow unstrung or at least loosened up a little, and the last couple of days he'd felt like he might be getting there.

It was because of her, Linda Lobo, dancin' lady. He liked looking at her, dancing with her, talking and laughing with her. He felt as if he might be getting to someplace better than where he'd ever been—her skin against his and her head tossing from side to side on the pillow, the push of her soft, round belly and grand breasts against him and the sound of his name as she whispered it over and over. Jack Carmine concentrated on her, on loving her so well, so desperately well, she'd go to Texas with him and never leave, never think about anything else but being here like this.

Two hours into that night, both of them half drunk with beer and each other, she had demonstrated the art of tassel twirling for him, which was more than enough to get things under way again, and him laughing and whispering as he came to her, "Let us all praise the wisdom of Carma." She arched her body, laughing at his words as she pulled him down and opened for him and took him into her.

CHAPTER SEVEN

New Orleans, October 27, 1993

"Oh, the shark has . . . pretty teeth, dear, and he keeps them a pearly white . . ."

The black woman, after walking forward and dropping dollar bills in Ariendo Vincent's money box, sang along with the alto saxophone as she returned to her chair. Just before she sat down, she glanced at Vaughn Rhomer as if she were not quite smiling but ready to.

The smallish round man in brown clothes and sensible shoes was watching her, studying her in profile, and she knew it. He'd pretended to be busy with other things, but he'd been looking at her since she'd arrived twenty minutes ago. She'd heard him when he'd fumbled the brandy order and felt . . . well, almost sorry for him, almost.

He was alone, and that was unusual. Most times they were with older women who wore their hair in tight curls. If not that, it was a group of them, conventioneers or football fans, behaving in loud and clumsy ways, mobs of slobs far from home and thus unshackled and

123

thus free to poke each other's arms while they leered at her. None of them could afford her body price. And she would not have gone with them if they could have met it. She had her own clientele, the reasonably elegant and wealthy gentlemen of New Orleans and points north who would call ahead before they came to town. They were mostly white and reluctant to be seen with her in fine restaurants, her color . . . her color. But in private rooms flowed caviar from bellies of Iranian sturgeon along with premium champagne from the bellies of Reims, and ordinarily they asked relatively little of her. Most of them just liked to look at her, to be around her, to smell the exotic scents she wore, to hear the voice like woodsmoke on a rainy night in deep autumn. The sex was usually in the category of expected and perfunctory.

But the round man in the sensible shoes had nice eyes. She'd noticed that when he had walked forward and put a carefully folded dollar bill in Ariendo's money box. He'd kept his eyes mostly on the ground during his walk but allowed them an angular glance toward her as he returned to his table.

She watched the smoke from her thin cigar, watched Ariendo Vincent ready himself for another song, and wondered what the man in brown clothes was thinking. Cohana Eliason, "Gumbo" to her friends, didn't really care what he was thinking, she just wondered. Other such men who had never been with a black woman were curious about the color of her in her secret places. Except for one man who had mentioned it to her, they never said as much, but they were curious. This man was probably curious.

She looked at her Cartier watch. The man from Boston would be here in two hours. Her notebook said he liked mild dominance, not much actual sex, and lots of

talk afterward about his machine tool business. The man
to her left, at the table by himself, was looking at her
again. She could sense it partially, and could see him a
little in her peripheral vision. What was on his mind?
What would he want? What secret fantasies danced behind those kindly brown eyes? It was a game she played
in her mind.

Vaughn Rhomer was still watching the black woman
and thinking about Walter Mitty. His kids had teased
him, said he was like Thurber's character.

"I am *not* Walter Mitty, whoever that is," he'd said.
"Who is he?"

Laverne had said Mitty was a guy who looked at mud
puddles and saw oceans, who would see a tiger when he
looked at Razberry. Vaughn Rhomer's friendly librarian
had found the story for him. He'd read it, thought about
it. The next time Laverne walked by and said, "How's
it going, Walter?" Vaughn had grabbed him by the arm.

"Let me tell you something, son. Maybe Walter Mitty
could see oceans in mud puddles, would look at Razberry and see himself facing down a tiger. But I see mud
puddles for what they are—mud puddles. And Razberry
is the family cat. I may be a dreamer, but I intend to
act on my dreams sometime, once I get you and your
two brothers out of this safe little nest and into the
world. I've tried to get all three of you hotshots to go
out there, but you won't."

"Dad, you're always talking about going *out there*.
Where is it, out there?"

Vaughn Rhomer had looked at Laverne for several
seconds before answering, trying to dig up a response.
Jack Carmine to the rescue, what Vaughn Rhomer had
heard him say once: "Some things, if you're dumb
enough to have to ask about them, you won't understand the answer, anyhow." He said that to Laverne.

Laverne had shaken his head, saying he had to meet some friends at the mall. He'd walked out, thinking the old man was strange, the old man who talked big about going out there but never went anywhere except to Best Value and garage sales. But he was a good father, Laverne knew that. Strange little old guy, but always there for you, *there* as in *here* and not *out there*. "Responsible" is the word he would have used if someone had asked him to describe his father. He'd decided to drop the Walter Mitty bit. The old man was right: somehow it didn't fit him. His father, Vaughn, was . . . coiled. Walter Mitty was not coiled. Simple—the difference—and profound. And a little unnerving. Laverne hoped things wouldn't change until he finished his B.S. in computer science. He wanted Vaughn Rhomer to just stay coiled and be *here*, not out *there*.

By God, Vaughn Rhomer knew he was not Walter Mitty. Hadn't he decided to make this trip alone, to use his two weeks of vacation all at once and drift south to warmer things? He'd spent hours in his basement room, studying maps and tracing routes, reading guide books, getting ready.

"What're you doing on your vacation, Vaughn?"

"Heading south . . . New Orleans."

"By yourself?" His co-workers were a little incredulous.

"Yep. Going to wander along, take my time. Going first-class all the way, staying at Holiday Inns on my way down. No cutting corners this time."

One of them laughed. "Don't be gone too long, Vaughn. All this talk about downsizing, your job might not be here when you get back."

Vaughn Rhomer wasn't worried about downsizing. Well, maybe a little. He was good at his job, but so was Arch Williams over at Fort Dodge, and they'd let him go when they'd reorganized that store, hiring younger fellows at lower wages. Younger fellows who were less likely to need medical care than older ones. But Vaughn Rhomer was only three years from retirement; he was guessing he could hang on that long.

He'd loaded the Buick's trunk with gear from his basement room. Knapsacks, canteens, first-aid kit, jungle hammock, and pertinent articles from his *National Geographic* files about the territory he would travel. After locking the house on Trolley Car Boulevard, he'd walked out back into high weeds. Razberry's grave was overgrown a bit, and he tidied it up, then stepped back, looking at the small marker he'd made from wood scraps and the words *Razberry Rhomer, 1978–1991*. He missed Razberry. She'd traveled far and well with him through long winter nights in Rhomer's Room.

His children had tried to persuade him not to make the trip. Their reasons were unclear both to them and Vaughn Rhomer.

"What would Mom think?" Louis had asked.

"About what?"

"About you just taking off like this."

"She'd probably worry, if she were still here."

"That's exactly what I'm talking about. Mom would worry."

Vaughn Rhomer had felt a twitch in his right cheek muscle and changed the subject. "How's your family, Louis? Lisa and the baby all right?"

"Oh, yes, they're fine. We're teaching Jennifer to say 'Grandpa.' "

"That's nice. Tell her Grandpa is leaving tomorrow for de land of cotton and points unknown."

Louis wouldn't give up. "But why New Orleans, Dad? That's a long way. Why don't you just go up to Clear Lake for a week or something?"

"If you can't ride with Bedouins or drink gin in the Raffles bar in Singapore while wearing a white suit and lemon–yellow tie, then New Orleans is next best." He'd known Louis wouldn't understand Bedouins or Singapore, and that's why he'd said it.

"Dad, now listen to me, do you *really* think you . . ."

"Good night, Louis. Take good care of my granddaughter. Talk to you when I get back." Vaughn Rhomer had hung up the phone and inventoried his gear stacked in neat piles around the living room.

The trip had gone well. He'd taken his time through the Ozarks, moving farther and farther into warm weather as he took the Buick south, stopping now and then to snap a picture with the old Rolleiflex he'd bought secondhand from a camera store in Otter Falls. The family hated the camera, fidgeting while Vaughn Rhomer would hold it waist high and look down into the viewfinder, shielding it from the sun. Marjorie complained and said it took too much time to get a picture taken. Nathan told Vaughn Rhomer the Rolleiflex was embarrassing, it was so old and out-of-date. Marjorie had purchased a Minolta point-and-shoot, which everyone liked a lot better.

The only bad part of the New Orleans trip had occurred in Vicksburg, Mississippi. He'd arrived at sundown, showered, and dressed in his new brown outfit, white shirt and tie included. Across the street from the Holiday Inn was a restaurant advertising genuine southern fried catfish. He'd decided on that and walked over to the restaurant, hoping they'd have some nice fresh vegetables to go along with the catfish. The dining area was decorated with buoys and fishing nets, and he'd been surprised to be the only person eating there. He'd looked out the window and waited for his food, watching cars pass by with noisy mufflers and heavily tinted windows.

While he was eating, a woman's voice shrieked continually from a bar area on the other side of a glass partition: "Sit on me, Knobby, sit on me, sit on me now!"

The bartender had kept saying, "Shsssh," but the woman had ignored him and shouted those same words again and again.

Vaughn Rhomer had planned a long, leisurely dining experience, but he'd eaten as rapidly as he could and did not enjoy his food, particularly the overcooked green beans and soggy hush puppies. Walking back to the motel, he'd thought about the proud heritage of the city, how the people had endured the siege of Vicksburg with style and grace and how far we'd come since that time— "Sit on me, Knobby!" for crying out loud, right in public.

The woman, Gumbo, glanced at her watch. She still had nearly two hours before the machine tool king would arrive with flowers in his hand. She turned slightly toward the little guy in brown, who was shooing a fly away from his espresso.

When Vaughn Rhomer finished waving the fly to more congenial hunting grounds, he looked up. The black woman was staring at him, and she was smiling now.

Vaughn Rhomer began to sweat beneath his clothes, which were too heavy for the thick New Orleans night. The images again, quickly now: a figure of steaming skin . . . spread-eagled wide . . . her writhing beneath your touch . . . You're either Walter Mitty or you're not, and the moment of truth is sitting eight feet away from you, Vaughn Henry Rhomer.

But the ambiguity, the lack of knowing what to do for sure. He'd only made love with two other women in his life, and one didn't count, since it had happened after a football game in high school and had lasted only thirty seconds. Thirty seconds didn't count as an experience. She'd been an alternate on the pom-pom squad, cheering when Vaughn Rhomer, second-string guard, had recovered the Waterloo East fumble on the seven-yard line. But she'd cheered even louder when, two plays later, Donovan Schuster—graceful, sleek Donovan Schuster—had leaped high and caught a pass for the winning touchdown. The newspaper account of the game had run a picture of Donovan's catch and wrongly identified Rollie Smike as the one who had recovered the fumble that made it all possible. Doris the pom-pom girl was not in Donovan Schuster's league, and she knew who had really recovered the fumble, so she decided to do it with Vaughn Rhomer as the next best thing. Yet in Vaughn Rhomer's book, it didn't count as a genuine experience. That left Marjorie, who drew back from the edges of anything coming close to sheer abandon, saying it wasn't ladylike.

But this woman, Gumbo, who was now staring at him and smiling, would know how to combine elegance with lubricious frenzy.

> *. . . it is important to understand women as more than simple variations on a theme. They are, in moments of undress and passion, quite different in kind, physically and mentally and emotionally. And each will have her own needs and her own ways of satisfying those needs. The male must be attuned to all of this and be prepared to accommodate her while yet experiencing his own pleasure. In and with a woman, in the sheer spirituality of the act, truth can be found that cannot be found in any other way—the*

woman's own truth, the man's truth. This
should all be remembered.

> Thomas Martin, Journeys, Vol.
> IV: The Orient *(London: Empire*
> *Publishing Ltd., 1927), p. 206.*
> *Read and copied in V. H. Rhomer's*
> *Notebook #11, 2/27/92.*

And, of course, we should discuss the spiritu-
ality of the Act itself. For that is what we all
seek, the spiritual sense that derives from the
oneness of man and woman. Therefore, we be-
gin with the idea of the sexual physical union
as something akin to a moment of religious reve-
lation. But to arrive at that moment, one must
expect the Act itself to last some time and never
be carried out in haste.

> Harry Stassen, The Complete
> Man's Guide to the Pleasures of the
> Tantra *(New York: Specialty Pub-*
> *lishers, 1977), p. 14. Read and*
> *copied in V. H. Rhomer's Note-*
> *book #11, 2/28/92.*

The black woman was still staring at Vaughn
Rhomer, and she was still smiling, and Ariendo Vincent
was blowing spit from his alto saxophone, but Vaughn
Rhomer didn't notice what Ariendo Vincent was doing
at that moment. Vaughn Rhomer was looking at the
woman and thinking about borders, about crossing
them. He could hardly believe it was him lifting his
brandy glass in salute and nodding to her. He could
hardly believe she was lifting her brandy glass in salute
and nodding back. And everybody remembers how
warm New Orleans was in October that year.

CHAPTER EIGHT

Iowa and Points South, 1986

Linda's mother leaned on the kitchen sink and looked out at Jack Carmine sitting on the fender of his pickup. "Where's this one from?"

"Texas. That's why we're goin' there."

"What's he do?"

"Got a little ranch where he stays winters, does wheat combining or lays gas pipe, summers." Linda was tugging a pair of new corduroys with an elastic waistband over Sara Margaret's bottom.

"Doesn't sound like much of a living to me."

Sara Margaret had her arms around her mother's neck, holding tight and looking over Linda's shoulder. "Who that man, Mommy?"

"He's a good friend of Mommy's, Sara Margaret. Here, stand up straight so I can tuck in your new flannel shirt. . . . Mom, where are her tennis shoes we bought when you came up to Dillon in August?"

"Over by the back door. She came in muddy yesterday." Linda's mother was still staring out at Jack Carmine, who had lit a cigarette and was scratching his cheek. "He looks kinda old."

"He's forty-seven."

"Looks older'n that in the face. What's this goin' to Texas all of a sudden all about?"

"Just seems like the right thing to do. He's a good man, Mom."

"I've heard you say that before, daughter. Several times before, seems to me. It's after two . . . gettin' a little late to start out yet today, isn't it?"

"Jack says we'll make Kansas City by dark, maybe even go on to Topeka if he's not too tired."

Jack was a little tired, in a good way. So was Linda Lobo, in a good way. They'd made love half the night and spent the morning in bed, talking and making love again. She had not come so many times in her entire life as she had in the last fifteen hours and smiled when she thought about it. High and letting down easy all at the same time, they'd ordered huge breakfasts from room service—eggs over easy, fried potatoes, toast— and sat cross-legged on the bed, eating and smiling at one another.

He'd loaded her new suitcase in the pickup's box, carefully placing dog food sacks around it and covering it with a yellow slicker he kept behind the truck seat. Linda was wearing new tan wool slacks, a red sweater with a white blouse under it, and the light mountain parka over it. She kept looking down at her new suede loafers with small tassels. She'd never owned shoes like that.

When she'd slid into the truck, Jack said, "Lookin' good, dancin' lady. What about little Sara Margaret, she need anything in the way of new duds?"

"Probably."

To the mall again for Sara Margaret clothes and a

bright red duffel bag in which to carry them. And a stuffed tiger Jack had insisted on buying. They'd swung off I-80 a little before two and come into the north edge of Altoona, where the house with gray shingles sat looking worn on an overcast day in late October.

"How long you known this Jack . . . what's his name?" Her mother had turned and was watching Linda stuff Sara Margaret's things in the red duffel. Sara Margaret sat on a kitchen chair, legs swinging, talking to her new stuffed tiger.

"His name's Carmine. Known him a while. Met him in Dillon while I was workin' at the chicken plant."

"That was a good, steady job. Hate to see you give it up just to go runnin' around with some crazy Texan." Her mother's last visit to Dillon had been in August, when she and Sara Margaret had ridden a Greyhound up to visit Linda. Linda had changed professions shortly afterward without saying anything to her mother about it.

"I told you what that work was doin' to my hands. They hurt every night from usin' that knife and workin' in the cold."

"Well, it was good, steady work, and that's hard to come by these days. Believe me, I done without plenty of times, and sometimes you got to put up with a little discomfort. He buy you those nice clothes you got on?"

"Yes," Linda said, brushing away a few strands of hair that had fallen over her face.

"Daughter, when a man starts givin' you presents right off, it's time to watch out. I notice you're beginnin' to look a little hard around the eyes, need to take better care of yourself."

Linda didn't say anything more. She zipped the duffel and straightened up, taking Sara Margaret's hand. "Here we go, Sara Margaret, for a ride in that nice truck out

there with that nice man. Hang on tight to your tiger
so it doesn't fall in the mud."

Her mother followed them out to where Jack was
sitting on the pickup's fender, kicking the heels of his
boots against the left front tire. He grinned and stood
down, a little uneasy at the truculent way Linda's mother
was looking at him. Linda handed him Sara Margaret's
duffel, and he put it under the yellow slicker, next to
Linda's suitcase.

Linda hugged her mother, who was looking as worn
as the house behind them, and it was plain on her face
she'd hoped her daughter might find better things in life
than she herself had. She knew about Linda's summer
nights with Lucas Mathen and had thanked God many
times for getting them all by that without a pregnancy.
And there'd been Wendell, and a string of others, and
then Gary. Jack Carmine didn't seem like much of a
rung up or down on any ladder. But at least he had a
place of his own, even if it was somewhere in godforsaken Texas. "You be sure to write or call, now. Let me
know how you're doin'," she said, bending over to pick
up a stray piece of shingle blown from the roof in a
recent windstorm.

"I will," Linda said, getting Sara Margaret centered
on the truck seat.

"Nice to meet you," Jack said, holding out his hand.

Linda's mother nodded and shook his hand for only
a moment. He looked kind of tired to her, and she
wondered why her good-looking, thirty-seven-year-
old, long-legged daughter couldn't have found something better. Jack backed the truck onto the dirt road,
and Linda smiled at the old cottonwood tree where she'd
had a tire swing in the warm days of her Iowa girlhood.
Her mother waved once, languidly, not smiling, and

went back to picking up bits of shingle as they rolled away.

"I never been south of Des Moines," Linda said, "except once when my high school class had a picnic at some park near Indianola. Or west of Council Bluffs or east of the Mississippi River, either."

They ate supper at a Hardee's in Kansas City, Sara Margaret sitting on her mother's lap, holding on to her tiger while Linda fed her a small cheeseburger and French fries. Jack and Linda kept looking at one another, smiling.

Back in the truck and heading for Topeka. Sara Margaret slept on the seat, her head on Linda's lap, while Jack's road tapes began and ended and started up again at low volume.

"I almost feel . . . well, kinda fatherly, seein' you and her over there," he said, coming up behind an eighteen-wheeler and swinging out to pass it.

"Ever been married, Jack Carmine?"

"Yep, about the time I was drinkin' beer and talkin' dirty back in '63. Stayed married, more or less, for seven of them years. She was pretty mad about me up and enlistin' in the army in nineteen and sixty-nine. She ran off with a dentist from Odessa while I was in Vietnam."

"Have any kids?"

"Yep to that, also. Got a son who's . . . let's see . . . twenty-five." Jack was holding tapes up to the dash lights. "Lookin' for one marked 'Emmylou' . . . here it is." Emmylou Harris came on singing about lonesome nights and cowgirls getting the blues sometimes.

"Ever see your son . . . what's his name?"

"Name's Tom. Last name's not Carmine, however, since my ex has done her best to completely stomp out any trace of me. I wanted to name him after the old diviner, Fine Daley, who convinced Poly there was oil under our ranch. That'd have made him 'Fine Carmine from Alpine.' Nobody else would hear of it, though. Used to see him every so often. He'd come down for a week or two in the winter when I'd be home. He's finishin' up learnin' to be a dentist and probably's pretty busy. 'Least he doesn't come to visit anymore. Haven't seen him for several years."

"How do you feel about not seein' him?" Sara Margaret sat up for a moment, and Linda helped her turn onto her other side, stroking her hair as she went to sleep again with her tennis shoes barely touching Jack's right hip.

"Oh, don't know. Like to see him now and then, I guess. Think about him. He seems okay, decently happy. Phones me once in a while, even though his mother says he ought to stay away from me. Says he's goin' to specialize in braces, whatever that's called these days. Hey, see that sign? Topeka's sixty-three exact minutes up ahead. We'll bed down wherever we can find somethin' tonight. Tomorrow night, if we get a real early start in the mornin', I got a treat for all of us."

"What's that?"

"Place near Calona, Texas. I'm keepin' it as a surprise."

"Well, that'll be welcome; I can't remember last time I was surprised by a place to stay. Did I hear you say earlier you have a brother?"

"Yep, Edward. Teaches the double-reed instruments at the University of Alabama music school. Haven't seen him for a long time. We're pretty different from one another; he turned out okay. How about you, ever been married?"

"Twice, I'm sorry to say. First time it was one of those teenage deals that was doomed to start with and hardly counts. Second time didn't work out, either. We just kept hangin' on 'cause of Sara Margaret and 'cause we couldn't think of anything better to do for sure, until he found someone else."

Topeka came up, and they stopped at a Ramada. The next morning they were on the road at sunup. The day drifted by, Jack driving, fiddling with his tapes, on silent running for long stretches and not saying much. Sara Margaret talked to her tiger and played "itsy-bitsy spider" with Linda. After Sara Margaret's nap in the afternoon, Linda read to her and pointed out the things they saw as Oklahoma fell behind and Jack took them west of Austin just ahead of sundown.

"Texas Hill Country up ahead, four hours more to the Calona good stuff. We'll raise Alpine tomorrow," he said, looking at downtown Austin in his rearview mirror. "To my way of thinkin', dancin' lady, somewhere out ahead, west of Junction, there's kind of a space-time curtain rifflin' in the wind. And out beyond that curtain blowin' around on the southern run of the high plains lies another land entirely: West Texas. You'll see what I mean before long. Different place altogether, and if you feel it, you'll live it and start believin' you're from a foreign country compared to everythin' else of an American nature."

After her second nap of the day, Sara Margaret was up and full of it when Jack turned off I-10 at a truck stop east of Calona. "You're not goin' believe this," he said. "Man had a dream, built an oasis right here in the middle of the Texas outback."

At night, the Best Western looked nice but ordinary to Linda. Jack got two connecting rooms and handed the keys to her while he drove the truck toward the end of the motel. "You can work it out accordin' to your motherly instincts, dancin' lady. Sleep with Sara Margaret, sleep with me, go back and forth from room to room."

Linda handled Sara Margaret while Jack carried in a suitcase and two duffel bags, then went back for the cooler. "Things are gettin' dangerously domestic when it takes more than one trip to unload the truck."

Inside the rooms were sliding glass doors. Jack was grinning when he swept back the curtains covering them. "Look at this, folks."

The motel was built around a huge atrium area covered with glass and filled with exotic trees and flowering plants. The three of them stood looking into the atrium, Jack pointing. "See, there's a nice big indoor swimmin' pool they keep at just below body temperature and a Jacuzzi off to one side. Looks like we got the place to ourselves. Me, I'm three minutes away from the water. I'll take little Sara Margaret out and leave you time for gettin' on your surprise."

Linda dressed Sara Margaret in a clean pair of underpants, saying, "This'll have to work for her swimming costume."

"It'll be fine," Jack said, standing there in a pair of dark green boxer trunks. He picked up Sara Margaret— "C'mon, muchacha, let's go swimmin' "—and went out through a sliding glass door, walking on flat stepstones winding through plants and trees, heading for the pool.

Linda could hear them laughing as she sorted through her suitcase. She peeked out and saw Jack Carmine bouncing Sara Margaret up and down in shallow water.

When she walked along the flat rocks leading to the pool deck, Jack had Sara Margaret on his shoulders, taking long, swooping strides in the water and singing,

"Jack's a good ol' horse if you treat him right / Jack's a good ol' horse who can run all night."

He looked up at Linda Lobo coming toward them and stopped singing. She was wearing a lavender bikini, cut low on top and high on the sides. He grinned. "Whoa! Takes my breath away, Miss Linda."

She smiled and pirouetted for him. "Anna Wilhelm said I should get this one. 'If you got it, flaunt it,' were her exact words. Not too much more here than my Rainbow Bar costume."

"Well, I've been in total agreement with Anna Wilhelm's advice all along, but never more than right this minute."

Linda sat on the edge of the pool, swishing her feet in the warm water while Jack leaned beside her, holding Sara Margaret, who was saying, "More horsey, more Jack horsey."

Later they ate Mexican food at the motel restaurant. It was after ten and Sara Margaret fell asleep on a high chair. They walked slow back to their rooms, Linda carrying her and humming, tucking her head against Sara Margaret's. Jack was practicing his Texas two-step as they walked, which hadn't improved since the last time he'd tried it.

Linda got Sara Margaret settled in bed and went into the next room, moving soft across the carpeted floor, smoothing back her hair as she walked. Jack had the sliding door open and was drinking a beer while he looked out at the darkened atrium area. She stood beside him and put her arm around his waist.

He smiled down at her. "How you feelin', dancin' lady?"

She grinned. "Real happy, cowboy. Feel like I've been transported to another world where there's only good things."

"Well, we'll put some amount of energy into keepin' it that way. How about another swim? We can leave Sara Margaret's slidin' door open and hear her if she needs anything."

"My suit's still wet. . . ." Linda stopped and noticed the little grin on his face. "You're not thinkin' what I think you're thinkin', are you, Jack Carmine?"

"All I'm thinkin' is that there's nobody out there and it's pretty dark. Pool closed at ten, but if we were to put on a couple of towels to get us from here to the water and be quiet once we're there, nobody'll notice. Just about pitch black except for those little lights at the far end."

Linda smiled at him. "You're a depraved man, Jack Carmine. But . . . more I think on it, more I like the idea, which I guess means I'm in that category also."

"I wouldn't have you any other way," he said, turning her toward him and sliding his hands into the back pockets of her jeans. "A rotten degenerate, is what Mama Pepito called me once when I was roostered up and whizzed a beer bottle through the front window of her equally degenerate little bucket of blood across the tracks in Alpine. But that was in my wild days. Calmer now, except when I'm within a hundred yards of you, as I'm steadily findin' out hour by hour."

Come the years later on Linda will look back and remember this. She'll remember being in the middle of her life in the middle of a warm swimming pool in the middle of Texas Nowhere, her long hair done up and her long legs around Jack Carmine and him talking soft about how things were going to be better from here on out. She'll remember that all she'd ever wanted was right there. In that transient moment, in that passing time, it had seemed that way . . . seemed that way.

CHAPTER NINE

West Texas, 1986

Dawn, and the moon sat full and fat on I-10, looking as if you could go right through it in a mile or two. Driving a pickup loaded with dog food and new clothes and maybe something better than what she'd had so far, Linda Lobo thought about what Jack had said yesterday, about this being another land entirely. She was used to green fields and towns that lay only a few miles apart, and the arid distances and high buttes out here made her feel small and vulnerable. It was no place to be running on empty.

While eastern commuter trains clacked toward the work of stocks and bonds and putting out magazines and designing clothes, it was quiet in West Texas on a Monday morning. Except for wind going by the truck window and the sound of the engine, and Sara Margaret talking to her tiger, and Jack Carmine trying to twist "Rainy Day Woman" out of the harmonica he kept in the glove compartment.

"Used to be able to play that one a little bit. Haven't been practicin'."

Linda watched a blue-and-white semi heading east on the other side of the median, its hood ornament catching the first slant of new sunlight, then looked at Jack Carmine over the top of her glasses. "Did you ever really practice it, the harmonica?"

"No, but I think about practicin' sometimes. That ought to count for somethin', make you better somehow."

He went back to playing, then stopped again and examined the harmonica. "This here's a workin' man's French harp. It's the only one I own, and it's in the key of E, which is the people's key. Heard that somewhere once, about E bein' the people's key. Now you'd think a workin' man's harmonica would just naturally want to play 'Rainy Day Woman' without any help from me, wouldn't you?"

Sara Margaret held the tiger on her lap and looked up at him, her face serious.

"Okay, muchacha, get ready to clap your hands," Jack said to her, and launched into "Pop Goes the Weasel," which he could almost get through except for a few notes here and there. Sara Margaret, her hair pulled back into a light blond ponytail, kept looking at him, holding her tiger.

Jack stopped, slapping the harmonica on his hand to clear the spit. "Say, mother of this girl, she know how to clap her hands at all?"

Linda laughed. "Of course. She's just overwhelmed at the music and is concentratin' on listenin'." She checked her mirrors and went around a Winnebago with Ohio plates, *The Roamin' Taylors—Jim and Lois* painted on the back.

"Well, I knew there was somethin'. . . ." Jack started

clapping his hands and singing, "All around the carpenter's bench . . . ."

Sara Margaret let a slow smile come over her face and
started clapping, too. Jack picked up the harmonica and
played the tune again, bobbing his head and stamping
his boots in time with Sara Margaret's hands. Linda
Lobo smiled and drove them on through a dawn that
was turning the high buttes red on their eastern sides
and sending the moon to where it goes before it comes
around again.

After a while Jack stuck the harmonica in his breast
pocket and said, "You know, there's somethin' about
that song . . . somethin'. Ain't no children's song at all
when you think about it, and ever since I was five years
old I been tryin' to figure out who's really doin' the
chasin'. When things're movin' in a circle like that, who
says the monkey's after the weasel, maybe it's the other
way around. More'n that, who's the carpenter and
what's he buildin'? That's what I keep wonderin'. And
where's he off to and leavin' his tools just lyin' there
while all this runnin' around his bench is takin' place? I
been thinkin' lately maybe he's sitting cross-legged on
the bench watchin' the chase down below him. The
weasel I can understand, but I never figured out why
the carpenter's got a monkey hangin' around his shop
. . . never figured that out. . . . How you doin', dancin'
lady, gettin' tired of drivin', while I talk nonsense?"

"No, I'm okay for a while yet. But now you got me
lookin' in the rearview mirror all the time to see if there's
any monkeys back there."

"They're there all right. Just can't see 'em most of
the time. Got to look kind of sideways quick, they live
right in the far corner of your eye. Best not to look,
though, it makes 'em mad if they think you're payin'
attention to 'em."

The billboard planted in the middle of America's big-empty read *Eat Beef—The West Wasn't Won on Salads.*

Jack took the wheel at Fort Stockton, saying he had to drive the last leg into Alpine, some kind of superstition, that if he didn't drive, he wouldn't actually feel as if he was there when he got there.

At first Linda was disappointed with the look of the countryside. Halfway through the morning Fort Stockton sprawled dry and dusty in brittle sunlight. Eight miles farther on Jack turned south on Route 67 and said, "See those mountains up ahead, that's where we're headed."

Linda Lobo tried to concentrate on the mountains, they looked serene, hazy, and blue in the distance, and she'd never truly believed there were mountains in Texas until that moment. But she was still thinking about monkeys and what Jack had said earlier.

Sara Margaret was lying with her head on Linda's lap, bored and sleepy from the hours of riding. Linda stroked the blond hair and looked straight ahead at the mountains. "Those monkeys you were talkin' about, Jack, kind of like thoughts that keep chasin' you, aren't they?"

"Maybe. What thoughts you talkin' about?"

"Thoughts about it all goin' fast. They won't leave me alone sometimes, remind me of the man who sold my mother a complete set of encyclopedias once when we couldn't afford a comic book. Thoughts that just keep rappin' on the door and then come on in when you're too tired to keep them out, and once they're inside they just keep talkin' until you feel like buyin' something just so they'll leave. Been gettin' those thoughts at the strangest times. Keep thinkin' about just what it is I'm doin' with my life."

"Like loadin' up and boltin' for West Texas with a man you hardly know?"

"Some of that." Linda adjusted Sara Margaret and put a boot on the dash. "Don't get me wrong, I've just spent three of the best days of my life with you, Jack Carmine. God, when I think about what we've been doin' with each other and what went on last night in the swimmin' pool, I don't care much about anything other than drinkin' beer and takin' my clothes off. But I got this little girl sleepin' here on my lap, and I don't see much out ahead for her the way I'm livin' out my life. Know what I mean?"

Jack grinned at her. "I surely do, Miss Linda. Used to feel that way myself until I kicked the encyclopedia salesman's ass out the door and told 'im not to come back. Told 'im I had a truck with new rear tires and a shirttail ranch and that was everythin' I needed."

"What age were you when you got that all settled?"

"Early twenties, I guess, give or take fifteen years."

Linda kept looking straight down the road while she talked. "You know, it's a damn vicious circle I'm caught up in—kind of like runnin' around some carpenter's bench—working hard just to keep me and Sara Margaret going and not enough time for putting down long, straight track that'd make things better tomorrow and the day after. I don't mind sayin' one of my main worries these past few months was that some savior of the people might see me dancin' in the Rainbow and try to take Sara Margaret away by declarin' I was unfit to be a mother."

Jack grinned. "You were safe. God looks out for the wayward and condemns the righteous. I stole that from ol' Poly Carmine. He used to say it at least once a day."

The mountains came closer, and the music kept playing. Sara Margaret sat up and rubbed her eyes. As they crossed the bridge over Antelope Draw, "Waltz Across Texas" came on the radio. Jack sang along with it while he tickled Sara Margaret with his right hand until she curled up with tears running down her cheeks. Linda Lobo listened to her daughter's laughter and thought just for a moment about what on earth she was doing here in a pickup truck with Sara Margaret and a man she hardly knew, headed for a one-horse ranch in Texas all the while she was thirty-seven and beginning to droop a little. And she was afraid again—the same come-and-be-gone-in-a-moment fears she'd had moving through the strobelights or with her hands buried in chicken guts—a woman on her own, a messy life behind and nothing she could see ahead of her that amounted to much in the way of a future for her and Sara Margaret.

"Hey, listen to this one," Jack said as a new song got under way. He turned up the volume.

> I came rollin' north from Texas
> Through a long yellow
>   summer,
> Swallowin' dust
> And ridin' big orange
>   machines.
> Breakdowns were my enemies
> Sundowns were my dreams.

"Hear that? That's my old buddy Bobby McGregor and his band. Bobby and me traveled fast and light together before he became a well-known singer of these songs he was writin' all the while we was goin' down the road. Used to sit in the backseat and play his Martin six-string, make up songs and write 'em down in notebooks. Haven't seen him for a long time now, since he settled down and got married, after which he got famous. What he's singin' about there is just the way it was when we pushed north on top of those big combines durin' the summers, runnin' up to Canada in the warm and driftin' south ahead of the cool. Like to do that again one of these years." His voice got a little softer. "Haven't heard from Bobby McGregor for some time."

Where 67 intersected with Route 90 running east and west, Jack leaned over the wheel and pointed right. "Alpine's that way eight miles." He pointed left. "The ranch is nine miles this way, so we're only seventeen miles from town, not countin' the little over two miles of road up to the house from the highway, which I guess ends up makin' us nineteen miles from Alpine if you want to be specific."

Linda stared west, toward Alpine. Down the stretch of highway there were mountains everywhere, one of them spindle topped, another divided into two separate peaks. And mountains straight ahead and behind her. Not the Rockies, not the high snowy places she'd seen in photographs. But mountains just the same, with the light a softer yellow now and the land looking buff colored, looking hard at first glance and yet forgiving in some other kind of way. She was thinking these were manageable mountains, mountains you could walk without special equipment, mountains that didn't dominate you.

Jack shifted and turned left on 90, running easy through the gears and looking around. "There's nothin' in the world like comin' home, especially when it's Alpine, Texas, full of the best and kindest people you're goin' to meet anywhere, with only a very few sons a bitches mixed in. This, I would say, dancin' lady, has got to be the finest place in the world in all respects, and I'm sure you and Sara Margaret are goin' to like it." He looked at her in that slow, easy, serious-come-wistful way of his, talking quietly. "I want very much for you to like it, 'cause I'm hopin' you and Sara Margaret will be stayin' on here for a long time."

"Why Jack call you 'dancin' lady,' Momma?"

Linda pulled Sara Margaret up on her lap. "I'll tell you later, sweetheart. Let's look at the pretty mountains now. See all those growin' things? Those're called cactus plants."

A Southern Pacific freight was running opposite them alongside 90, heading west toward Alpine, five engines pulling a hundred cars and moving fast.

"Look at the ol' SP," Jack said. "She's gatherin' up her skirt and gettin' up enough steam to make it over Paisano Pass other side of Alpine. Long trains out here, not like the little short-hauls back in the Midwest. Saw one on the Houston–El Paso run come through once with thirteen engines and four hundred and thirty-four cars."

After two miles Jack slowed down and turned off the highway onto a dirt road running back into the mountains. Over the road was a metal arch with *Circle-C Ranch* scrolled at the top. The left footing of the arch was bowed out in a peculiar shape.

"What happened there?" Linda asked, pointing at the bow as they passed under the arch.

"I was afraid you'd ask that." Jack was trying to miss the potholes and rocks in the winding dirt road and was only partially succeeding, the three of them bouncing up and down, lurching left and right. "The truth of it is, that's a remnant of my wild and squandered youth, which it turns out was an accurate . . . preview of my adult years. . . . Jesus, got to get this road fixed, makes you sound like you're stutterin' just tryin' to talk. Earl and me and Shy, that's an earlier dog we had, were comin' in late one night after an evenin' of honky-tonkin' through the countryside. Shy was sober, Earl and I were the other side of crazy, as usual. Earl was drivin' and kind of drifted off to the left as we passed through the gate, hit it pretty good. I was only fifteen then, and Poly cast a hard eye on carousin' of any kind, he was a fairly straight hombre, 'cept when he was courtin' Rainy and got her pregnant with me, as she tells it. Anyway, on that night Earl gets out and looks at the gate all bent and skeejawed there in the headlights and says, 'Aw, sheeit, Jack, Mr. Carmine's gonna let me go for sure now.' And I'm sayin', 'No, he ain't, Earl Chavez, 'cause I'm drivin' the rest of the way up to the house and tellin' all concerned it was me that hit the damned thing.'

"Rainy was waitin' for us when we pulled in the yard, big ol' new crunch in the left fender of that Ford pickup, which had a lot of crunches in it anyway. But Poly could spot a new crunch in anything from two hundred yards out with his unaided eyes.

"No point in just passin' over it, I figured, since somebody was goin' to eventually see what we'd done to the gate. I'm soberin' up pretty fast by then and say to Rainy that I hit the gate and how sorry I was about doin' it. All she said was, 'Better get to bed. I've got a feeling there's going to be a lot of work to be done around here, starting tomorrow.'

"Next morning, Poly comes up from the gate and tells me the fence line over Little Horse Mountain— that's the big blue fellow you see right ahead of us— needs replacin' and that I'm assigned to do it. I spent the rest of the summer workin' fence up one side and down the other of Little Horse Mountain, all by myself in the Texas sun. Poly got busy with another crusade, and Rainy said she wasn't gettin' the gate fixed, lettin' it stand, in her own unique way of puttin' it as another monument to the stupidity of all the male Carmines she'd ever met."

More bumps and lurches, across two cattle guards, rusty wire curled on the ground, an empty Lone Star beer bottle sitting on a wooden fence post.

"So I'm up there on Little Horse Mountain workin' while Earl's doin' okay around the barn and cattle pens, and my younger brother, Eddie, is sittin' in the livin' room practicing his oboe and tauntin' me when I came draggin' down those evenin's when I didn't camp up on the mountain. He stopped the tauntin' after I told him I was goin' to be hammering fence posts with his oboe, startin' the followin' day, which he sensed wasn't an entirely idle threat if I got in just the right mood. The one good part of all this is that Earl never forgot about me takin' the blame, and we buckled up close for life, close as two partners in crime can get."

"That was awfully generous of you, Jack, takin' the blame for what happened."

"Wasn't generous at all. If I was goin' to get out and around, I needed Earl to drive, since I was only fifteen and wasn't supposed to be drivin' anyway. It was a straight-ahead calculation of income and outgo, the purest kind of rational thinkin' in spite of my condition that night."

Linda Lobo smiled. "I still think it was generous. . . . You shrug off credit too fast, Jack."

"There's the house," Jack said as they rounded a clump of desert candle and the road straightened out to the south, still climbing upward at a pitch of four degrees, past cattle pens and chutes and wrinkled gray dung. "Earl must have the stock up in the back pasture. I called him and said I was bringin' guests and to get things cleaned up and move his brown ass out to the rooms attached to the barn."

"See, already Sara Margaret and me are disruptin' your lives, just like I said back in Minnesota."

"Listen, me and Earl lived in those rooms for three years together; ain't nothin' at all wrong with 'em, suit 'im just fine. I'll go down and help him fix the place up nice and neat, which'll be nicer and neater than it ever was in olden times. Get 'im a small fridge and make sure the little wood stove works; he'll be a light rider down there, just wait and see. By the way, first thing we got to pick up in town is a couple of broad-brimmed hats for you ladies, 'cause the high-desert sun down here'll turn you old before your time if you're not careful. Beats hell out of deep snow and cold wind, however . . . least *I* think so. Wait'll you see first light come up over the Glass Mountains there to the east, you can see sunrise from the main bedroom without ever gettin' out of bed.

"Hey, here comes ol' Hummer, recognizin' the truck and the crazy man drivin' it." The brown dog came running along the road toward them, tongue hanging, tail wagging. Jack leaned out the window and shouted, "Hummer boy, how you doin'? Good to see you, pleased you made it through another summer."

Hummer barked and ran alongside the truck for a few yards, then sprinted on ahead toward the house. The house where Linda would lie in bed with Jack Carmine, drinking coffee and watching sunup crawl over the Glass Mountains. Where the wind would come at dawn and die later in the morning, leaving only the slightest trace of breeze in long grass and scrub cedar and mesquite. Where the silence would close around when she stood by a fence line or sat on the porch. She came to almost fear the quiet, so quiet, such big-space silence, she could imagine hearing the blue mountain laurel struggling to flower in the spring or the beat of a hawk's wing two miles off. The lack of any sound pressed upon her until she felt as if she might implode from the pressure of it.

She never quite got used to the silence, the sound of nothing, and holding her breath, she would wait for the rumble of a train down by the highway or a blow of wind that would set the grass to bending.

She learned how to repack pumps reaching down fifteen hundred feet for water, Jack grinning at her as they worked. "Now, see, you're a town girl, Miss Linda. You turn on a faucet and never think about where the water comes from, somebody somewhere's handlin' all that. Out here, water's everything. We turn on a faucet and think about how the pump's doing five hundred yards out in the brush, wonderin' if it's still going up and down or does it need greasin' or repackin', and we use our gray water to feed the garden when it's planted, which it never is anymore. I'm showin' you how to repack the pumps in case they need it while I'm gone sometime and maybe Earl ain't available for whatever reason I can't imagine at the moment. Anyway, certain things are worth knowin', and repackin' pumps is one of 'em."

With Jack Carmine, the surprises went unbounded. On a Friday in high summer he brought home an air mattress from Morrison True Value, the store Jack called "the best supplier of anything and everything you could ever imagine wantin'—pumps and toilet seats and everyday dishes, not to mention guns and pool cues and Merle Haggard tapes. If they ain't got it, they get it in a day or two; one of the last great stores anywhere."

"What're we supposed to do with that?" she asked, staring at the package—"Camper's Queen-Size Air Mattress."

Jack wiggled a cigarette between his front teeth. "When the moon's high and the weather's good, I thought we might go up on Little Horse Mountain and fool around. Leave Sara Margaret in Earl's charge. Go native, as it were."

"Jack Carmine, you *do* get ideas, and overall, I like most of them. What about rattlesnakes, though?"

"The buzzworms are the least of our worries. They won't bother us if we don't bother them. Besides, if one crawls across you, just lie still and pretend it's me doin' somethin' wholly different and exotic to you; that'll set you free, turn you into a buffalo gal. If that don't ease your mind, I'll take along a belly gun with some number six shot cartridges in it and fire in the general direction of nothin' from time to time."

And on nights when the moon was high and the weather good, they took the air mattress and drove Poly Carmine's 1959 Toyota Land Cruiser as far up Little Horse Mountain as it was able to go. After that they climbed, Linda Lobo carrying the air mattress, Jack Carmine carrying a cooler full of beer and a portable radio with a tape deck in it. Big moons came over the Glass Mountains while the radio played and Texas Jack Carmine talked soft to the dancin' lady while he touched her. On top of him at dawn, with the sun in her face, with the sun on his hands and his hands on her breasts, in those times her fears were someplace else, and there on Little Horse Mountain was the only place she could imagine being.

"Got an idea, going into Morrison's," Jack said one Tuesday morning, and lit out for town. Two hours later she heard the pickup grinding along the east side of the ranch house. In the back was an aluminum stock tank, on the front seat was an electric trolling motor and some other gizmo, which she found out later was a fish cooker. Linda went outside, wiping her hands on a dish towel and watched Jack and Earl wrangle the tank out of the truck bed.

"Now what?" she asked, Sara Margaret standing beside her.

The Jack Carmine grin. " 'Now what' is one of the smaller strokes of technological genius to hit this place in some time. It's a surprise, of sorts, so I'd appreciate it if you'd go back inside and promise not to peek till I say it's all right. Sara Margaret's good at keepin' secrets, so she can go down to the barn with Earl and me while I figure out the rest of this contraption. Got it three-quarters worked out, figure out the rest as I go, which is the way good things get done. Grand design requires too much thinkin', spend all your time thinkin' when you should be doin' and never get around to the doin'."

For the next hour the pickup came and went, and she heard voices through the screen.

Jack: "Damn, pinched my finger."

Earl: "Jack, you're crazy as your daddy."

Jack: "Earl, stick that loose end of the hose in here and turn on the water."

Earl: "Jack, you're *crazier'n* your daddy."

A half hour later, two sounds. First, the low burble of the trolling motor. Second, the hot roar of propane heating the fish cooker under the tank.

He'd called to her through the kitchen screen, "Okay, you can come out now and view genius at work."

Jack was sitting in the stock tank, swimsuit on and smoking a cigar, *North Stars* cap turned sideways. Earl was leaning against a desert willow, arms folded and shaking his head.

Jack waved his hand expansively. "Welcome to Jack's Jacuzzi or Earl's Low-End, High-Desert Spa, depending on what name you like best. Okay, swimsuits everybody, the water's fine."

Earl didn't own a swimsuit and was too modest to wear one if he'd had one.

"That's all right, Earl, just get in with your jeans and workshirt on. Gotta take your boots and socks off, though. The masseuse comes at four, aerobics start at five, and facial packs will be applied this evenin' after a supper of Jell-O and lettuce. By tomorrow we'll all be beautiful and younger than springtime."

Sara Margaret sat on Linda's lap. Earl, in shirt and jeans and looking embarrassed, sat across from them. Jack sat near the controls for the motor and propane. All of them were sitting on cement blocks. Outside the tub, within Jack's reach, was a bucket full of ice, beer, and a Coke for Sara Margaret.

"This is goin' to take a little tweakin' and a couple extra motor batteries for long sessions, but it'll work," he'd said, handing out drinks to everyone.

They sat there, all of them laughing after a while, laughing at Jack and with Jack. The trolling motor burbled, the propane burner roared occasionally, and a Tuesday in West Texas moved along on its own terms.

There were nights when the javelinas came. The wild pigs were black and hunched, lethal looking in the darkness, moving fast and oblivious to or simply unafraid of either humans or dogs. Some of the boars had curling, three-inch tusks and ran to seventy pounds or more. Earl claimed he'd seen one that went over ninety. They looked even bigger moving under the yard lights, bristles extended, like mutant rats from some old horror film. At suppertime, a week after Linda first came to the ranch, Earl mentioned casually to Jack that the javelinas had become a problem again and that he'd seen some other tracks, big tracks, by one of the water tubs a quarter mile away.

"Lion?" Jack asked.

"I'm guessing that. The sign was pretty well trampled down by other animals. Droppings nearby looked suspicious, however."

"What's this all about, lions—what kind of lions?"

Linda was wondering just where in the hell she had landed her and Sara Margaret. Iowa seemed a long way off.

Jack grinned and pointed at his plate. "You know, these frijoles are so good, they jump right off the fork at you." He took a bite of the beans, chewed, and swallowed, looked up at her. "Mountain lions. We got three dozen kinds of potential bad out here, and Earl's talkin' about one of 'em—mountain lions, pumas, catamounts, whatever you call 'em they're all the same thing. They usually stay back a few miles on the other side of Little Horse Mountain, but occasionally they range down here. They don't bother much, usually leave the cattle alone. If it's an old one that can't hunt too well anymore, might be a problem. I'd keep Sara Margaret close to the house for a few days till we see what's happening."

"What about the . . . what're they called?"

"The javelinas?" Earl said.

Linda nodded.

"Wild pigs. They smell garbage or feed or droppin's from the pecan trees or Hummer's dog food if we don't put it up evenin's. Seem to have a real taste for dog food. They don't tend to come after human bein's unless they've got babies around, though a friend of mine got treed by a pack several years ago. But they're hard on dogs; local vet earns a fair part of his livin' fixin' up dogs torn apart by javelinas. They're rough cusses, aggressive, particularly when there's a pack of 'em and especially when they got young'uns with 'em."

Earl started smiling wide, and Jack said, "Now, Earl, c'mon now. You're not goin' to tell that story, are you?"

"Yep, too good not to tell." He grinned at Linda Lobo. "Twenty years ago, *mas o menos*, we was havin' a bad javelina problem, they was in the barn damn near every night after somethin' or other. I was sittin' on the toilet in my rooms attached to the barn when all hell broke loose one evenin'. Our old dog Shy was pretty well gone in years, but she was howlin' like a curly wolf. Next thing I know the toilet bowl exploded right under me. I didn't know what was goin' on, damn near fainted and had to rest my head on the sink for a long while just to recover and wonderin' if I'd done that. Then I noticed the hole in the wall right next to the toilet bowl. Seems Jack had led a javelina just a little too much, and the bullet came right through the barn wall into the apartment. Couldn't bring myself to sit again for the next four days."

Linda Lobo had got the image and held a napkin to her mouth, laughing at what she saw in her mind and the look on Earl's face as he told the story. Sara Margaret laughed, too, though she wasn't quite sure why.

Jack ran his tongue around the inside of his mouth. "That's Earl's version, and it wouldn't stand up under cross-examination by a boy lawyer. Truth is, I didn't lead 'im too much at all; somebody'd been fiddlin' with the damn sights on the Winchester, that's what."

A few nights later Linda was sitting on the back steps, pointing out the Big Dipper to Sara Margaret. Hummer lay beside them and suddenly brought his head up, starting into a low growl and then moving across the rumpled bricks of what used to be a patio. He'd entered long grass forty feet away, barking hard, and ten seconds later came backpedaling out of the grass. She saw it then, the black shape coming toward them across the patio, tusks curling out of its jaws. The javelina stopped twenty feet away and looked at her, ignoring Hummer.

She fumbled open the screen door, dragging Sara Margaret inside. Jack was already heading in her direction, the .30-30 Winchester saddle gun in his left hand. "Javelina?" he said.

She nodded, shaking.

Jack levered a brass cartridge into the rifle and grabbed a flashlight. "I don't like shootin' anything I don't have to, but I also don't like bullies, and those goddamn pigs'll bully you if you let 'em. Never figured out whether they're brave or blind or just dumb."

He kicked open the screen door and swept the yard with his light. Hummer came back on the steps, and Jack squatted down, saying, "Good boy. . . ."

"Nothin' there," he said, coming inside. "Sure it was a javelina?"

"Yes, it was big and black, and it came right toward us. Jack, how dangerous are they?"

"Well, they don't respond real well to a whip and a chair. Like Earl said, they'll tear hell out of dogs. Poly claimed he'd once heard about a pack of 'em eatin' somebody's kid—five-year-old boy—down near Presidio, and Earl tells that story about a friend of his bein' treed. Hard to say. I don't like the sons a bitches, myself. Don't blame you for bein' scared. Rest easy, Earl and I'll take care of 'em."

Later that same night Hummer started up again, the pitch of his bark escalating second by second. Linda lay in bed and listened, afraid for Hummer and wondering just how well she fit in this big, rough country. In the darkness she felt Jack get up and heard him pulling on his boots and jeans, zipping a leather jacket over his bare chest. Hummer's bark suddenly changed to a squeal that sounded as though he'd been hurt. She swept the curtain aside and saw a pack of javelinas moving past the window, only three feet away.

"Goddamn 'em, they're after Hummer," Jack said, running now, the saddle gun in his hand. He jammed Smyler Carmine's old Colt Army .45 in his waistband and swung open the front door.

"Jack, be careful, there's a whole pack of them and they're big."

"Where are ya, Hummer?" Linda heard him say quietly.

Jack went across the gravel parking area, down toward the barn where lights were blinking on in Earl's apartment. Suddenly he sat down in the gravel and braced the rifle on one knee, holding the barrel of it and the flashlight with his left hand. And then she saw the javelinas—eight or ten of them—moving like a black herd of something from your childhood night dreams, moving through the beams of his flashlight and into the broader beam of the yard light. One of them was much bigger than the others.

The crack of Jack's rifle was louder than she expected, and she jumped when fire came out of the barrel and the sound rolled over her an instant later. The largest of the black shapes went down, oaring the dust with its feet. The rest began running for long grass behind the barn. Jack levered in another cartridge without taking his eye from the rifle sights and fired again. After that it turned quiet, except for Sara Margaret crying in the back bedroom. One of the downed javelinas got halfway up, struggling to drag its paralyzed hindquarters toward the brush. Jack walked over and finished it off with Smyler Carmine's .45.

He came into the house, laid the rifle and pistol on a chair, and went back outside, calling for Hummer. After a while the dog limped toward the front door.

"Let me look at you, fella."

He examined the dog and stood up, closing the door. "He's all right. Hummer's got guts, but he knows when to back off. Got a little cut of some kind on his right paw, but he's fine otherwise."

Jack went into the bathroom, staying there for a

while. Linda heard him vomit hard and the toilet flush. He brushed his teeth and slid into bed, reaching for her hand.

"I hate killin' anything, makes me sick to my stomach," he said.

That's all he said, but she could tell he lay there for a long time before he quieted himself and began snoring softly. The next morning Earl tied ropes to the javelinas, one of which was the "second-biggest boar I ever seen," he said later, and dragged them into the brush, the javelinas sliding and bumping along behind Poly Carmine's Land Cruiser, leaving a trail of blood in the dust.

Linda Lobo had come to West Texas, and West Texas had come to her across the patio, with three-inch tusks that would now bleach in the high-desert sun. On the night Jack killed the javelinas, she lay next to him and looked out toward the Glass Mountains, at the big Texas sky with stars all over it. She'd turned thirty-eight a week earlier and had been wondering again if it all came down to this and nothing more. The last letter from her mother said Gary had seen the light and wanted to get back with Linda again. Her mother thought that was a good idea for Sara Margaret's sake, but Linda had shaken her head in disgust when she read the letter.

Listening to the sleeping sounds of Texas Jack Carmine, she reached out and touched his hair, feeling a little guilty somehow. After a while he rolled on his side and was quiet. Out in the yard she heard Earl's footsteps on gravel, and later on a coyote howled once in the far distance. It was dead silent then, and Linda Lobo stayed awake for a long time.

CHAPTER TEN

New Orleans, October 27, 1993

The dog standing outside the Cafe Beignet and looking in at Vaughn Rhomer was thin and mostly brown with white markings on her face, a product of uncertain parentage and desultory matings over the last two hundred years in the alleyways of New Orleans. She weighed a pound under thirty and had lived the four years of her life beneath a rotting pier east of the French Market, using the survival skills her mother had taught her and passing on those skills to five litters of her own pups—an open garbage can, handouts from tourists, an occasional dead fish killed by ship propellers. In the last three days she'd come to know Vaughn Rhomer and watched now as he lifted his brandy glass and returned the black woman's salute.

On the first day, Vaughn Rhomer had merely watched the dog sniffing along the river's shore and thought if her legs had been any shorter, she'd have qualified as a large caterpillar. On the second day, he'd whistled softly and said, "Hello, puppy." On the third,

this morning, he'd brought an extra beignet to the riverfront and looked for the dog. She'd come along after
a while and taken the beignet from his hand while he
sat on the wall, dangling his feet above the shoreline and
looking across the water toward Algiers, remembering a
favorite passage from his notebooks.

> *That's all I ever thought about for a long*
> *time, about the going, and early on it never*
> *mattered where. From the beginning, and I see*
> *this clearly now, my work in photography was*
> *partly a passion and partly a vehicle for travel-*
> *ing. And yet I've seen a thousand places—more*
> *than that, probably—where I'd wished I had a*
> *separate life for each of them so I could settle*
> *down and live there, so I could get to know some*
> *people well, as others have done, as most have*
> *done. I could have run a general store in that*
> *dusty little hillside town in Nevada; joined the*
> *ashram in Pondicherry, India; or opened a ga-*
> *rage in a mountain town in southwest Texas or*
> *raised sheep in the Pyrenees or become a fisher-*
> *man in some Mexican beach village.*
>
> *The cut is double and hard either way, a*
> *matter of tradeoffs. The road versus the settled*
> *life. I'd never thought much about that until I*
> *was in my fifties. I met a woman then, and I*
> *would have thrown aside everything for her, the*
> *road included. But there were things in the way*
> *of us, and that was my one chance, and afterward*
> *I went back out on the road with my cameras.*
> *In my later years I've given up the traveling,*
> *yet I am still alone. All those years on the road*
> *(plus my own reclusive and somewhat antisocial*
> *nature, I suppose) has not equipped me for be-*

coming close to people. The woman, the woman—she was my one chance at what I'm talking about and yet there was no chance at all with her, as I think back on it.

So, all those years when you were reading beneath a yellow evening lamp and wondering about the far places and maybe wishing to visit them, the places where I've been dozens of times, I was passing by your window and wishing just the opposite. I was wishing for your chair and your lamp, your family and your friends. It was probably a rainy night when I went by your house, my gear on the seat beside me, looking for a motel that wouldn't injure my expense account too badly. I would have found one and slept and moved on the next morning, remembering your yellow evening lamp.

> *Excerpted from Robert L. Kincaid, "The Cost of Going," in Michael Tillman (ed.),* Collected Essays on the Road Life *(Denver: Rocky Mountain Classics, 1992), pp. 314–315. Complete article originally published in* The American Traveler, *July 1980, pp. 43–49. Passage copied in V. H. Rhomer's Notebook #11, 3/12/92.*

Vaughn Rhomer had felt a nudge at his left elbow and looked down. The dog was pushing her nose and then her upper body between his arm and his leg, resting that way on his lap and licking the powdered sugar from her jaws. He'd noticed the sores on her head and ears but petted her anyway, avoiding the sores and wondering what kind of salve would heal them. And she'd lain there for a long time, enjoying the feel of his hand on her and perhaps not recalling if anyone had ever petted her before.

Tomorrow he would have to begin the journey home. But this afternoon he'd gone by the A&P on Royal Street and bought a can of dog food. In one of his rucksacks was a military-issue P-38 can opener, and before leaving, he intended to visit the riverfront and give the dog something nourishing as a parting gift.

Ariendo Vincent began to play a slow waltz in E-flat Vaughn Rhomer had never heard before, but the song was as soft and warm and round as the New Orleans night. Off to one side, the dog watched as Cohana Eliason put down her brandy glass on the marble tabletop, rose from her chair, and held out her arms to the kindly man who brought extra beignets to the riverfront. Vaughn Rhomer stood and moved slowly toward the woman, while the brown-and-white dog lowered her head and trotted south toward the river.

CHAPTER ELEVEN

New Orleans, October 27, 1993

If you could have danced only one dance in your life, it should have been with a woman named Gumbo, in New Orleans, when the weather was warm in late October and Ariendo Vincent played his alto saxophone in E-flat major. The sixtyish man knew how to waltz, he'd done it with Marjorie many times to the music of Art Whalen's Rhythm Kings on Friday nights at the VFW. The black woman draped her shawl over her left arm and put her hand on the man's shoulder, surprised at how lightly he moved and how well he felt the meter.

If Ariendo Vincent could have smiled and played alto saxophone at the same time, he would have done it, understanding in the way of a street musician who had seen it all in a life on the concrete that something fine and special was taking place before him. He played the song and played it again, did a variation on it for the third chorus, stringing it out, letting it run, watching the small man dressed in brown smile at Cohana Eliason, watching her smile back at the man.

There are those who dream and those who go out there, those who only watch as a woman dances through firelight while rivers flow and turtles sleep and a very few who rise to dance with the woman before she has gone to where rivers go until they cycle back to run again. Vaughn Rhomer had risen, had broken the latch and gone out there. Somehow Cohana Eliason knew that, somehow Ariendo Vincent knew that. And Vaughn Henry Rhomer, traveler of the far places only in his mind until this moment, knew it most of all. He danced the woman out onto the sidewalk, past Ariendo Vincent, toward the big river and back again, sweeping her in wide turns through the night with her shawl flowing out behind her, pleading with all the forces of light and darkness and shades in between to never let it end, to let the music run like all the rivers and come around to run once more in a cycle that would go on and on.

CHAPTER TWELVE

West Texas, 1987

When the fiddler hit the first three notes of "Faded Love," Jack Carmine stood up, looking for Linda Lobo. She was talking to people farther down the table, and the path to her face was a ragged caravan of Lone Star beer bottles, some empty, others on their way to that happy condition.

Jack had to shout over the music. "Bob Wills!" he said.

Linda put one hand to her ear and gave him a questioning look, so he escalated, making up in decibels what he lacked in diction. **"Bob Wills . . . it's the old Bob Wills song!"**

He motioned toward the dance floor of the Alpine Civic Center, and she followed him. Jack took her into his arms. "Like the way you smell, Miss Linda, that the new perfume you bought downtown the other day?"

She nodded, looking up at Jack Carmine's face under the black Stetson. "Jack Carmine, you must know just about every country song ever written."

"No, there's four or five I can't recall. Know this one, however. Those first three notes are what you might call a signature. Everybody down here recognizes the first three notes of 'Faded Love.' 'Least the older folks do."

As the fiddler drew out the ending of the song, the band switched gears and rolled into a faster number, one of Waylon Jennings's songs. Jack took Linda around the floor, singing along to the music, "Out in West Texas, Bob Wills is still the king . . ."

There were two things Linda Lobo came to like about West Texas. First off, as Jack had said, it seemed like visiting a foreign country with a way of doing things all its own, a culture hooked deep into the traditions of ranching and droughts, of bar fights and empty drill holes and marriages that worked or didn't. Second, the men danced, *really danced.*

She looked forward to the occasional dances in town, drinking and talking more than she usually did, making up for the long periods of solitude on the ranch. Jack knew everybody. She'd watch him leaning against a post or against the bar, shaking hands and grinning. People liked Jack Carmine; he talked their language, he was one of them. Now and then a woman would take hold of his arm, looking up at him and smiling, saying things Linda Lobo couldn't hear. She'd feel a little jealous when that happened, watching Jack talking easy with another woman his age and imagining the two of them doing things in some pickup truck, years back down the line.

But Jack wasn't jealous. The men liked to dance with Linda, always asking Jack's permission before they asked her. He'd tip his Stetson and say, "It's up to Miss Linda, but I'm warnin' you, she's more than you can handle out on the dance floor."

That wasn't necessarily true. Some of the men were a lot better than she was, moving in an intense, soulful way, taking her through wide, complicated turns with fancy footwork, always on the beat. By midnight things would heat up, the band running at high volume and people moving fast under the civic center lights. You had to keep up or get run over. Sweat trickled down Jack Carmine's face as he danced Linda around the floor, a bottle of Lone Star stuffed in his back pocket, his right hand stuffed in her back pocket, a little off the beat but having fun.

Midnight, the band playing hot and hard with the pedal steel guitar fairly screaming, two hundred pairs of boots and a hundred Stetsons rising and falling and turning toward the morning. Afterward she and Jack would drive the pickup back to the ranch and fix egg sandwiches. Jack Carmine would lean against the kitchen door frame, egg sandwich in one hand and a bottle of Lone Star in the other. He'd look up at Little Horse Mountain out back and say, "It's as pretty here as it's ever goin' to get any place, dancin' lady."

Four months after Linda Lobo came to West Texas and the days began to warm in early March, Jack started talking about big orange machines, about riding them north, talking about fields of wheat that ran yellow and ready in autumn when the Canadian sky was cobalt blue. The ranch wasn't big enough to support them, he said, and he had to get out and bring in a cash crop of some kind that would take them through the next winter.

Linda suggested maybe he could find work closer to Alpine and that she could waitress or something so Jack wouldn't have to ride the combines north. She knew, though, it was something more than money; it had to do with Jack Carmine and whatever it was that sent him out there.

But he fought back the road, saying there was Sara Margaret to think about and Earl had to see to the cattle, so there'd be nobody to take care of her while Linda was working. He looked around that first summer and hooked on with a construction crew at the local college, making a lot less money than he could have made riding the combines.

He came home tired in the evenings. "I'm carrying lumber in and out of classrooms where I used to sit twenty-five years ago, some sense of a full circle there and not much progress when you think about it."

"You never said you went to college. What were you tryin' to be?"

"Teacher. I experienced some momentary wobble toward idealism for a short time, just before I lurched back the other way for good. Hard to be better than we want to be, I guess. On the other hand, goin' to school started to feel like gettin' directions in Wal-Mart after a while: Turn left at wallpaper, right at housewares, third shelf from the top."

Linda was finishing up drying dishes, stepping over Hummer as she moved from sink to cupboard. Jack sat at the kitchen table, an old door laid over sawhorses. Outside, Rainy Carmine's last pecan tree was trying to come into blossom, and there was the distant sound of a bird in the direction of Little Horse Mountain. The kitchen door was an abstract in peeling white, though Jack had been promising to scrape and repaint it, which he never got around to doing, or fixing the broken spring that kept it from closing tight. Said he'd paint the door but liked the spring the way it was.

"I sometimes think about goin' to college," she said over her shoulder. "When I was up in Dillon I thought about movin' back to Altoona and goin' to the junior college in Des Moines."

Jack Carmine picked up a salt shaker and examined it, balanced it on the back of his right hand and moved the hand slowly back and forth across the table. "Why, and for what reason?" He picked up the pepper shaker and duplicated what he'd done with the salt.

"Just think somehow it'd make me more of a person, able to do things on my own."

She could see cuts on his hands while he fiddled with the salt and pepper shakers. She'd always noticed how big his hands seemed compared to the rest of him. His hands and his face somehow were older than the rest of his body.

"Well, if you can carry it off without bein' changed too much, you'll come out all right," he said. "It's a paper world now, I guess. Get the graduation paper in hand, get a certain kind of job payin' pretty well while sittin' on your ass lookin' at more paper before you give the paper to someone else who's sittin' on their ass lookin' at paper."

He'd come close to the image she sometimes saw in her mind. She saw herself going to class and then eventually wearing a cap and gown on a warm May afternoon when some elderly man would hand her a diploma that said she was smart and could get a good job. She imagined air-conditioned offices and, if she thought hard enough on it, could see herself walking through those offices, briefcase in hand and well dressed, knowledgeable, and respected.

High school had been okay for her, she wasn't dumb, she knew that. But college? College had always seemed like something other people did, the group in high school that carried books home at night and got A's on tests and worked on the yearbook. She'd been part of another group, the ones who'd never thought much about the future, figuring it would all come down to marriage and babies anyhow. She'd waitressed in a downtown cafe after school and summers, serving up meat loaf and hamburgers, knowing the men from the cement plant were watching her and talking about her breasts and long legs and high ass. Instead of school, she'd focused on Lucas Mathen in those days, on what they were doing in the grass of Hayes Park or in his car when the weather turned cold. The future had seemed a long way off in the '55 Ford he was customizing— the dash lights soft and the radio playing and her laying her blouse on the steering wheel while he was touching her all over.

She closed the cupboard and folded the dish towel on the counter. "You went to college, Jack."

"For a while I did that, then decided not to do it. Somethin' wrong with the way we organize school, sort of like we're developin' only part of the human bein', some little tiny part up here"—he pointed to the left side of his head—"while the rest of whatever makes us up—the music and hands and feet parts—are cryin' out, 'Hey, what about me?' "

"So where's that leave things?" Linda Lobo asked.

"Don't think we ought to give college degrees to anyone who can't run a table saw or hasn't rode a combine north through the summers or can't overhaul a truck engine out in the backyard. Ought to put some qualifier on diplomas, somethin' like 'Limited to Thinkin' about Certain Things—Pretty Sunups and Other Useful Stuff Excluded.' Ever wonder why schools get vandalized but dentist offices don't? Somethin' in all that someone ought to figure out after a while. You're doin' fine, Miss Linda, but if you want to go to college, well, there's one right down the road in Alpine where I'm carryin' lumber. You can sit in one of those chairs with initials carved on the arm of it and

I'll wink at you as I lug two-by-fours in and out and past where you're sittin'. Might bend over and do somethin' soft and sweet to the back of your neck as I slip by, just to make sure you're not forgettin' the important things while you're learnin' how to shuffle paper."

Linda stood by the sink and looked out through the screen door. "Well, I'll think about it, that's all. Seems pretty scary, but I might try it sometime. Saw a TV program a while back about a lot of older women goin' to college, worked out okay for them, I guess."

Jack danced over to her. "Only scary part is you might lose all the good things you are. Let's drive into town, drink some beer and break some pool cues at the Crystal. Goddamned Billy Leaton beat me at eight-ball two weeks ago, got to sharpen up my useful skills 'fore they run off on me completely."

On a Friday night in July, Linda Lobo first saw Jack go into one of his spells, staggering around outside the house in the starlight, yelling incomprehensible words about Leon taking the red away and shaking his whole body as if he were firing an imaginary machine gun. She didn't know what to do and could only scream his name, asking for God's sake what was the matter. Earl came running from the barn and grabbed hold of Jack, trying to lay him down and get him calmed, but Jack fought with him and tore away. Earl stood off to one side near Linda, and they watched the pickup bounce down the dirt road toward the highway, the taillights rising and falling like the man himself.

The following day: her boot heels across the dark pine floor fifty times to the front windows, the kitchen, the back steps, the front windows again. At lunchtime she took ten minutes to make Sara Margaret's sandwich, spreading peanut butter and mayonnaise across the bread, moving the knife with precision, covering each slice and every corner with uniform thickness as if she were finishing a fine piece of cabinetry. Sara Margaret ate her lunch, stretching her arms as wide as they'd go while telling Linda about the "great big worm with a funny-looking tongue" she'd seen near the garden that morning. Linda drank coffee and didn't pick up on what Sara Margaret was saying, even when Sara Margaret flicked her tongue in and out as a demonstration of what she'd seen. When Sara Margaret asked where Jack was, Linda only said he'd gone off for a while and would be back soon.

Early afternoon, Sara Margaret napping, loud tick of the Regulator clock from the kitchen, and no other sound. Linda sat in the living room and stared at the empty fireplace. She moved to the bedroom and lay there for hours, listening for a pickup truck that didn't come.

Around seven Hummer started barking. Linda was in the kitchen and walked through the living room to the front porch, watching the trail of dust following Jack Carmine as he drove along the dirt road toward the house. That night they danced in the living room and then straight out the open front door. They danced down the steps and kept on dancing down the road with Waylon Jennings fading as they went, Jack talking about getting out the air mattress and going up on Little Horse Mountain to watch the sunrise and maybe going to Mexico in a month or two.

That autumn Jack smiled at her across a dinner table in the Holland Hotel. She was wearing the black dress he'd bought her exactly one year earlier.

"Make it kind of an anniversary of sorts," he'd said a day earlier. "I'll clean up the truck, you put on your black dress, and we'll go somewhere nice, down to the hotel if it's okay with you. I'll even put on a white shirt and tie, do it up right."

As it turned out, the white shirt was beyond rescue and the tie was lost. "That damned tie used to be here, know I had it 'cause I kept it around for funerals. Went to the funerals, never went to the lunches afterwards. Come to think of it, last time I saw the tie Hummer was wearin' it on the occasion of a shoot-out of some kind. Don't matter, I'll shine my custom-mades and put on my Stetson, look just fine in a West Texas kind of manner."

They stayed all night at the hotel, and when he grinned and asked if she wanted her own room, she smiled back at him as she'd done a year earlier. "Not on your life, Jack Carmine . . . not on your life. Not tonight." Those were the good times, when he was the best there ever was for her.

But there was some long, slow, downward slide to Jack Carmine that was inexorable. No matter what she or Earl or anyone else might do, Jack's fall had a momentum of its own, governed by whoever sat on the carpenter's bench and watched the circle race below. His spells started coming more often, every few weeks—suddenly, unexpectedly, for no reason anyone could see or predict, he was driven to tears and frenzy by his recollections, by the roar of his chop-chop chronicles. Shouting about babies on razor wire and how you could sweep a rooftop with a machine gun just like you were using some giant push broom, he'd stagger around the yard with a bottle of Lone Star in his hand, his arms in a position of holding the .50-caliber and jerking his body from its imaginary recoil. Yelling then about scalp hunters and back shooters and for Leon to take it away, to take the goddamn red away, and she would grab his arm and scream at him that for chrissake, Leon wasn't listening anymore.

And he'd scream back at her, "It's the killin', don't you see that? I've killed every goddamned thing that ever got close to me, babies and women and anything else that fuckin' moved through my sights."

Afterward she would lie quiet in bed and hear his footsteps on the porch, walking up and down. The sound of his voice was low and mantralike, mixing a poet's words with his own: "It was like this, you see: From my mother's sleep I fell into the 'state,' and I hunched in its belly till my wet fur froze. . . . You see— it was like this: From my mother's sleep . . ."

In the dark, hours later, the quiet shuffle of bare feet and a nightshirted Earl gently laying Jack Carmine on the bed beside her, Hummer following along. If whatever was ugly and misshapen inside him could not be appeased with words and touching, she'd hear the truck heading out. He'd be gone sometimes for days, and nobody knew where he went or why he went for sure, except Earl Chavez, who one day came to the porch steps and told her all he knew about Jack Carmine. And even Earl Chavez didn't know the whole story for sure.

After the fifth of Jack's spells in less than three months, Linda was sitting on the front porch through a late afternoon, rocking in a cane chair older than she was. Back and forth she went, slowly and with a mindless precision, looking north and down the road. It seemed more and more her life was being spent looking north for Jack Carmine, for the dust cloud that would follow him when he had temporarily shed his demons and would come up the dirt road, cleansed and ready to dance again.

A small stone beneath one of the rockers vaguely

annoyed her, but she was too tired to adjust the chair or move the stone. An intermittent breeze from the west became interested in a loose strand of her hair and blew it first across her cheek, then back the other way, until she tired of the game and pinned it up. Hummer snoozed off to one side, and Sara Margaret was building something out of old bones in the gravel area below her. Linda Lobo had turned thirty-nine the previous week.

A quarter mile off to her left she saw Earl Chavez leave the barn and start walking up toward the house, the house that Jack owned. This was Jack's country and Jack's shirttail ranch, and they all were living on what Jack brought home. Jack-the-strong, sometimes, who could handle whatever came down the road toward him. And Jack-the-desert-willow-branch, sometimes, who bent in a curve upon himself, rolling on the ground and calling for Leon to take the goddamned red away.

Earl Chavez was a hundred yards out, taking off his hat and wiping his forehead with a bandanna.

The stone beneath the rocker gave up and turned to grit that blew across the porch floor when the next breeze came around. Linda Lobo had been drinking a lemonade, but her stomach didn't feel like lemonade, and she leaned forward to set the glass on the porch railing. Her heartbeat altered, increasing and settling back again, worrying about Jack Carmine, and worrying about herself and Sara Margaret all at the same time. The two of them, Sara Margaret and her, they were like what? . . . something alone and out of place . . . like sea birds circling in the middle of a high-desert nowhere, running out of water and running out of time, living the days and nothing else.

She held her hands in her lap, then used them to smooth her hair, then laid them on the chair arms as Earl Chavez said, "Afternoon, missy."

"Hello, Earl." She didn't feel much like talking and barely got the words out.

The two of them sat there, she on the rocking chair, Earl on the steps. Both of them staring down the ranch road toward the highway, saying nothing. The house faced north and squatted low, red-brown adobe with a thirty-degree pitch on the metal roof. At one time there had been terracing made out of railroad ties and rocks, from the gravel parking area up to the front door. The terracing had crumbled some, and the flower beds were empty. But it still made a pleasant approach with three tiers leading up from the gravel, and Linda Lobo had wondered in the beginning what kind of flowers might grow on the terraces, if anything could grow in dry dirt sprinkled with broken glass.

From the front porch of the house you looked down toward the highway and the Southern Pacific tracks two miles away. If the wind was right, the rumble of the freights reached all the way up to the house. Beyond the tracks and highway was the lower edge of the great Permian Basin, stretching away under yellow sunlight up into middle Texas. Earl Chavez sat on the top porch step and looked north toward the highway where Linda Lobo was looking.

Earl took a drag on his Camel and cleared his throat, threw the cigarette away, spat in the dust. He didn't look anything like what Linda had expected when she'd first come to the ranch. She'd expected an overweight, kindly Mexican with a round, shiny face, the way she'd always thought about Mexicans based on what she'd heard. But Earl Chavez was thin like Jack and only two inches shorter, with muscled arms and shoulders underneath his snap-button western shirt and straight, honest eyes. She'd watched him ride and noticed how smooth he sat a nine-year-old gelding named Cactus, how easily he moved among the cattle, making them do what he wanted.

Without looking at her, he said, "Missy, it's your right to know, so I will try to tell you part of the reason why Jack is the way he is."

He swung around and leaned against a post, glanced at her for a moment, then concentrated on getting a mesquite thorn out of his boot sole. After that, he draped one arm across a folded knee, looking sometimes at the porch floor, sometimes straight at her as he talked.

"You see, missy, Jack's always played a lone and somewhat dangerous hand as a matter of both nature and policy from the day he was born. I was eighteen, then, and had just started workin' for Mr. Carmine. I recall Jack sayin' once, 'Earl, I should've come into the world with a warnin' label attached: For Temporary Use Only, Some Assembly Required.' "

A half mile to the northeast, three buzzards were circling the corral area, backdropped by a gray curtain of rain ten miles farther out.

"Looks like Marathon's goin' to get rain. We sure could use it here," Earl said before going on with his story.

"Don't let Jack fool you, missy. He's got this tired old cowboy way about him sometimes, talks his own special brand of West Texas and pretends he doesn't know much about anything. But Jack, he got Mr. Poly Carmine's brains. Eddie junior got something else, the hearin' and playin' of music, probably from Mrs. Carmine—she played the piano real well, you know.

"One thing that's always bothered Jack is how Mr. Carmine let the ranch go. Jack's always loved this place, wanted to do nothin' else but raise cattle, build fence, and all the rest that goes with ranchin'. From the time he was about eighteen he hardly ever said anything to

Mr. Carmine. Funny thing is, I don't think Mr. Carmine ever noticed.

"After Jack got out of high school he roughnecked up north in the oil patch for a few years. After that he started into college here for another few years before droppin' out. Studied history. He liked learnin', but he never much liked school. He was just too damn restless, I guess. When he quit college, the draft board began takin' a serious interest in him because of all the young fellows we was sendin' over to Vietnam, though he probably was safe due to the fact he was married and had a son.

"But, see, Jack had met a man in Wichita during one summer when he was workin' north on a combine crew. The man was a Vietnam veteran who'd lost both his legs to a land mine and was awful bitter about the whole thing. He and Jack talked for a long time about what was goin' on over there. Jack was pretty fascinated by it in spite of lookin' at this man in a wheelchair."

That fit, Linda Lobo thought. That fit Jack Carmine and all he ever was. Jack Carmine liked edges, borders, liked to poke at the boundaries and see what was out there as a way of forgetting who he was and where things might be taking him.

Sara Margaret had gone out of sight around the porch, and Linda called to her, "Stay out in front where I can see you, Sara Margaret."

Earl spat in the dust again, ran the back of his hand across his mouth. "After droppin' out of school Jack worked on the ranch and sometimes drove combines or laid utility wire for about three years. He was pushin' thirty at the time and kept talkin' about Vietnam. One day, Jack and me rode up on Little Horse Mountain and talked for a long time. The entire town, of course, was in favor of stoppin' communism in its tracks right there in the Vietnam jungles, but that didn't have much to do with his thinkin'. I recall him sayin', 'Earl, there's a whole lot goin' on over there in Southeast Asia that a man ought to see, participate in history, as it were, instead of just readin' about it. Got nothin' to do with keepin' the world safe for democracy, far as I can tell, just somethin' worth lookin' into.'

"Few months before his thirtieth birthday, in that ol' Jack Carmine way of his, he just drove over to El Paso and enlisted. That was in the summer of '69. Damned if I ever know how he got through basic trainin'. Jack never has done well with orders. What was it he used to say? . . . said he had a built-in taste for anarchy of all kinds. I asked him what he meant by that, and he said he liked situations where the borders weren't in sight and you had to go out and find 'em or make 'em up yourself. He got in some trouble durin' basic trainin', hit a drill sergeant or something. Spent some time in the stockade for it, I know. But Jack's always been a dead shot when he isn't drinkin', and he always was good at fixin' cars and trucks. So I guess, figurin' he had some skills the army needed, they let him out, punched him the rest of the way through basic trainin', and shipped him right off to Vietnam.

"He didn't come back for nearly six years, took his leaves somewhere out there in that part of the world. Kept reenlistin' on the promise he could stay in Vietnam, which of course the army was more'n happy to accommodate. Most of the boys wanted to get right home soon as their tours were finished. Not Jack. He'd write these general-type letters, implyin' he wasn't doin' anything very dangerous, but he was. Jack and I've been amigos for a long time, and when he first came back we talked a lot about what went on over there. Far as I know, he's never talked about it to anyone else.

"He'd say, 'Earl, you're not goin' to believe this . . . ,' then he'd tell me some other little story about the things he saw. I had a hard time acceptin' everything he said, but he swore it was all true and just as he'd seen it. Things like machinists bein' asked to make shiny metal swagger sticks for officers instead of fixin' Howitzers like they was supposed to, about how you could buy American M-16 rifles and other military equipment in downtown Saigon from people sellin' stuff on the street, how a lot of the boys was smokin' dope and others who were shootin' their officers in the back durin' firefights.

"But there was something about it that held Jack there, even after he'd been hurt. You know that scar on the back of his right shoulder? Tells people it was a huntin' accident. It ain't. It's shrapnel—case of ammunition in a helicopter got hit and blew up the helicopter just as it was landing. Blew Jack right out the door or he'd have been killed, so he said. But he said Vietnam was as close to true confusion as you'd find on earth, and that's what held him there. He called at Christmas one time and Mrs. Carmine asked him when he was comin' home. Jack said to her, 'What am I supposed to come home to, a wife that's run off with a dentist from Odessa? Come home to a ranch that don't exist anymore and layin' utility wire and goddamned folksingers?'

"The whole business turned out to be kind of a time bomb. None of it seemed to bother him while he was doin' it, but it's caught up with him here later on. That's when he has one of these come-undones of his and starts hollerin' for Leon to do somethin'."

Linda asked, "What's a steel guitar player from Bob Wills's old band got to do with those feelin's of his?"

"He ain't talkin' about the Bob Wills 'Leon' when he's goin' crazy. Jack was a machine gunner on helicopters for a long time. Flew right at the end with a pilot named Leon Carmichael. It's *that* Leon he's talking about. Somehow he thinks this Leon Carmichael can fly him away from what's eatin' up his heart, just like Leon flew him and the other boys out of trouble in Vietnam.

"There's one thing happened toward the end that, more than anything else, feeds the animal eatin' him alive. He only mentioned it once. I was holding him in my arms over by the barn on one of his specially bad nights while he was lyin' on the ground looking up at me and kind of babblin'. Seems this thing occurred during the final evacuation of Saigon. He was on the last helicopter ever to touch down in Vietnam, pullin' some hard-pressed marines off the roof of the U.S. embassy. Jack won't even mention it when he's straight, so I never learned the whole story. But Bobby McGregor, that singer friend of Jack's was there and saw it, and he won't talk about it, either. Whatever it was, it was somethin' bad that kind of put the finishin' touches on Jack Carmine.

"If you want to know where he's gone right now, I'd say it's one of two places. Sometimes he drives down across the border to Ojinaga and gets stone drunk for a day or so. If he's gone more than two days, I generally figure he's gone up to Wichita and had a long talk with that fella that lost his legs in Vietnam. He does that every year or so. Sometimes the two of 'em catch a plane for Washington, D.C., and sit by the Vietnam War Memorial for days at a time, runnin' their hands across the names of all the fellas they knew over there who never made it back. Wherever he goes, he'll come back and'll seem just fine till it all starts up again in a month or two or a day or two.

"I'll tell you this, missy. Jack Carmine has a lot of bottom to him, he can work harder than any three men and he'll make you laugh and he'll never let you down when times get hard. And I can tell he cares for you in a way he's never cared for anyone else—not even close. But you stay with him and you're takin' on a life of pain for yourself and the muchacha. He's always been restless, and now there's this thing from his Vietnam days that's mated up with the restlessness and created somethin' that even scares me. And like I said, me and Jack have been amigos for a long, long time. Used to be he had these spells only every few months. But in the last years they been comin' more often, though he held 'em off pretty good for a while after you came along. I keep thinkin' he'll go completely around the bend one of these times and none of us'll be able to help him get back."

Sara Margaret came running to the porch, carrying the skull of a young javelina. "Look, Momma, you can see the teeth and everything."

Linda Lobo held the skull in her hands and rocked slowly, looking down at the skull.

After a while Earl stood, hitched up his jeans, scuffed his boot in the dust. "He'll come back, missy. He'll come back sometime. He always does. He's got nowhere else to go."

Earl went down the dirt road. The low sun moved his shadow over cactus and dust as he walked, until he reached the corrals and disappeared in the complex of board fences and metal chutes.

CHAPTER THIRTEEN

New Orleans, October 27, 1993

Ariendo Vincent gave the waltz a long, slow ending, repeating a phrase over and over, letting the sound of his horn fade away in increments so small there was no space between them. Sensing this, Vaughn Rhomer and Cohana Eliason brought their dance to a close. With Ariendo Vincent drawing out the last note of the song, Vaughn Rhomer took the woman through one last, slow turn. As he did, she gracefully swept her umbrella and purse from the table.

"I must go now," she said, there in yellow and white, smiling as the music ended. "You dance beautifully, and perhaps another time we will ask Ariendo to play for us."

For a moment Vaughn Rhomer wanted to cry out to her, ask her to stay, to let him buy a brandy for her. But old travelers know when the dance has ended, when the time for parting has come, and Vaughn Rhomer was now an old traveler. He bowed slightly and said, "Thank you," said only that and stood there, brown cap in both hands. She nodded to Ariendo Vincent, who was smiling, too, looking first at Vaughn Rhomer, then nodding to Cohana Eliason as she looped the shawl about her and went into the night.

Vaughn Rhomer placed a five-dollar bill in Ariendo Vincent's money box.

"Take care, mon," Ariendo Vincent said quietly. "Hold on to whatever you had for that moment."

Back in his room, Vaughn Rhomer couldn't remember walking to the hotel, couldn't remember coming up Toulouse. He ordered a good cigar and brandy from room service, the same brandy he'd drunk at the Cafe Beignet, and stood on the small balcony cantilevering out behind the French doors in his room. Vaughn Rhomer was smiling, couldn't stop smiling.

He leaned on the balcony rail and looked up at the New Orleans night, cigar in one hand, brandy in the other. And nodded to himself.

CHAPTER FOURTEEN

Charlotte, North Carolina, Late October 1993

The auditorium dressing room was newly painted mint green and lined with mirrors. If Bobby McGregor got in just the right position, he could see all sides of himself at once and thought that wasn't a bad thing to do as long as you didn't look too close. Better than the years of country bars and cheap hotels, though, tuning up in dirty toilets or roachy kitchens where cooks and waiters dodged your guitar neck and wished you'd get the hell out of their way.

Lester Virdeen stuck his head through the door, "We're goin' on, Bobby. See you in a few minutes."

The rest of the band was standing in the hall behind Lester, all of them wearing jeans and boots, powder blue shirts and black bandannas, gray Stetsons.

Bobby McGregor took his 1957 D–28 Martin out of its case. "Give me an A, Lester."

Lester Virdeen plucked his fiddle.

"Bow it for me, will you."

Lester tucked the fiddle under his chin and bowed it while Bobby brought the Martin's A string up a notch.

"There it is, A-440 and hummin'," Lester said. "How you doin', okay?" Lester Virdeen was smiling. He was nearly seventy years old and still played some of the hottest fiddle in the business, along with acting as surrogate father for the younger guys in the band.

"I'm fine," Bobby said. "How's Glen, his stomach get squared away?"

"Well, he's stopped throwin' up, at least. Little flu or food poisonin' or somethin'. These young guys stay up late drinkin' too much and eatin' junk food. Keep tellin' 'em this ain't no damned vacation trip and they ought to live on the road like they do at home."

Bobby grinned. "Maybe they do."

Lester shook his head in a way indicating agreement and disapproval at the same time. "Like I told you once, the best and simplest band wouldn't have anyone younger'n sixty in it. Anyway, Glen'll be all right once he gets to beatin' on his snare and thinkin' about music."

Bobby nodded. "Go out there and lay it down, get 'em ready."

"We're on our way." Lester swung the door shut and walked off.

Twenty seconds later a roar came through the heavy curtains and down the hall as the band went on stage.

Bobby McGregor worked along the twelfth fret of the Martin, using harmonics to fine-tune it.

"Yeah," he said, responding to a knock on the door.

A young man with a bad complexion poked his head in. "A photographer from the *Observer* is here and wonders if he can get a couple of photos."

Through the open door Bobby McGregor heard his

band moving into the warm-up song, Lester Virdeen pushing his electric fiddle hot and hard on "West Texas Roads."

"Okay, tell 'im I've only got about two minutes, though." Goddammit, he thought, they always wait until the last second, the time when your gut is tight and your hands are sweating enough chemicals to eat right through the guitar strings. He set the bottle of Miller on the floor behind his leg.

The photograp:her came sliding and banging sideways through the door, carrying a camera bag, a Canon 35-millimeter and flash unit hanging from around his neck. Out on stage Maclean Stockton was coming into his solo as Lester finished up, playing the pickup notes perfectly, then stomping on his volume pedal and making the Fender Strat cut like a knife in the upper registers. Bobby McGregor smiled to himself. The band was getting tighter and tighter as the tour went on.

"Just a couple of shots, Mr. McGregor." The photographer was working fast, winding a new roll of film into his camera. "Didn't know we were going to cover your concert until a half hour ago."

In the near distance the band was playing clean and tight. Maclean Stockton rolled into that syncopated cross-picking he threw in now and then, eighth-note licks he'd picked up from Jessie McReynolds's mandolin style. Bobby had tried to learn how to do that but couldn't get it up to any kind of speed. Maclean Stockton never went to the dentist and didn't finish high school, but he had a wrist like a chain saw and quick-twitch muscles you only get from good genes and practice.

Bobby pointed down at the bottle of Miller. "I'll appreciate it if you keep the beer out of the photo."

"No problem. Just need a couple of head shots. I'll get the rest during the concert."

The motor drive on the camera whined, the flash recycled and fired again.

Behind the photographer's words, down the hall and out on stage, Jimmy Gonzales came in on pedal steel.

"I've got about thirty seconds," Bobby said to the photographer.

"Just a couple more, please."

Bobby was shaking his head, smiling and thinking all photographers were pessimists. Always just a couple more, then a couple more after that. He stood up, slung the Martin over his shoulders, and fished in his jeans pocket for a flat pick. "That's it, got to sing some songs."

"Thanks very much, Mr. McGregor. Break a leg."

As the band pulled off a jazzy variation on the shave-and-a-haircut-two-bits ending, with Lester and Maclean playing together in thirds, Bobby McGregor checked to make sure his fly was zipped, then walked into applause and spotlights. He tipped his Stetson to the crowd, raked his flat pick across the strings, and nodded to Lester Virdeen. Lester tapped his bow four times, the drummer following him on the snare drum's rim, and they were off and rolling, the pedal steel laying down a carpet you could walk across on an autumn night in Charlotte, North Carolina.

> If I had it all to do over again
> I'd do it just the same
> Except for all the times
> I treated her so badly. . . .

Two hours later they closed with the new song. It had come on the charts a week ago and was already up to number fifteen.

"Bandit," Charlotte Concert.

Bobby and harmonica only. Nice, easy 4/4.

She used to call him "Bandit,"
for reasons of her own.
And she almost always smiled
when she'd say it.
She'd say, "Bandit,
let's wash the pickup,
you can take me out to dinner,
and I'll wear a pretty dress . . .
. . . for your pleasure."

One-measure lick by Fender Strat, full band comes in, pedal steel up front.

So come on, Leon   *—Hard two-beat*
play it again,
make it sound like a knife,
scrapin' down across the wind
that blew up from Texas
on the shoulders of the rain
with dust on its clothes
from ridin' lonesome trains.
Play it like the sound
of a long fall from grace
puttin' slits around your eyes
and cracks upon your face
that used to grin at everything
till everything got hazy
from the holes in your life
when the times drove you crazy.

Slow fade back to Bobby & harmonica.

She could do the Texas two-step
to the music of Bob Wills
And she liked the twirlin'
lights of the oldtime ballrooms,

but she got tired of dyin' days
and lonesome for another life,
she got tired of dyin' dreams
and old guitar tunes.
So come on, Leon . . .

Bobby McGregor played a bass run Maclean had shown him, said, "Take it away, Lester," and stepped back from the microphone while the band slid into the instrumental break.

Saigon, just after dawn on April 30, 1975. Eleven marines left on the roof of the American embassy, the last human pieces of America's great and holy and futile safari in Southeast Asia. Passing around a bottle of Johnny Walker Black and coming down off methedrine and the major saying the chopper pilots might have forgotten they were still up there on the roof and the VC moving into central Saigon from all directions. The major saying the marines might have to climb down the embassy's rocket shield and fight their way to the sea. Fat chance, Bobby McGregor thought back then.

People trying to toss babies over the embassy wall, begging the Americans to take them. Babies—hung up there on the concertina wire and screaming. A young marine saying, "The major's right, they goddamn fuckin' forgot us, they're just goin' fuckin' home and leaving us here."

Packs and fire extinguishers stacked against

the rooftop door and hundreds of Vietnamese who were being left behind pounding on the door, yelling and shouting, trying to get on the rooftop, the door about to come off its hinges. Bobby McGregor remembers clicking off the safety on his M-16 and pointing it at the door when the major said, "Got to buy us some time, pile 'em up when they come through that goddamned door." Bobby had spent two years in 'Nam without ever actually killing anyone. But he was going to do it at that moment. He didn't like the idea at all, but he was ready to do it.

Then over burning-smoke-city-Saigon and through the glare of red sun came a lone CH-46 escorted by six Cobra gunships, the Cobras bobbing and weaving like dragonflies through the haze. "Tear gas," the major yelled, and they dumped it down the stairwell and around the roof, which was a stupid thing to do since the rotor blades pulled it right back toward them and into the chopper. Bobby McGregor running for the helicopter door and ducking as the chopper's machine gunner opened up at a sniper in a building across the street. That image especially hangs on, the gunner, an older guy with a hard face and sunglassed eyes and helmet pulled low—the perfect killing instrument with both hands on the gun and nothing distracting him except tears running down his cheeks from the gas. Chopper lifting off, Bobby still trying to climb in, legs dangling, gunner grabbing the back of Bobby McGregor's flak vest and yanking him full into the chopper. Name stenciled on the gunner's uniform: Carmine.

Jimmy Gonzales brought them out of the instrumental break, gave Bobby McGregor a nice fat pickup note on the dominant seventh, and Bobby came back in on the vocal:

> She liked the sound of steel guitars
> And rain on ol' tin rooftops,
> She cried at sad movies
> When they were over.
> And I liked the way she tasted
> In the dead, low heat of summer,
> Kind of a floatin' mix of her perfume
> And the scent of new-mown clover.
>   So come on, boys . . .

The encore was another of Bobby's songs, "Saigon Red." His agent hated the song and said it ought to be dropped from the repertoire, too damn long and too damn sad, bringing up things people wanted to forget about. Bobby kept it in and stumbled a bit on the words as he always did, seeing that moment after Jack Carmine had pulled him into the chopper. Turning and looking as the gunner opened up: gunner's body shaking with the recoil of the .50-caliber, ammo belt feeding into the .50 like the fastest snake you've ever seen, blowing apart a woman and baby as the door came off its hinges and people surged onto the roof. The .50 had suddenly stopped, and the gunner named Carmine never fired another round all the way out to where they landed on the *Midway*. He and Jack had become close friends later on, but neither of them had ever mentioned what happened that morning on a Saigon rooftop.

The obligatory interview afterward, Bobby putting the Martin back in its case.

"Yeah, it was a real nice audience.

"I don't know why they like the songs, they just like 'em, that's all. I try not to think about it, might just go away if I think too hard on it."

The reporter was confused, scribbling, "People like the songs because they're good songs." That'd sound all right, make him sound like he was bragging. She'd been seven years old when Jack Carmine was yanking Bobby McGregor into a helicopter. Aside from that, she didn't care much for Bobby McGregor or his music.

Bobby McGregor standing, leather guitar case slung over his left shoulder, answering the last question. "We go on to Dallas from here." He walked down a dark hallway and wondered about Jack Carmine, about how he was doing these days.

CHAPTER FIFTEEN

New Orleans, October 28, 1993

Vaughn Rhomer organized his gear and called down for a bellman to help him with it.

"Got quite a bit of luggage here," the bellman said politely. "Must be traveling for a long time."

"Yessir, quite a while, quite a while," said Vaughn Rhomer, dressed in khaki pants, a blue cotton shirt with genuine horn buttons and epaulets on the shoulders, and his speed-lace boots with nonslip lug soles.

He paid his bill and drove out of the hotel garage at 7:45 A.M., turned left on Toulouse and headed toward the riverfront. On the seat beside him were a can of dog food and his P-38 can opener.

Sitting on a bench near the river, he looked for the dog, but she wasn't anywhere in sight. That was okay, he enjoyed watching the river traffic, the big ships with names such as *Alexander's Unity (Valletta)* headed down the river and out there. He walked along the shore, looking for a small shell or rock he could take back as a memento for Mary Harding, the Otter Falls

199

librarian who had helped him with his files. She was about his age, single, and he'd considered maybe asking her out for dinner sometime, especially after she'd said how much she admired him for making this trip alone.

"It's a good thing you're doing, Mr. Rhomer. My husband and I used to travel a lot before he died. I miss the traveling, but I don't feel like going alone or with other women." She'd told him that while he was at the library doing research on New Orleans.

Vaughn Rhomer was concentrating on the river's edge and didn't notice the dog until he heard a small sound and saw her sitting ten feet to his left, looking at him.

"Hi, puppy," he said, and opened the dog food, digging it out of the can with his Master Mechanic belt knife. Jack Carmine had sent him the knife years ago after Vaughn had admired the one Jack carried. He put the food on a square of Hardee's wrapping he found in a nearby trash can, cleaned his knife on the grass, and pushed the food toward the dog.

She looked up at him, still sitting ten feet away, uncertain. He tossed her a piece of the food, and she shied at the quick movement of his hand but returned and sniffed the food before eating it in one gulp. He pushed the Hardee's wrapper closer to her and grinned when she came over to it, rolling her eyes up at him from time to time while she ate.

Upriver a thousand miles was Best Value and vegetables that surely would be in a mess by the time he returned. It was time to be heading out. He took a long, deep breath, looked at the river, then at the dog, and stood up. "Good-bye, girl, take care of yourself."

The dog had finished eating and followed him, a few steps behind at first and then beside his pant leg as he walked. He reached the Buick, took out his keys, and squatted down, stroking the dog. Then, with no hesitation, he unlocked the passenger-side door and patted the seat. "Come on, girl, let's get out of here."

The dog looked up at him, wagging her tail. He patted the seat again. "If you're coming along, better get in."

With her short legs she wasn't much of a jumper, but she made it to the floorboard of the Buick, then climbed on the seat. Vaughn Rhomer went around the car and got in behind the wheel, looking at the dog, the dog looking at him. He smiled and started the engine, moving past Jackson Square and up Saint Peter. Farther up, he crossed Rampart to where Saint Peter and Basin Street became one for a short distance. Hot-pink azaleas were blooming in a park just on the other side of Rampart, and he pointed them out to the dog, who was sitting quietly on the seat, looking sometimes out the side window, sometimes over at Vaughn Rhomer. Where Saint Peter divides from Basin and heads north, he saw the sign pointing to I-10. "That's us," Vaughn Rhomer said. "The Big Road out in front, girl."

Rush hour had passed, traffic on the interstate was light as Vaughn Rhomer's nonslip boot sole pushed the accelerator and took the Buick west on I-10. Past the airport and into the countryside. The road was mostly bridges of one kind or another traversing swamp and bayous. No clouds, except some light, feathery ones far and low in the west, small white birds on the water or feeding along the shorelines and mud flats. White cranes wading, green-and-white sign, *Lake Pontchartrain.* Another sign: *The Bonnet Carre Spillway.*

"Don't have names like that in Iowa," Vaughn Rhomer said, pointing at the signs. The dog wagged her tail and panted.

Home, heading home. Empty house, Marjorie gone,
company downsizing and replacing older fellows with
younger ones.

Light ripples on Pontchartrain, electric towers
marching across the lake, eerie-looking chunks of drift-
wood floating and dead trees standing in the water.

Signs:

Exit 210, 55 North, Two Miles—Hammond
Entering St. John Parish

Vaughn Rhomer was two minutes short of turning for
home, for Trolley Car Boulevard and Rhomer's Room,
when the morning news on National Public Radio mentioned the name of Thomas Martin. Vaughn Rhomer
leaned forward and adjusted the tuning, turned the volume up.

> One of England's literary charlatans died
> yesterday. Thomas Martin, who had been con-
> fined to a wheelchair since childhood, wrote
> a series of fictional adventure-travel books in
> which he purported to have explored exotic
> and unknown places. The Explorer's Society
> had condemned what they called his "outra-
> geous claims and patent lies," but people none-
> theless enjoyed Martin's writing and pretended
> it was true, even when they were aware it was
> fiction. Thomas Martin, who traveled only in
> his imagination, was eighty-seven when he
> died.

Not everyone had known Thomas Martin's writings were fiction. Vaughn Rhomer looked at the dog
and then slowed the Buick, stopping in the breakdown
lane. The sign said *Emergency Parking Only*, and

Vaughn Rhomer mumbled, "This might be an emergency."

He pulled out his Rand McNally road atlas from beneath the front seat and studied pages toward the end of it before putting the map back under the seat and sitting there for a full two minutes, both hands on the wheel and looking straight west on I-10. Once when he'd asked nephew Jack about what kinds of road maps were best, Jack had said, "You don't need no road maps, Uncle Vaughn, you just go."

North lay Mrs. Butro and young women in next-to-nothing shorts who moved by his vegetable counters. North lay downsizing and the grave of Razberry Rhomer and children who would visit and say, "Jennifer, don't touch Grandpa's radio with your sticky hands." Vaughn Rhomer didn't want to be a grandpa, didn't want Jennifer's sticky hands on his World Traveler radio.

He waited for a break in the traffic and pulled out on I-10, coming up to speed.

Exit 210, 55 North, One Mile—Hammond

Sixty seconds to the exit now, then up 55 to St. Louis and Route 61 North after St. Louis. Vaughn Rhomer mentally counted his money and estimated he had a little over two thousand in cash and traveler's checks. The day was Thursday, he had to be back at work on Monday. Doing what? Captain Turnip goes back to what? Yellow evening lamps, safety. Celery Man returns. Grandkids, the BBC at midnight, a long gradual decline into senility or its old-folks-home equivalent. A slow waltz in E-flat major was going through his head, and he saw the face of a woman named Gumbo, and he heard Ariendo Vincent saying, "Hold on to whatever you had for that moment."

Vaughn Rhomer looked at the dog, she looked back at him. He grinned at her. "Mexico . . . how's that sound to you?"

He pushed the Buick up to seventy and took out a cigar, cracking the window a bit so the smoke wouldn't bother the dog. He looked over at her. "What do you think about the name 'Bandida,' suit you? Like it all right?" The dog grinned at him. "It's settled, then, Bandida it is. We'll get you a kerchief to wear around your neck—pretty one, yellow, maybe."

He went by the exit to 55 North, accelerating even more, racing under a sign,

Baton Rouge—Straight Ahead

"We'll get some medicine for your head and ears in Baton Rouge, Bandida, and then you'll be ready for all the places we're going to see. Hope you don't mind if I dance with a few señoritas . . . or maybe it's señoras for me, maybe even invite the nice librarian back home to visit us in Mexico. Good, I didn't think you'd mind. We'll go through Alpine and see if nephew Jack's home, drink some good liquor and tell stories, then over to Taos and drop in on Lorraine for a day. After that, we'll beat south and visit all the little Mexican beach towns, go wherever the highway goes, eat shrimp on the sand and drink beer, listen to the sound of mariachis and swim in big surf at night."

He located a veterinarian's office in Baton Rouge and got some salve for Bandida's sores. "She's had a rough life," the vet said. "Get her spayed as soon as you can."

On the outskirts of Baton Rouge he bought a Styrofoam cooler and ice, two six-packs of Corona, ten cans of dog food, and an *LSU Tigers* cap.

As he drove west, he could still smell the scent of Cohana Eliason's perfume, remembered the waltz in E-flat major, and began to hum it. "Dancing with

Gumbo," is what he'd named the song. The sign going by on his right read *Houston, 321 Miles*.

Three hours down the road, Vaughn Rhomer was in Texas and rolling easy toward Beaumont. A construction crew was doing something in a field off to his right. The sun was up hard now, and Vaughn Rhomer pointed toward the workmen. "That'd be hot work out there, Bandida. Tough, hot work, hate to do that kind of work in my older years. Looks like they're laying pipe or something."

A hundred yards out in the field, the crew boss was saying something, and a man leaned on his shovel, watching traffic on the highway. He was stripped to the waist and sweating, barely noticing a dog leaning out the passenger-side window of a blue Buick heading west. His cap was faded and pretty well gone to where old caps are bound to go, but he'd found it in a closet last spring. It carried the logo *North Stars*. The man bent over and coughed hard, almost to the point of retching. He straightened up and wiped his arm across his forehead, pulled the cap down, took another shovelful of dirt.

CHAPER SIXTEEN

Flight 402, La Paz, Mexico, to Dallas,
October 28, 1993

"Well, I'm a'sittin' down inna San Antone, waitin' on an eight o'clock train. . . ." The Marshall Tucker Band pushing hard, coming through the woman's earphones before being interrupted by an announcement from the flight deck. The pilot said they were on schedule and were presently heading northeast over the Davis Mountains. She tilted up her sunglasses and looked down through the clear, high-desert air as the music came back. "Gonna work a week, make a hundred dollars, hit the road again. . . ."

From thirty-eight thousand feet she could make out a long freight working its way through West Texas while Marshall Tucker and the boys kept moving. Down there someplace, almost directly beneath her, were nearly two years of her life blowing around in the beige dust and brown hills—"I don't want you to think you're the first one to leave me out here on my own. . . ."

Earl and Hummer and Cactus. She wondered about them, hoping they were doing well, they'd all been pretty old when she was down there with them.

The man in the aisle seat leaned over her and looked down. Hot fiddle, electric guitar, and flute taking a long break in the song, singer back on. "Aw, if you wrote all the women's names down and let me pick one out . . ."

He was saying something to her, and she lifted the earphones away from her head, "I'm sorry, what?"

"I said I didn't realize there were mountains in Texas. Can't be much, never heard about them. Sure is nothing else out there, one of the great empty spaces of America." She nodded. He straightened his tie and went back to reading.

She looked again at West Texas floating by under the wings and turned up the volume on the Marshall Tucker Band steaming toward the end of things. "No, it ain't gonna be the first time this ol' cowboy's spent the night alone. . . ." The music—the kind of music that gives you a feeling of moving fast and leaving things behind, of trying on another life without actually going out there and doing it. Music giving you the deep down sense of turning wheels and long winding trains headed west through the desert night, starlight on all the rails ever laid with good intentions . . . wheels, rubber tires running easy through some October past, silver coin in the air—"Call it"—Gitchee Gumee up ahead and then turning left into Little Marais, lobster and a nominal birthday cake and Jack Carmine looking silly with a propeller on his head . . . sitting with him cross-legged on the bed of a Holiday Inn, eating eggs and toast, laughing while he waved a fork and told another of his endless supply of stories and her looking at him and remembering a night that had ranged over the spectrum of gentle depravity—she and Jack Carmine—rising toward him over and over, pushing her belly and breasts against that thin body of his that was brown on his face and arms and pale otherwise, and doing with him just about everything possible for a man and woman to do with one another, moving from softness to a fierce, wild hammering at each other and then back again to easy words and quiet touching, and thinking if things kept going on this way, she might have to consider putting the word "love" back in her vocabulary sometime.

Jack Carmine, talking soft to her in those moments, telling her what she'd wanted to hear, that things were going to be better from here on out, that naked and crazy like this she was the best there ever was among all the women who had ever lived, and she wanted him more in those old Octobers than she'd ever imagined wanting anyone before or since. Jack trying to pull "Rainy Day Woman" out of his harmonica and wrapped up in a blanket with him on Little Horse Mountain and drinking Lone Star at sunrise, Jack saying, "Damn, there ought to be some way to preserve a mornin' like this, put it up in a mason jar or whatever so you could take it out and look at it whenever you wanted."

The flight attendant was handing out hot towels in the first-class cabin. Her name was "Elena," according to her name tag, and she was telling the couple behind them that broiled salmon was one of the choices for lunch. She'd be bringing menus in a few minutes.

Mark Elwin wiped his hands on a towel and looked over at the woman beside him. "You all right?"

"Yes, fine." She was, mostly.

She was seven years beyond Northern Food Processors and the Rainbow bar and her first trip down the far roads of West Texas. A little heavier now, age and the ordered life pushing her in that direction. Four years ago she'd started taking classes at the Des Moines Area Community College, some vague and stumbling attempt at turning each day into something with more promise than the last. Mark Elwin had been a guest lecturer on insurance, and they'd talked afterward about what a single woman with a child might need in the way of life insurance. He'd called the following week, asking her to go out with him. It went on from there; they'd gotten married a year later, and he was a good man, good to her and Sara Margaret, decent in bed and in a lot of other ways. He'd encouraged her to continue with college, saying it was what she needed, and besides, the wife of a vice president of a major insurance company ought to have a college degree. Taking classes and being available when he wanted her to travel with him was difficult. Still, she made it work, and in eighteen months she'd get her degree in American studies from Drake University. She already knew the title of her senior paper: "Leon McAuliffe: The Steel Guitar and Western Swing." Mark Elwin had asked why she wanted to write on something so foreign and obscure, and she'd said only that the music of Bob Wills and his Texas Playboys had been a seminal step in the development of American music.

There was something about it all, however, a kind of fragile sincerity cutting through her life, the overtones of a dishonest bargain. Always she had this sense of belonging to another existence, slightly insecure in the world through which Mark Elwin traveled with ease. She'd mapped onto Jack Carmine's world without any problem, country music and Lone Star beer, old pickup trucks and West Texas highways, "Faded Love" and a hundred Stetsons moving under the Alpine Civic Center lights. She understood Jack Carmine had been a logical extension of her growing years, of Lucas Mathen and customized Fords, of serving up meat loaf and cheeseburgers and not thinking much beyond where she was at the moment.

Now it was plans laid out months ahead of time. It was the Plaza in New York and dinner at the best restaurants, it was the symphony orchestra that Mark said they should help because Des Moines ought to have a symphony orchestra. She remembered sitting in a meeting where the financial problems of the orchestra were being discussed and for some reason thinking of Jack Carmine and imagining him there beside her. Jack in a flannel shirt and torn jeans and old boots, leather wristband, workingman's harmonica tucked in his right breast pocket. She'd smiled then and laughed quietly to herself, thinking what Jack might have offered in the way of solving the orchestra's budget problems: "Easy, take a capitalist's point of view and make the whole shebang more efficient—speed up the line, play Bach a lot faster." After that he'd have pulled out his harmonica and played "Buffalo Gals" while doing a syncopated shuffle out the door of the meeting room.

The late Octobers, mostly, in the years after, that's when she turns and looks inside while she looks southwest: in the car in the rain and wipers going, in the backyard with autumn smoke from leaf fires a block or two away, in her bed and the sound of other breathing next to her. And sometimes—the late Octobers, mostly—she tries to make it all come back again, missing Jack Carmine and wanting it all again, wanting to grab Sara Margaret and run like leaf smoke for the high desert, make the left turn west of Fort Stockton and drive sixty miles toward the sweet Texas high country that seems even sweeter from a distance. Wanting it desperately in her mind, wanting it in reality and not wanting it, simultaneously.

Texas Jack Carmine, a mirror of sorts, reflecting back clear and bright the sum of what your mother warned you about, and in that way showing you other possibilities all at the same time. Texas Jack Carmine, in his own way, caring more than anyone else would ever care for her. She remembers him leaning against his truck, black Stetson pulled down to the top of his sunglasses, wearing a clean shirt and jeans and a shine on his custommades, waiting for her to come down the ranch house steps in her black dress the first time they'd gone into town for dinner.

She'd stopped on the porch and turned for him, saying, "Well?" Jack had reached in and honked the truck horn as a way of applauding, then walked up and swung her down from the porch, carrying her toward the truck and kissing the side of her neck, whispering in her ear, "Dancin' lady, you're all I could ever have imagined wantin'. I'm takin' you out for an evening of undiluted good times followed by a night of unequaled debauchery only you and I are capable of. Even dusted off the truck seat for you."

He'd lifted her into the truck and shut the door, stood there looking in at her, the same little boy expression on his face she had come to know when he was looking at her in moments such as these, as if he'd been given something and cared for it so much, he couldn't stop worrying someone might take it away. He'd taken out his harmonica then, saying, "I wrote a song for you, first and only song I ever wrote. Been sittin' down at the barn practicin' three weeks just for this occasion. Call it 'Dancin' on Little Horse Mountain.' " He'd stood there with dust on his custom-mades, Stetson pulled low, and played a simple melody he got perfect as far as she could tell.

When he'd finished, he grinned and said, "You've just witnessed Jack Carmine at his absolute musical best. Probably never get it exactly right like that again."

"Bandit," she'd said quietly, reaching out the truck window to touch his face, "sometimes you're a genuine wonder."

Jack Carmine had grinned at her, looking out from under his black Stetson and, as usual, fighting to hang on all the while he was hanging on. On the way to town, driving into a Texas sundown, they'd held hands and smiled at one another. And staring first down the highway, then over at her, he'd said the same words he often used when he was feeling like that: "You take my breath away, dancin' lady." She'd squeezed his hand tight when he'd said it.

Her early days in West Texas had moved by quiet and easy. Days that felt like they were longer than in other places, and it had made her life slow down and seem longer, too. Days and weeks and months, the brown dust, the wind, the silence. Linda had planted a garden and Earl took Sara Margaret riding on Cactus, propping her up in front of him on the saddle and letting her hold the reins. Jack had mended fence and fixed pumps, and they'd spent long nights together in bed, drinking Lone Star, making love, and laughing at the moon.

If it had gone on that way, she might have made it through Jack's bad moments. She might have stayed on and maybe helped him get through it all in some way. But as time went on, there'd been fewer trips to Little Horse Mountain with the air mattress, the black dress hung in a plastic bag in the closet, and there were long periods when he didn't talk to anyone except to say that money was short and he was going to look for better-paying work than he could find around Alpine. Sometimes he'd taken the one burro on the place, loaded a pack on it, and spent days in the canyons with his saddle gun. On mornings when the wind was up and dawn boiled dark red over the mountains through rain squalls, she'd lain in bed and heard the distant sound of the rifle bouncing off mountains and down the canyons.

Earl had told her, "Jack's got this idea you're not happy here because of the javelinas. Says he's cleanin' them out, once and for all, hunts only after dark using a flashlight. Hard to say how many he's killed, lot of 'em. Cuts the ears off and shows 'em to me when he comes back, keeps the ears in gunnysacks down at the barn. Seems to have temporarily substituted killin' javelinas and throwin' up afterwards for thrashin' around on the dirt and hollerin' for Leon. Same thing, though, far as I can tell by lookin' at his eyes."

Jack Carmine, she'd imagined him up there in the canyons, carrying the saddle gun and wearing his old sheepskin vest, moving through the mesquite like the big diamondback rattlers that hunted only at night. She'd imagined black shapes running through his light and Jack following them down the sights of his rifle, levering brass cartridges and firing, firing again, and again. . . .

In the summer of her second year on the ranch, Jack had told her all the javelinas had been killed and she didn't have to worry about them anymore. He also said he'd got on with a combine crew heading north. They'd argued about it, Linda saying he wouldn't be back for months and how that wasn't fair to her.

She'd gotten mad for the first time in a long time and slammed a frying pan down on the stove. "This has nothin' to do with money, Jack, this has to do with Jack

Carmine just needin' to go off somewhere. I think Rainy was right, all you Carmines are crazy. She may have put up with it, but I'm not about to much longer."

"Well"—Jack had leaned against the refrigerator, thumbs hooked in his belt and a strange, hard look on his face—"first off you need to understand that Rainy Carmine was not an entirely innocent bystander in whatever afflicted this outfit over the years. When the dust was risin' and the shit flyin' around here, she'd be more'n lookin' out for herself and be right in the middle of it with her own contributions."

He'd finished up the argument by saying, "Dancin' lady, I've taken care of the javelinas for you. Now I'm goin' out to get us some money so I can take you down to the hotel in style. Iron up your black dress and get yourself ready, I'll be back before you know it. Maybe we'll drift down to Mexico and lie on the beaches for a while."

She'd watched the pickup hit Route 90 and turn right. And Texas Jack Carmine had headed out to ride the big orange machines another time, ride them north into the autumn. He'd sent postcards for the first two months:

Hang in there, Dancin' Lady, I'll be back in late October. And, Wheats yellow, skies are blue. Breakdowns are my enemies, sundowns are my dreams.

He'd called from Wichita and farther up, moving toward Canada, asking about her and Sara Margaret. "I sent a thousand to the First National in Alpine; go buy somethin' nice for yourself and the muchacha. I care for you, Miss Linda."

Thirty-nine, headed for forty. She'd made an appointment at the college in Alpine and talked to a woman who counseled what were called "mature students." Yes, all was possible, and financial aid might be available. But Linda noticed how young the students looked, had second thoughts, and went back to the ranch to work in her garden, pulling weeds and thinking about long, straight track and that Sara Margaret would be ready for kindergarten next autumn.

Jack hadn't taken care of all the javelinas. In August, just at sundown, she'd been cleaning the house and thinking she hadn't heard from him for almost three weeks. Sara Margaret had been playing somewhere out back when Linda had heard a sound on the front porch. A boar had been right there on the porch, snuffling around, pushing its snout against the screen. She'd taken Jack's saddle gun down from its pegs, thumbed back the hammer the way he'd shown her, and shot the javelina through the screen. It was a gut shot, and the boar had taken a long time to die, making horrible sounds, fighting for its breath while bleeding and defecating all over the porch, scraping its hooves on the boards and trying to get up. She'd watched it die and had thought it was looking in at her all the while it was dying.

After that she'd sat at the kitchen table for three hours, holding an ice pack against her cheek where the rifle stock had kicked her because she hadn't tucked it tight against her the way Jack had said to do, thinking as hard as she'd ever thought in her life. Thinking about options, about getting older and getting nowhere, about Sara Margaret being ready for kindergarten and growing up alone out in the high desert. Twice she'd walked into the living room and looked out at the boar lying in its clotted blood on the porch. Then she'd packed the suitcase Jack Carmine had bought for her almost two years earlier and gathered up Sara Margaret's things. The following afternoon Earl had driven them into town in Poly Carmine's old Land Cruiser, sitting with them in

the double-wide trailer serving as a Trailways bus station. It was the rainy season in southwest Texas, and a
summer storm had moved through while they'd waited.

After the storm the highways had been wet and shiny
for a little while, the bus wheels making a hissing sound
on the pavement as they carried her and Sara Margaret
east on Route 90,

> past the 67 intersection,
> past the *Circle-C* arch with a bow in it,
> past Little Horse Mountain,
> past the black dress that still hung in the ranch
> house closet where she'd left it draped in
> plastic,
> past where she'd been at another time in her
> life.

Sara Margaret had kneeled on the seat next to Linda,
watching the ranch entrance go by. "Why we leavin'
here, Momma?"

Linda had spoken quietly, her voice sounding as tired
as she felt. "Sara Margaret, it's time to get on with our
lives before both of us get too old for gettin' on with
anything."

Sara Margaret had her serious face on. "What about
Jack and Earl and Hummer and Cactus? What about
them? They comin', too? They comin' to Iowa? When'll
Earl get to take me ridin' on Cactus again?"

"I don't know, sweetheart. I don't have everything
figured out yet. Wish I did, but I don't. Why don't you
look at the comic books I bought you at the drugstore."

Sara Margaret had sat down and concentrated on the
seat in front of her, hands in her lap and not saying
anything.

Linda had looked up the dirt ranch road as the bus
went by it, turned and watched until Little Horse Mountain was out of sight. She'd taken hold of Sara Margaret's

hand then. "I don't know how many last planes out there are, Sara Margaret, but we keep catchin' them one after the other, thinkin' all the time the next one is the last one. Seems like makin' things better always involves leavin'. Someday maybe it'll all settle down. . . . It's just got to settle down."

In the darkness later on that night, Sara Margaret had fallen asleep with her head on Linda's lap while the Trailways plowed through West Texas and on toward Dallas, where they'd made a connection for Des Moines.

She never knew Jack had come looking for her. When he'd called the ranch a week after she'd left, Earl Chavez had tried to be vague about Linda's whereabouts. Finally he'd said, "She's gone home, Jack. I think you ought to consider just leavin' her alone."

Jack had driven south all of one night and most of another day to Altoona. But Linda's mother had lied and said she had no idea where her daughter was and that Jack could take his damned ol' pickup and get off the property.

He'd wandered around Altoona for a while, thinking he might see her and try to explain things, get her to reconsider, then head on back to Texas with her and Sara Margaret. At dusk he'd bought a six-pack of Bud and pulled into a place called Hayes Park, sat there on the fender of his truck for a long time, and listened to the locusts, which were a sure sign of autumn coming on. Around ten o'clock he'd headed out for Alpine.

Linda never quite sorted out her feelings about Jack Carmine. Early on they had something to do with being wild and free, her final run toward taking life as it came and making love at dawn on mountaintops. He'd taught her something about the road life, about its pleasures and its costs. And he'd given her something else, hard to say exactly what it was, but it had begun with the black dress. She'd felt it the night he'd bought the dress for her, something to do with thinking better about yourself. Texas Jack Carmine had a way of making that happen and making it stick.

There were times afterward when she'd felt guilty about the way she'd pulled out on him. In one of those times she'd written a long letter to him, addressed it to "Mr. Jack Carmine, General Delivery, Alpine, Texas" and tried to explain everything. She'd intentionally omitted her return address and mailed it from the Plaza Hotel in New York when she'd gone there with Mark Elwin on a business trip.

Jack Carmine never read the letter. He knew what it would say without looking at it, had guessed how the song would end from the moment Linda Lobo came out of an Otter Falls dressing room in a black dress. Jack carried the letter in the back pocket of his jeans for three days, thought about burning it, then buried it instead, far up one of the canyons behind the house.

When Bobby McGregor did a concert in Des Moines, Linda had called around to various hotels until she'd located him. They'd first met when Bobby played El Paso. He'd had his wife, Sharon, with him on that tour, and the four of them drank and talked half the night. Bobby and Jack did most of the talking, reminiscing about big orange machines and bars in Shreveport and the time Jack got out in Cheyenne and went to Mexico.

"Yeah, and he never sent any damn Polaroids like he promised," Bobby had said, glancing at Linda Lobo, wondering if all that seemed to lie beneath her clothes was really there and envying Jack Carmine, who knew for sure.

"Never had time to take any pictures." Jack had grinned. "Too busy doin' the things most people only take pictures of."

Sharon had rolled her eyes, listening to the good ol' boys talk about the good ol' days.

Five years later in a Des Moines coffee shop, Linda and Bobby had talked about the weather and things in general, then drifted over to the subject of Jack Carmine and stayed there. Bobby had said he understood how she felt, why she couldn't hang on with Jack. Said he'd gone through a lot with Jack and finally had to get away from him the same way Linda had. To Linda Elwin it had all seemed sensible and correct when they talked about it that way, in the daylight, in Des Moines, a long way from Little Horse Mountain and dancing down the road with Waylon's music coming out the ranch house door.

Each of them had told their "Jack" stories, the funny ones, and admitted the more they talked, the more Texas Jack Carmine became larger than life, out of all proportion to the man himself. And in a strange fashion, the stories remembered themselves.

Bobby had offered her tickets for the concert, but Linda Elwin had declined politely, saying her husband didn't go out much in the evenings except for the symphony. Bobby had grinned and said he understood, looked at his watch and said he had to hustle over to the auditorium for a sound check, that he was breaking in a new harmonica player and had to run through a few things with him.

After Linda had paid for the coffee, they'd shaken hands out on the sidewalk and then for reasons neither of them had to explain, they'd come together and held each other close.

Linda Elwin had looked up at Bobby McGregor and said, "I miss him sometimes, Bobby . . . really miss him . . . miss that life . . . part of it, at least, the wildness, the unpredictability."

He'd nodded and kept holding on to her, looking into her face, smelling her and thinking she didn't smell like a city woman. She smelled of all the highways that ever ran through spring and summer toward sad-eyed endings, and, goddammit, at that moment he got close to saying things he shouldn't say but wanted to. He'd let it go, kept it proper, and didn't say he wanted to see her naked just once in his lifetime, that he'd be complete after that and never ask for one more thing from whoever hands things out. Sometimes later on he wishes he'd said it; he'd felt at that moment she might just have done it, gone to his room and taken off her clothes in some kind of reaching back, some kind of tribute to the world of Jack Carmine and a reclamation of who she still was, deep down.

And she might have, if he'd asked. Linda Elwin understood men and sensed by the look in his eyes what Bobby McGregor was thinking about. She probably wouldn't have done it, but she might have, and later on she was glad he hadn't said anything.

Driving home that day, Linda had thought about Sara Margaret and how she never asked anymore about Jack and when he might come by and play his harmonica for them. But a few months ago she'd noticed a bandanna folded neatly on Sara Margaret's bureau. Jack Carmine had given it to her one day all those years ago when the dust was up and the West Texas sun was like a propane torch. He'd untied the bandanna from around his neck and said, "Loop this around your head, muchacha. Give you some protection from the elements." They'd walked a long way that afternoon, up into the canyons, Jack carrying Sara Margaret on his shoulders when they'd turned for home.

Looking into the sun on her way out to West Des Moines, Linda Elwin had tears in her eyes, just a few at first. She pulled the BMW into a supermarket parking lot and cried hard for several minutes, not even sure why she was crying. But it had something to do with harmonicas in the key of E and high-desert roads, something to do with Little Horse Mountain and warm swimming pools in the middle of goddamn Texas-Nowhere. It had to do with the illusion of freedom, with an image that kept coming to her over and over in recent years—just hauling off and ending up in some cheap hotel in a dusty little Mexican village where you'd never been, getting drunk on hot cactus liquor and getting wild-warm-wet-crazy, screwing your head off for days with somebody whose name you didn't even know. It had to do with pulling out on Jack Carmine the way she had and deals you lived with because it was the best thing for you and Sara Margaret.

But time is an old lens of amber, and as you look down the barrel of it, good things get remembered and bad ones left behind. The good images stay, as if they were suspended somehow in a mason jar, like Jack had said about sunrises one time. She keeps them there in the jar and sometimes in the late Octobers, especially in the late Octobers, takes them out and looks at them. And those some years later on a jet heading for Dallas, she remembered her first trip to Texas with Jack Carmine, called it back up and held it in her mind, smiling. Music playing—Waylon and Merle and Emmylou, highway music—and being in the floating middle of exactly no place at that time, but more than good enough back then, it seemed, and a whole lot better than where she'd come from. It had been late October, and she'd headed into a warmer sun with Texas Jack Carmine, traveler of the summer roads, rider of the far places.

Mark Elwin glanced up from his broiled salmon.

"You got a great suntan in Cabo San Lucas. Looks good on you, goes well with that lavender outfit you bought."

"Thanks." She smiled, happy to be with him.

Down below, West Texas was falling behind the 737.

Over I-10 and Vaughn Rhomer.

Heading for Dallas.

Des Moines after that.

Home.

At the Dallas–Fort Worth Airport, she and Mark waited for their Des Moines flight. Mark was reading an article about new findings in life expectancy while Linda sat beside him and watched passengers going back and forth to wherever passengers go before they come around again. The tall man in cowboy boots, leather guitar case over his shoulder, walked down the corridor and glanced at her. She smiled at Bobby McGregor and almost said something. He slowed for a moment, saw the man sitting beside her, and nodded, quickly touching the brim of his Stetson before going on.

CHAPTER SEVENTEEN

West Texas, October 28, 1993

Vaughn Rhomer stopped for the night in Katy on the outskirts of Houston. He smuggled the dog into his room and ordered pizza from the restaurant next door. The following morning he and Bandida were on the road before sunup and around noon picnicked at a rest stop outside of Junction.

Vaughn Rhomer waved his sandwich and said, "This is called the Texas Hill Country, girl; one of the prettiest places anywhere, so people say." The dog was busy eating her sandwich and didn't respond.

He thought about his words: "So people say." Hell, *I* can say it, he was thinking, I've been here and not just heard about it like before.

At an outdoor phone he called Otter Falls and talked to the manager of Best Value.

"You're *what?*" Bert Freeder asked, hearing the *whoosh* of West Texas wind coming down the line from Vaughn Rhomer's end.

"Just what I said, I'm quitting. Have them draw up

my retirement papers, I'll let you know where they can send the checks."

"Jesus Christ, Vaughn, we can't get along without you here. You can't be serious, anyhow, just haul-assing out for Mexico at your age. I'll hold off on the papers for a week or two, let you get over whatever's eating you."

"Bert, mail the papers in. I won't be coming back. Good-bye, I'll send you all a card from Mexico." Vaughn Rhomer hung up the phone.

An hour before sundown he stopped at the intersection of Routes 67 and 90. Years before, Jack Carmine had drawn him a map of how to find the ranch in case Vaughn Rhomer ever got down that way. Vaughn Rhomer had studied the map, memorizing it, just in case. He turned left on 90, drove a little ways, and found the bent arch: *Circle-C Ranch*. He drove slowly up the dirt road toward an old ranch house turning a color somewhere between red and pink in late sunlight.

No answer at the front door, none at the back screen door.

"Jack?" he called. Bandida looked up at him. "Well, door's open, so I'm sure Jack won't mind if we go in and make ourselves at home for a while." Bandida followed him into the kitchen.

It all seemed familiar to Vaughn Rhomer. Jack had told him stories about life on the ranch, and Lorraine had written occasionally about what things were like in West Texas. He noticed the kitchen table right off, an old door laid across two sawhorses, and remembered Jack telling him how that makeshift table came to be.

"See, Poly had his papers all over the table all the time. Rainy complained about it, but he just kept tellin' her life was too short to always be puttin' things back in their proper containers. She kept warnin' him to get the damned table cleaned off so we could have a sit-down supper just one time, instead of everyone standin' around the stove with plates in their hands. Said there wasn't even space to play poker and she was goin' to do somethin' drastic if he didn't clean it off.

"One evenin', Poly was off somewhere fightin' another one of his battles, and she just boiled over, got red in the face lookin' at the table piled about two feet deep with maps and legal documents. Made all hands and the cook move the table out back. It was a heavy bastard, solid oak that had come down to us from Grandpa Smyler, like everything else. We all stood around and watched, too afraid to say or do anything while Rainy got a bucket of coal oil from the barn. You guessed it—she burned that goddamned table and all of Poly's crap stacked on it. While it was burnin', Rainy went in the house and brought out a pack of marshmallows, made us all find sticks and toast 'em right then and there, said that's all she was fixin' for supper that night. Local fiddler even wrote a song about the event, called it 'The Night They Burned the Table.' "

Vaughn Rhomer ran his hand across the door that had become a table and looked around. Guns: lever-action rifle on pegs above the door, pearl-handled revolver hanging in its holster from a nail. Old pistol. He touched the scarred ivory grip with his finger.

The house was dusty, the stove hadn't been cleaned for months, years probably, and it was quiet outside except for a sweep of wind that would come for a few seconds and then die away.

He walked into the living room and looked at the worn leather furniture with wide wooden arms. The room was dim, almost dark, and smelled of long-ago woodsmoke from the fireplace. Vaughn Rhomer imagined Jack and that pretty woman he'd brought through Otter Falls seven years ago—Linda Something—sitting here, talking by the fire. A large bedroom opened off the living room; Vaughn Rhomer couldn't help but go in. Jack had mentioned how you could see sunrise over the Glass Mountains from his bed, and Vaughn Rhomer wanted to see just once what mountains would look like through bedroom windows.

A long closet ran half the length of one wall, doors swung open. On the floor was a pair of battered female-size cowboy boots with run-over heels. A few wrinkled shirts hung on the wooden bar next to something black in a plastic bag. He fingered the dusty bag and saw it contained a woman's dress, a fancy one. On the back of a high Spanish-style chair was a beanie with a propeller attached to it. The wind came from the north through an open window and lifted stiff, yellowed curtains, spun the beanie's propeller three-quarters of a complete turn before it stopped.

Vaughn Rhomer heard the crunch of rubber tires on gravel outside, went to the back door and out on the porch. Around the corner of the house came a Mexican man in jeans and boots and a crinkled hat with a buzzard feather in it.

The man said, "Howdy, can I help you?"

"I'm Vaughn Rhomer, Jack Carmine's uncle, from Iowa. Just passing through and thought I'd stop and say hello."

The man held out his hand. "Oh, yeah, Jack's mentioned you in complimentary fashion a few times. My name's Earl Chavez, worked for the Carmines nearly fifty-five years. Not much to do now, look after a few cattle is all, but Jack's good enough to keep me on."

"Is Jack around?"

"Nope, sorry. He's off somewhere workin' on a crew

layin' gas pipe or somethin'. Come on in, though, I'll fix us some beans and eggs if you're hungry."

Bandida lay on the floor while Earl Chavez and Vaughn Rhomer talked late into the night. Around two o'clock, after beans and eggs and several drinks of after-supper whiskey, Vaughn asked whatever happened to the dog, Hummer, Jack used to talk about.

"That ol' dog died four years ago," Earl said. "Buried him by that fallin'-down oil derrick out back. He'd pissed on it enough times I figured he'd laid some kind of claim to it. I've stashed a note among my things askin' Jack to bury me out there also, right beside Hummer for about all the same reasons."

Vaughn Rhomer nodded while Earl Chavez squinted at him through eyes bloodshot from years of dust and looking into a hard sun for stray bulls. "Life been pretty good to you, Mr. Rhomer? If you don't mind me askin'."

"About all you could expect, I guess," Vaughn Rhomer said, thinking he must seem awfully soft and pink next to Earl Chavez. Earl Chavez, in his faded red-and-green-striped shirt with snap buttons and a frayed collar, was at least ten years older than him but still looked hard. Vaughn Rhomer noticed how big and muscular his forearms were. "How about you, Mr. Chavez?"

"Pretty much the same . . . about the same." Earl was looking down at his hands on the table, using each to massage the other as he talked. "All cowboys hope to get a place of their own sometime, but cowboyin' doesn't allow for makin' enough to get one. End up with bad knees and arthritis in these ol' hands from wranglin' cows and sendin' 'em to city folks who think beef is raised in plastic packages in the back room of a grocery store."

He held up his hands and showed gnarled, swollen knuckles to Vaughn Rhomer, then looked down at the table and spoke quietly. "Days kinda go by one after the other, and pretty soon your life is gone and you're right where you were all those years ago. Find yourself givin' up on gettin' done what you said you were gonna do fifty years ago. Fellow named Sam and I were talkin' about that the other day. Sam got it about right, said, 'Except for low wages and endin' up with nothin' but a beat-up body after fifty years of hard work, cowboyin' is the best life there is.' Jack offered to cosign a note with me years ago when a little place the other side of Alpine came up for sale. But I was afraid I couldn't make a go of it, and it scared me to think Jack might lose what's left of the Circle-C here if things went bad for me, so I let it go by."

Vaughn Rhomer looked down at the table where Earl Chavez was looking and thought about his Best Value pension plan. It wasn't a great plan, but it wasn't bad, either. Enough to get by on easy if you lived quiet and cheap in some Mexican beach town.

Sometime before dawn, Vaughn Rhomer asked about the woman, Linda Something-or-other. Earl Chavez poured them each another drink of whiskey and said, "I don't want to say too much, that's kind of Jack's private stock, and I ought to leave the tellin' to him if he's so inclined. She was the best, I'll say that. And she was just about the only thing Jack ever really cared for. I liked her a lot, too . . . really did . . . liked her a lot. Those were some of the best days we ever had around here. Liked her little girl, also. I used to take the muchacha ridin' with me, sit her right in front of me and let her hold the reins . . . never had any kids of my own. Wonder now and then whatever happened to them . . .

hope things worked out for them . . . Miss Linda and the little girl." He looked to his left, out the kitchen window at first light coming up over the Glass Mountains, remembering better days when a woman's blouses fluttered on the clothesline, when there was a garden with tomatoes in it and a little girl rode out with him to check on the cattle.

Bandida began to growl, got up and walked stiff-legged over to the screen door. When her growl got louder, Earl Chavez flexed his stiff fingers and took down the Winchester from its pegs. He booted open the door and stood on the back porch with the rifle dangling from his right hand. Vaughn Rhomer went out and stood with him.

"Goddamned javelinas," said Earl Chavez. "Jack claimed he'd killed 'em all one time about six years ago. He didn't, I can tell you that much, Mr. Rhomer. Jack's done a lot of things in his life, but he never killed all the javelinas. They're goin' to outlast all of us. Guess they're stayin' out in the brush this mornin' and not comin' up to the house." He smiled at Vaughn Rhomer and nodded at Bandida. "She'd make a good ranch dog. A little short in the leg, but I can tell she's got some heart to her."

Vaughn Rhomer squatted down and stroked Bandida. After a while he stood up and reached out his hand. "Mr. Chavez, it was a pleasure meeting you. I got to be moving on. Thanks for the whiskey and good conversation. And please tell Jack I stopped by to say hello. Tell him also that when you last saw me, I was headed for Mexico."

Vaughn Rhomer began walking toward his car. He turned and said it one more time. "Mr. Chavez, be sure and tell Jack I was headed for Mexico. Tell him I was alone, except for my dog, and I wasn't sure when I was coming back. Also tell him thanks for showing me the way. He'll understand."

Earl Chavez nodded, "Jack has a way of doin' that, showin' others the way. I'll be sure and tell 'im, Mr. Rhomer. He'll be pleased you stopped by even if he wasn't here. Not too many people are tryin' to look up Jack Carmine these days." He opened the kitchen door and turned to spit over the back porch railing before going inside.

West of Alpine the Southern Pacific was moving alongside the highway, picking up speed for the run over Paisano Pass. The moon sat full and fat down Route 90, and somebody was singing a song on the radio, Jimmy Somebody-or-other; the beat of the song matched the train wheels turning. Vaughn Rhomer didn't know the song or the singer, but he hummed along and tried to pick up some of the words, something about following the dancing life.

EPILOGUE

In the words of Bobby McGregor:

Things kind of run together when you get into your forties, events and people bleed over into one another and smudge up some. But last Christmas, Christmas of '93, that's pressed sharp, tooled clean and hard in the special place where we tuck away what's worth hanging on to. I remember Elena. Elena and the sound of my boot heels.

We'll take the boot heels first. They're leather, and they've clicked across the tiled floors of more airports than I care to think about, fast-fading echoes of a life on the road. A year ago: O'Hare, in Chicago, and the click again. Steady, long-legged meter, trying to catch the last flight out for Sioux Falls on Christmas Eve.

O'Hare had gone down two days earlier while a big storm moved through. I'd sat it out in Atlanta, waiting for Chicago to open up. The southeast weather was quiet, so the band had made it back to Nashville okay. We'd shaken hands, said good-bye, while they loaded gear and Christmas presents into airport vans. Long way, two months of planes and applause and warm-

233

colored lights in my eyes. And the songs—the sweet, sad curl of old lamentations all the singers sing in one way or another. Charlotte, Dallas, Denver, Houston, Orlando, Memphis, on and on, ending the string in Atlanta.

I was thirty-six hours late into O'Hare and moving fast. Down the escalator from the C concourse, underground and heading toward the F gates. The Martin six-string rode in a black leather bag slung over my left shoulder. Behind me the Samsonite case I was towing clicked, too, over the floor tiles. Little wheels and boot heels, the syncopations of my days now.

Two minutes from F6, "Silent Night" came over the sound system, Perry Como on the vocal. Perry, the old smoothie, and telling me all was calm, calm and bright. Boot heels, little wheels, all the infants across all the years, but only one so tender and mild, the rest were cranky and crying while mothers rocked them in airport restaurant booths, near the Polish sausage machines.

As it turned out, I could have taken it easy, walked slower. United was running late and wouldn't leave for Sioux Falls until eleven-twenty, things still backed up from the storm. Out on the tarmac the big planes looked like giant insects crawling around among piles of dirty snow.

The high arc, then, out to where the West gets under way. We bumped down in Sioux Falls, all fourteen of us, a little before one. After eight weeks in the lot, the pickup was covered with snow and ice, cold and stiff and starting slow. I took it into the country, along the dirt road, and turned up the lane. Lights were on, house-sitter left fourteen pages of phone calls in the log and a note: "Everything's okay. Had the furnace people out to fix the blower (they'll send bill). Black Cat is fine, he misses you, I think. Merry Xmas.''

I took out a Miller's and sat at the kitchen table, twisted off the cap, and drank half the bottle in two long swallows. Black Cat came down the stairs, talking cat talk, jumped on my lap. Last entry in the phone log: "12/24, 7:15 p.m. Sharon from San Miguel Allende— 'Merry Christmas. Call if you want.' " She'd left a number in Mexico. The divorce had come through two years back, but we still kept in touch, financially and otherwise. It would take the Denver and Houston concerts to keep her well provisioned and hid up in San Miguel for the winter.

Too late to call my mother out in Belle Fourche, three hundred miles farther west. I snuffled through piles of mail and gave up when I came to a manila envelope marked "Enclosed is your individually personalized custom-made product." I couldn't recall ordering anything.

I've never been much for holidays, for celebrating them. Still, there's something about Christmas Eve, I guess, and the dull thump of unwelcome solitude was starting to hurt a little. Aloneness, which I like, was drifting over into loneliness, which I don't. Christmas Eve carries baggage with it, maybe a hangover from my boyhood when my mother's house was warm and smelled of December cooking.

Phone rang. Sharon, I figured, trying once more with her ritual and perfunctory Christmas call. There was loud music in the background of wherever the phone was located. Just the music at first, and shouting, no voice on the line.

Then: "BOBBYBOBBYBOBBY, THAT *YOU?*" Jack Carmine, Texas Jack. I hadn't heard from him for years.

"Jack, good to hear your voice," I said, and meant it. "Where'n hell are you?"

"The Crystal—Alpine—havin' one hell of a party, leavin' a trail tonight even old hounds could follow."

Jack, shouting, voice Texas drawled and tequila slurred. "Merry Christmas, old buddy-Bobby." The tequila took away the *t* and *m* in "Christmas" when he said it.

Jack, laughing: "Heard your new song on KALP yesterday—sounds better'n I remember you; must be your band. Know most of the words already. I recall you were kickin' around that idea fifteen years ago while we was supposedly headin' for Bakersfield and I got out somewhere in Wyoming. Sang little bits of it back then . . . that's right, ain't it? That's the song, ain't it? Hey, heard that song called 'Bandit'? It's my life story, Bobby. Know the song I'm talking about?"

I knew the song, I'd written it—song about a woman pulling out and a man remembering her: "She used to call him 'Bandit,' for reasons of her own. . . ." Jack's story, my story: "Is that her I see dancin', out along the highway? / No, it's just the heat waves risin' from the West Texas blacktop." I was thinking the good ol' boys were getting older, but they weren't so good on Christmas Eve anymore, just older. And alone. Older and alone, part of some other world that was dying and wouldn't come again. Good ol' boys, listening to the fading sound of distant trains, like passengers left at the station.

"Bobby, hope you're not too amplified these days. Liked the way those old pickers'd lift their six-strings and play right through the mike. Saw one of these new guys on TV the other day, sort of a round-faced guy with a Stetson, had a head-mike thing wired to him, looked like he was takin' calls at a mail-order outfit. Hope you don't get to that point, Bobby."

I didn't say anything, didn't have a chance to say anything. Jack was running off words without leaving any spaces.

"Jesus, Bobby, remember the good days, damn, weren't they good, Bobby? Pushin' those big damn orange combines all the way from Texas to Saskatchewan? Remember that time snow caught us at Weyburn and we had to cut all night?"

I waited until he stopped, then said I remembered, told him the wild days were good days, and took another hit of beer, petting Black Cat while I talked. Down the line he started coughing hard, almost choking, and I asked how he'd been doing.

His voice was froggy, with a deep scratch in it. "Been a little under the weather for a few months, got this goddamned cough that won't go away and leave me alone. Think I'm feelin' better somewhat, 'least tonight I am. It's gettin' down to last things, Bobby, cold coffee mornin's and warm beer afternoons, but nothin' the matter right now a little tune-up won't fix."

A woman's voice came on the line and Jack yelling behind her, telling her to give him the phone back. She screamed, *"He just needs another tequila!"* and hung up.

I sat there for a while and thought about Jack. Missed him, traveled with him in the early years, liked him, loved him, maybe, if men can love in that way.

Thinking some more about Jack Carmine and how he set us all free in one way or another. Just being around him did that to some people. He loved us in a special way, and we knew it, and in doin' so taught us to think better of ourselves. Showed us how we might be worth more than we'd ever seen in ourselves and got our thoughts moving on toward where he could never go or wouldn't have wanted to if you'd have asked him. He set the rest of us free while he was strugglin' to get there himself and never made it.

Hard to say, in the end, whether he failed us or

whether it was the other way around. I used to think it was the former, but I been changin' my mind a little over the years. Goddammit, though, he was tough to deal with sometimes, and most of us got pushed away . . . or maybe . . . maybe we just out-and-out ran, tryin' to get some distance between ourselves and what was inside of Jack that scared us. Or sometimes, and I'm speakin' about as honestly as I can here, I wonder if we were just afraid that helpin' him when he needed it took up too much of our time and energy when we could've been doin' other things. When it comes to love and caring there are no easy releases, and it'd take a big trowel to spread the blame.

But I still remember him in that black Stetson of his, smokin' one of those thin cigars and leanin' against a building in Ojinaga back in the late seventies, grinnin' and sayin', "Bobby, I do believe we're goin' to be all right, we're goin' to make it just fine." I asked him what he meant by that and he just shook his head and started dancin' down the street, doin' that little shuffle he was always doin', wavin' for me to follow him. I caught up with him, and he kept on grinnin', said, "Let's do somethin' that'll give us some stories to tell before senility slaps us upside the head." We were both wearing old suit coats we'd bought in a Mexican used-clothing shop, and he grabbed hold of my sleeve, draggin' me into another one of those end-of-world joints he favored.

That's how I try to remember Jack, leaning kind of cool and smart-ass against an adobe wall in a border town. Like to think of him that way instead of the way he's become from what I hear, looking ten years older than the fifty-four he'd be by now. Forgetting his own rules, pawin' around for turmoil, drinking way too much, and breaking up his hands fighting his way

through most of the bars from West Texas to Saskatchewan, crying sometimes right in the middle of when he's
tearing a place all to pieces. Word is that the combine
crews won't take him on anymore, too much trouble.

Aside from 'Nam, I knew Linda was part of the reason
why he was hung out and strung out. After she packed
up and left, Jack completely lost control. The women
pulling out . . . Linda, Sharon . . . looking for something better than Jack and me. Can't blame 'em, I sup-
pose. I could have called her, Sharon in San Miguel,
and said something about having a nice holiday, but I
didn't. I knew she'd be with somebody but would pretend she wasn't.

I thumbed Christmas cards: my mother, my agent,
my lawyer, the fan club, couple of musicians I know.
Hallmarks with tender verse, tender and mild,
"boughten cards" as my dad used to call them.

My agent had enclosed a review with his card.

Bobby McGregor's recent concert here was
a puzzle. You watch him come out on stage,
lean as a ten-penny nail, looking undernour-
ished, spotlight raking across his long, brown
hair. I wanted to like it, to like him, but
there's something very strange going on in
his voice, his eyes. Some hint of a deathlike
something that's marching toward him, some
harbinger of tragedy, something about rain
on lonesome highways and gray on the soul
that made this reviewer depressed and wishing for a good ol' rock 'n' roll Christmas
song. . . .

I tossed the clipping aside. They just never get it.
They never understand it's the sense of tragedy that

makes the music come. The singers curve in from some other place, riding some far-back arrow that carries us and sadness along together. We know the arrow ain't going nowhere but down eventually, and that's why we sing what we sing and why we sing the way we do.

The reviewer should have gone to see *The Nutcracker.* Happy stuff, kids and merry feet in toe shoes. Some wear toe shoes and believe things will turn out all right with a little tinkering. Some wear cowboy boots that go click and believe differently, believe you just go out there and see what happens while there's time. Like one of my songs says, "Some reach for the latchkey, others reach for the rains / Some run for the fireside, others run for the trains."

Two o'clock rolled by, and I kept drinking beer and petting Black Cat, loneliness laying hard and heavy on me. Wind came up outside and more snow on the way, that's what the flight attendant had said. Her name was Elena Martinez. She had long black hair with a few random gray streaks and pulled it back in a French twist, one of those things women can do with their hair. Never had figured out how they carry that off, how women could get all that hair gathered up neat and tight with a comb in the back, just one or two strands drifting loose, which kind of adds to the overall effect. Jack Carmine once said he liked the way a woman's neck looks when long hair is swept away from it, only a strand or two still lying on the skin. I remember him saying in that context, perfection has its flaws, but flawed perfection—a loose strand of hair on the skin of a woman's neck—now, that has a peculiar kind of force to it.

Elena had sat on the seat arm across from me and said she was from L.A. but had to spend Christmas Eve at the Holiday Inn in Sioux Falls. She was somewhere in her forties and a little worn from serving too many bad meals and showing too many people how oxygen masks work. And she wasn't one bit happy about laying over in the Dakotas. I said I didn't blame her, said that or something equally inane just as the pilot came on and announced we were getting ready to land. Elena had moved along the aisle, making sure everybody's seat back was in the upright position, tray tables locked. She'd been standing at the door when I exited and wished me a Merry Christmas.

Two-thirty, night going by. I lowered Black Cat to the floor, unzipped the leather case, and took out the Martin. I bought it used. It's been with me twenty-five years and scratched up pretty bad, but it has a bass like distant thunder. I played a run down into G and started singing quietlike, "Her slender brown hands make the sign of the cross / And gracefully light the pine-scented candles," wishing I could get the damn song finished. I'd been working on it for the last month in hotel rooms.

The old days—I started thinking about the old days again. About Jack, about long yellow wheat bending in big snow just south of Weyburn and Jack's voice on the CB that night: "Hang in there, Bobby. Stay on the cut, I'm just off to your left and movin' fast, see your headlights sometimes when the snow lets up for a minute."

Jesus, the years seemed to be running by. Too fast. Charlotte one night, on to somewhere else the next. Too fast. Or, looking at it from another angle, maybe not fast enough, not fast enough to get me through before I'd be old and in the way. Garth Brooks and Bobby McGregor this year, somebody else coming right along after that. What the hell, Bob Wills nailed it down somewhere around 1935 when he was telling Leon McAuliffe how to handle instrumental breaks: "You smile at me when you take it and smile when you give it back and play like hell in the meantime." That's about it, taking it and giving it back, playing like hell and smiling whether you feel like smiling or not. Leon and Lester, all the others, taking it and playing it and moving on when you're finished. As Jack used to say, "Bobby, after a while we're all missing in action."

Two forty-five. Beer bottles on the table, four of them, the rubble of a lonely Christmas piling up.

Jack . . . Jack Carmine and Linda A-Something. I've never gotten past Linda. She's the seventh chord I can't get resolved. I thought about calling her. Nights like this you get all down and alone and start wanting to talk to the past, see if those you knew are still out there and okay. Let the sound of their voices tell you it's more than a dream, that you were actually in some other place a long time ago when it seemed like it all might run forever.

I imagined what her husband would say after she hung up. "Who'n hell was that in the middle of the night?"

"Oh, just some guitar player I used to know. He called to wish me happy holidays."

Bad idea, calling Linda. Bad ideas seem to hide somewhere in beer bottles.

Aw, but Linda-Linda, put on your boots and jeans. We'll go to Texas, pick up Jack Carmine, and head down to Mexico. . . . On second thought, no Jack this time. Just you and me. Just one time, you and me by ourselves. Get rid of your city clothes. Better yet, get rid of all your clothes, get drunk and crazy and shake it in my face, on the bed or on the floor or sitting on a dirty bathroom sink like the Ojinaga whores used to prefer it. Wouldn't matter, and I could give it all back smiling after that.

I got the number for the Crystal Bar in Alpine and

dialed it. No answer, party over, evidently. I looked at
the phone for a moment, then checked the book and
dialed again. Elena Martinez's voice was just this side
of sleepy, but she could be ready in twenty minutes if
I wanted to pick her up.

Some reach for the latchkey, others reach for the rains.
Maybe it's possible to do both on Christmas Eve. Elena
was waiting in the lobby when I pulled up at the Holiday
Inn. She hurried out and climbed in the truck, wearing
black wool slacks and a white turtleneck under her coat.

"How're you doing, cowboy? Nice of you to call. I
was just sitting there drinking Scotch and watching *The
Nutcracker* on television. My mother used to take me
to see it every Christmas. Ever see it?"

"Once," I said. "On television."

"I saw you walking off the plane with a guitar. You
a musician?"

"Sometimes, when I'm runnin' for the trains, ridin'
the big arrow toward places unknown."

She looked at me in a curious way. "What are you
running for tonight?" Her voice was quiet, a little Spanish tinge holding on from way back, and she looked
soft and pretty in the dash lights.

I turned on the wipers and said, "Tonight, I'm runnin'
for the fireside, hangin' on to the latchkey, gettin' off
the great, sad arrow for a while and intendin' to grin
just a bit if it's at all possible."

"Well, Bobby McGregor, I'm not sure I know what
that means, but maybe we can make it possible." I could
tell she was smiling.

Snow was falling hard when we went up the lane six
miles from town. We sat in my kitchen for a while,
a man's kitchen, plain and way too functional, I was
thinking. Somehow the presence of a woman changes
your way of looking at the world, gets you away from

pure, hard function and more in the direction of things less well defined, a little more softness and form to offset stark practicality. I've never figured that out, either. Makes you wish for a little vase of flowers on the table or some nice blue curtains on the windows instead of only sun-bleached shades. Of course, that's just my opinion and probably isn't widely held in these days when we're not supposed to see much difference between men and women. Jack Carmine and me, I guess we were born to live in other times; maybe we do.

Elena and I stood on the back porch, watching the snow, watching our breath in the cold. She put her arm around my waist and looked up at me. I touched her hair, feeling the comb, letting my hand run down along her neck, feeling her skin. I'd been humming the melody to "Bandit" but stopped when she looked up at me.

She leaned against me and put her head on my chest, watching the snow and speaking so quietly, I had to lower my head to catch her words. "I have a winter heart in these years of my life, cowboy. . . . I always . . . always somehow feel like I'm a long way from home, especially tonight."

I told her I was a long way from home, too, in some other kind of way. Said I felt like I was getting more in that direction as the years went by. Said I kept hearing distant thunder, like the Martin's bass strings. Elena said she knew what I was talking about, only for her it was the sound of big surf along the Mexican coast. We held on to each other for a long time, snow angling down through the yard light and drifting a bit before tailing off toward morning.

Overall, things turned out pretty calm, reasonably bright. When your heart has turned all the flat colors of winter, sometimes you reach for the moment. Sometimes you do that, looking for the warm again, trying to get back home again without getting lost in far-deep snow out in strange country, out in a place where nobody understands your words and cannot point the way for you.

On the twenty-sixth I leaned against the bathroom door frame and watched Elena fix her hair. She smiled at me in the mirror. "What are you thinking about?"

I grinned back at her. "Just always wondered how women do that, get their hair up in a French twist; I guess that's what it's called. Now I know."

Elena Martinez left for the coast in early afternoon. Me and Black Cat headed out for Texas an hour later—wanted to introduce him to Jack Carmine before all of us got too old for running, before the thunder got too loud, before the arrow started its long fall toward final things, toward sadness and all that.

"Jingle Bell Rock" was playing when we hit the Kansas line, Black Cat on the seat back behind my head, purring. I thought of Elena, hoping she'd made it home all right for the holidays. We'd exchanged phone numbers, promising each other we'd try to set up something when I played Bakersfield in April. If not Bakersfield, then Phoenix a week later, or maybe San Diego in May, crossing paths out there on the road. Maybe a visit at my place when summer was here again and Black Cat would lie on the porch railing before the sun was high. I told her that would be a good time to visit, in summer, when the night breeze would come all the way from Montana and riffle the blue curtains I was going to put up in the kitchen.

Then I started thinking about how we love so timidly, except for those Christmas Eves when the great arrow halts its flight for an hour or two, suspended up there by a voice of a woman who also flies alone and hears the sound of big surf along the Mexican coast. A woman who whispers your name over and over again in the darkness while holding on to you, holding you close and warm enough that you think maybe distant thunder and the roll of big oceans can be put off for a while. A woman named Elena, who understands the sweet, sad curl of old lamentations flowing from a winter heart, who has slender brown hands and makes the sign of the cross before making love.

I stopped thinking after a while and concentrated on driving. Shifted gears and cut west at Oklahoma City with Amarillo up ahead. Listening to Guy Clark singing on the radio, ". . . got these lines in my face tryin' to straighten out the wrinkles in my life," and believing Guy Clark got it just about right. Stomped my boot down hard on the accelerator, petting Black Cat and heading for Texas, looking for Jack Carmine, who's spent his entire life hearing thunder louder than anyone's ever heard and keeps pushing the big arrow downward at an ever-faster clip while the rest of us are just trying to slow it up for an hour or two.

Locate Texas Jack Carmine, go down to Mexico again, and listen to some border music. Lie on the beaches . . . buy some alligator boots and a couple of secondhand suit jackets, wear black Stetsons and lean smart-ass against adobe walls . . . smoke little cigars and tease the señoritas. Take some Polaroids, just to prove we did it one more time before we got too short. Show the pictures to grandchildren if we ever have any and ever see 'em if we do have 'em. Brag a little bit, tell 'em we did that . . . tell 'em me and Texas Jack Carmine went to Mexico one more time and talked about where the moon goes before it comes around again.

Maybe write a song about it.

ACKNOWLEDGMENTS

All of Bobby McGregor's songs are fictional, as are all the writings appearing in Vaughn Rhomer's notebooks.

The Saigon evacuation scene, though fictionalized here, is based on the following sources: John Pilger, *The Last Day* (New York: Vintage Books, 1975); David Butler, *The Fall of Saigon* (New York: Simon & Schuster, 1985); Clark Dougan, David Fulghum, *et al.*, *The Fall of the South* (Boston: Boston Publishing Company, 1985); "55 Days of Shame," *Newsweek*, April 15, 1985, pp. 47–53. John Ketwig's fine book . . . *and a hard rain fell* (New York: Macmillan Publishing Company, 1985) was especially helpful in better understanding Vietnam from a GI's point of view.

The following was taken from Randall Jarrell's poem, "The Death of the Ball Turret Gunner": "From my mother's sleep I fell into the State / And I hunched in its belly till my wet fur froze." Randall Jarrell, *The Complete Poems*, New York: Farrar, Straus & Giroux, 1969.

The quote involving Bob Wills's instructions to Leon McAuliffe on instrumental breaks is from Charles R.

Townsend, *San Antonio Rose* (Urbana, Ill.: University of Illinois Press, 1976), p. 125.

The description of Ben Carmine's clothing is based on information in Elton Miles, *Tales of the Big Bend* (College Station: Texas A&M Press, 1976).

Thanks to Wayne LaCox, drummer, guitar player, and friend. More than twenty years ago he gave me a choice phrase for this book. I wrote a song around the idea and sang it many times, playing a red, electric Gibson guitar, standing in front of Wayne's drums. I've forgotten the song over the years, but I remembered the phrase.

Thanks to Sam Cavness, one of the last cowboys, who has taught me a lot about the cowboy life. And to Carl Lewis, who actually built "Jack's Jacuzzi."